ICE

ICE

Vladimir Sorokin

Translated from the Russian by
Jamey Gambrell

NEW YORK REVIEW BOOKS   **nyrb**   *New York*

THIS IS A NEW YORK REVIEW BOOK
PUBLISHED BY THE NEW YORK REVIEW OF BOOKS

Published in the United States of America by
The New York Review of Books
1755 Broadway
New York, NY 10019
www.nyrb.com

Library of Congress Cataloging-in-Publication Data

Sorokin, Vladimir, 1955–
 [Lëd. English]
 Ice / by Vladimir Sorokin ; translated by Jamey Gambrell.
   p. cm. — (New York Review Books classics)
 ISBN-13: 978-1-59017-195-0 (alk. paper)
 ISBN-10: 1-59017-195-0 (alk. paper)
 I. Gambrell, Jamey. II. Title.
PG3488.O66L413 2006
891.73'5—dc22
                                2006021077

ISBN 978-1-59017-195-0

Printed in the United States of America on acid-free paper.

1 3 5 7 9 10 8 6 4 2

Contents

Out of whose womb came the ice?
And the hoary frost of heaven, who hath gendered it?

Job 38:29

Part I

Brother Ural

The new warehouse of Mosregionteletrust.

A dark blue Lincoln Navigator drove into the building. Stopped. The headlights illuminated: a concrete floor, brick walls, boxes of transformers, reels of underground cable, a diesel compressor, sacks of cement, a barrel of tar, broken wheelbarrows, three milk cartons, a scrap heap, cigarette butts, a dead rat, and two piles of dried excrement.

Gorbovets leaned on the gates. Pulled. The steel sections aligned. Clanged. He slid the bolt shut. Spat. Walked to the car.

Uranov and Rutman climbed out of the car. Opened the trunk. Two men in handcuffs lay on the floor of the SUV, mouths taped.

Gorbovets came over.

"The light turns on somewhere here." Uranov caught the string.

3

Ice

"Can't you see?" Rutman pulled on a pair of gloves.

"Not too well." Uranov squinted.

"The main thing is we hear it!" Gorbovets smiled.

"The acoustics are good here." Tired, Uranov wiped his face. "Come on."

They dragged the captives out of the car. Moved them over to two steel columns. Tied them tight with rope. Took up positions around them. Silently stared at the bound men.

Five people were visible in the headlights. All of them were blond and had blue eyes.

Uranov: 30 years old, tall, narrow shoulders, a thin intelligent face, a beige raincoat.

Rutman: 21, medium height, skinny, flat-chested, lithe, a pale unremarkable face, a dark blue jacket, black leather pants.

Gorbovets: 54, bearded, not very tall, stocky, sinewy peasant hands, barrel-chested, crude features, a dark yellow sheepskin coat.

The bound captives:

1st: around 50, stout, ruddy, well-groomed, wearing an expensive suit;

2nd: young, puny, hook-nosed and pimply, black jeans and a leather jacket.

Their mouths were taped with semitransparent packing tape.

"Let's start with this one." Uranov nodded toward the heavy guy.

Rutman took an oblong metal case out of the car. She placed it on the cement floor in front of Uranov, and opened the metal locks. The case turned out to be a mini refrigerator.

Ice hammers, two of them, placed head to tail, lay inside: long, rough wooden shafts, attached to cylindrical ice heads with strips of rawhide. Frost covered the shafts.

Part I

Uranov put on gloves. He picked up a hammer. He stepped toward one of the bound men. Gorbovets unbuttoned the fat man's jacket. He removed his tie and yanked his shirt. The buttons popped and scattered, exposing a plump white chest with small nipples and a gold cross on a chain. Gorbovets's coarse fingers grabbed the cross and jerked. The fat man gave a low moan. He began to make signs with his eyes. Rolled his head back and forth.

"Respond!" Uranov cried aloud.

He swung the hammer back and hit him in the middle of the chest.

The fat man moaned louder.

The three stood still and listened.

"Respond!" Uranov commanded again after a pause. And again he hit him hard.

The fat man's insides growled. The three froze, and listened.

"Respond!" Uranov hit him again, harder.

The man moaned and wailed inside. His body shook. Three round bruises appeared on his chest.

"Lemme whack the fucker." Gorbovets took the hammer. He spit on his hands. Swung it back.

"Respond!" The hammer crashed into the chest with a juicy thud. Splinters of ice scattered.

And again the three stood stock-still. They listened. The fat man moaned and shuddered. His face grew pale. His chest began to sweat and turned purple.

"Orsa? Orus?" Rutman touched her lips uncertainly.

"That's his guts grumbling." Gorbovets shook his head.

"Lower, lower down." Uranov nodded in agreement. "He's empty."

"Speak!" Gorbovets roared and hit him. The man's body jerked. It hung feebly from the ropes.

Ice

The three moved very close. Turned their ears to the purple chest. Listened carefully.

"Guts growlin'..." Gorbovets exhaled sadly. He swung back.

"Reee-spooond! Reee-spond! Reee-spoond!"

Bang. Bang. Chips of ice flew out from the hammer. Bones cracked. Blood began dripping from the fat man's nose.

"He's empty." Uranov straightened up.

"Empty..." Rutman bit her lip.

"Empty, the motherfucker..." Gorbovets leaned on the hammer. He was out of breath. "Oof...goddamn...how many of you empty ding-dongs they gone and multiplied?"

"It's just a bad streak," Rutman sighed.

Gorbovets slammed the hammer on the floor with all his strength. The ice head shattered, shards of ice flying everywhere. The torn straps of rawhide fluttered. Gorbovets threw the handle into the refrigerator. He picked up the other hammer and passed it to Uranov.

Uranov wiped the frost from the handle, staring gloomily at the fat man's breathless body. He turned a heavy gaze to the young man. The two pairs of blue eyes met. The captive thrashed and began to wail.

"Don't be scared, kid." Gorbovets wiped drops of blood off his cheeks. He held one nostril, leaned over, and blew his nose on the floor. He wiped his hand on his sheepskin coat. "Sheesh, Iray, it's the thicksteenth thumper we've bashed, and it's another beanbag! What kinda friggin' luck is this? It's a regular evacupation, I tell you. The thicksteenth! Another empty dingaling."

"Could be the hundred and sixteenth." Uranov unbuttoned the jacket of the second captive.

The young man whined. His rickety knees knocked together.

Rutman began to help Uranov. They tore open the black T-shirt with the red inscription WWW.FUCK.RU. Shivering under the shirt was a white bony chest covered with spotty freckles.

Uranov thought a moment. He handed the hammer to Gorbovets.

"Rom, you do it. I haven't had any luck for a while."

"Okeydoke..." Gorbovets spat on his palms. Pulled himself up. Swung back.

"Re-SPOND!"

The icy cylinder hit the frail chest with a whistle. The captive's body jerked from the blow. The three listened closely. The young man's thin nostrils flared. Sobs broke from them.

Gorbovets sadly shook his shaggy head. He drew the hammer back slowly.

"Respond!"

The whistle of air splitting. A sonorous blow. A spray of ice splinters. Weakening moans.

"Something...something..." Rutman listened closely to the black-and-blue chest.

"Just the upper part, the upper..." Uranov shook his head.

"It's thumbsing...I don't know...maybe it's in the throat?" Gorbovets scratched his reddish beard.

"Rom, again, but more precise," Uranov ordered.

"How mush more precise can ya get..." Gorbovets swung back. "Ree-spond!"

The chest cracked. Ice scattered on the ground. A bit of blood spattered from the broken skin. The young man hung limp from the ropes. His blue eyes rolled back. The black eyelashes fluttered.

The three listened. A weak staccato grumble sounded in the boy's chest.

"It's there!" Uranov twitched.

Ice

"Lord almighty, bless the Light!" Gorbovets tossed the hammer aside.

"I was sure of it!" Rutman laughed joyfully. She blew on her fingers.

The three pressed against the young man's chest.

"Speak with your heart! Speak with your heart! Speak with your heart!" Uranov spoke in a loud voice.

"Speak, speak, speak, come on little man!" Gorbovets mumbled.

"Speak with your heart, with your heart; speak, with the heart..." Rutman whispered joyfully.

A strange, faint sound came and went from the bloody, bruised chest.

"Speak your name! Speak your name! Speak your name!" Uranov repeated.

"Your name, little fella, tell us your name, your name!" Gorbovets stroked the young man's fair hair.

"Your name, say your name, speak your name, name, name..." Rutman whispered to the pale pink nipple.

They froze, transfixed. They listened closely.

"Ural," said Uranov.

"Ur...Hurrah, Ural!" Gorbovets pulled on his beard.

"Urrraaaal...Uraaaaal..." Rutman's eyelids closed in joy.

They began fussing about happily.

"Quick, quick!" Uranov pulled out a coarse knife with a wooden handle.

They cut the ropes. Tore the bandage from his mouth. Placed the young man on the cement floor. Rutman dragged a first aid kit over. He found the smelling salts and brought them over. Uranov placed a wet towel on the battered chest. Gorbovets supported the young man's back. He shook him carefully.

Part I

"Come on now, little guy, come on now, little one ..."

The boy's whole puny body jerked. His thick-soled boots thudded against the floor. He opened his eyes. Inhaled with difficulty. He passed gas and whimpered.

"Now—there, there. Go ahead and fart little one, go ahead and fart ..." In a single swoop, Gorbovets lifted him off the floor. He carried him to the car on his sturdy, crooked legs.

Uranov picked up the hammer and knocked the ice onto the floor. He tossed the shaft in the mini refrigerator, closed the top, and picked it up.

They settled the young man on the backseat. Gorbovets and Rutman sat on either side, propping him up. Uranov opened the gates. He drove out into the dank darkness. He climbed out and closed the gates, got back in behind the wheel, and steered the car along the narrow, uneven road.

The headlights illuminated the roadside and remaining patches of dirty snow. The glowing clock face showed 00.20.

"Your name—is Yury?" Uranov glanced at the young man in the rearview mirror.

"Yu ... ry ... Lapin," he said with difficulty.

"Remember, your true name—is Ural. Your heart spoke that name. Up until today you were not living, just existing. Now you are going to live. You will have everything you want. And you will have a great purpose in life. How old are you?"

"Twenty ..."

"You've been sleeping for twenty years. Now you've awoken. We, your brothers, awakened your heart. I'm Iray."

"I'm Rom." Gorbovets stroked the boy's cheek.

"And I'm Okam." Rutman winked at him. She pushed back a lock of hair from Lapin's sweaty brow.

"We'll take you to a clinic where they'll help you and where you can rest."

Ice

The young man cast an exhausted glance at Rutman. Then at Gorbovets and his beard.

"But... I... but when will I... when... I have to—"

"Don't ask any questions," Uranov interrupted. "You're in shock. And you have to get used to it."

"You're still just a weakling." Gorbovets patted his head. "Get yourself some shut-eye, and then we'll have a talk."

"Then you'll find out everything. Does it hurt?" Rutman carefully placed the wet towel on the round bruises.

"It... hurts..." The young man sniffled. He closed his eyes.

"Finally that towel came in handy. I keep wetting it and wetting it before every hit. Then—it turns out that it's just one more empty. So you have to go and wring the water out!" Rutman laughed. She embraced Lapin carefully. "Listen... it's so cool that you're one of us. I'm so glad..."

The SUV banged over the potholes. The young man shrieked.

"Slower... don't gun it..." Gorbovets fiddled nervously with his beard.

"Is it very painful, Ural?" Rutman spoke the new name with pleasure.

"Very.... Oooowww!" The young man groaned and cried out.

"That's all, that's it. No more bumps from here on," said Uranov. He drove on, carefully.

The car emerged onto Yaroslav Highway. It turned and took off toward Moscow.

"You're a student," said Rutman affirmatively. "Moscow University, the journalism school."

The young man moaned in response.

"I studied too. In the economics department of the Pedagogical Institute."

Part I

"Whoa, man alive!" Gorbovets pulled on his nose. "Messed yourself didja! Got scared, little one!"

A slight smell of excrement came from Lapin.

"That's completely normal." Uranov squinted at the road.

"When they hit me, I squeezed out some brown cheese, too." Rutman looked straight at the young man's thin face. "And I let go a stream of hot water, quietly. It was great. But you..." She touched him between the legs. "You're dry in front. Are you Armenian?"

The boy shook his head.

"But there is something from the Caucasus?" She ran her finger down Lapin's hook nose. "Maybe from the Baltics—no? You have a beautiful nose."

"Don't come on to him, you horny she-goat, he don't care about his nose right now," Gorbovets grumbled.

"Okam, call the clinic," Uranov ordered.

Rutman took out a cell phone and dialed.

"It's us. We have a brother. Twenty. Yes. Yes. How long? Well, in about..."

"Twenty-five minutes," Uranov said.

"We'll be there in half an hour. Yes."

She put the cell phone away.

Lapin leaned his head against her shoulder. Closed his eyes. He sank into oblivion.

They drove up to the clinic: **7 Novoluzhnetsky Prospect.**

They stopped at the guard booth. Uranov showed his pass, then drove up to a three-story building. Behind the glass doors stood two hefty orderlies in blue robes...

Uranov opened the car door. The assistants ran over with

a gurney. They lifted Lapin out of the car. He woke up and moaned feebly. They placed him on the stretcher. Strapped him down. Rolled him inside the clinic door.

Rutman and Gorbovets remained by the car. Uranov followed the stretcher.

A doctor was waiting for them at reception: a plump, stooped man with thick graying hair, gold-rimmed glasses, a meticulously trimmed beard, and a blue robe.

He stood next to the wall, smoking. He held an ashtray.

The orderlies rolled the bed up to him.

"The usual?" asked the doctor.

"Yes," said Uranov, looking down at his own beard.

"Complications?"

"It appears the chest bone cracked."

"How long ago?" The doctor took the towel off Lapin's chest.

"About . . . forty minutes ago."

A female assistant ran in: medium height, chestnut hair, a serious, high-cheekboned face.

"Excuse me, Semyon Ilich."

"Okay, then . . ." The doctor stubbed out his butt and set the ashtray on the windowsill. He leaned over Lapin, touching the swollen, bright purple chest. "Right, first of all: our cocktail here is glowing in the fog. Take care of him. Then do an X-ray. And then bring him to me."

He turned sharply and headed for the doors.

"Should I stay?" asked Uranov.

"No need to. Come back in the morning." The doctor left.

The assistant tore open a hypodermic. She attached the needle, broke two ampoules, and drew the liquid into the hypodermic.

Uranov ran his hand over Lapin's cheek. Lapin opened his

eyes. He raised his head, looked around, and coughed. Then he jerked away from the stretcher.

The orderlies fell on him.

"Nnnnooo! Nnnnno! Nnnooo!" he cried hoarsely.

They held him down to the bed. Began to undress him. The odor of fresh excrement rose from him. Uranov exhaled.

Lapin wheezed and cried.

One orderly wound a tourniquet around Lapin's thin forearm. The assistant leaned over it with the needle.

"There's no need to suffer..."

"I want to call hooooome..." Lapin whined.

"You're already home, brother," said Uranov, smiling.

The needle entered the vein.

Mair

Lapin awoke at three in the afternoon. He lay in a small twin bed. The ceiling was white. The walls were white. There were semitransparent white curtains on the window. On a white bedside table with bent legs was a vase with a spray of white lilies and a white fan, turned off.

Next to the window, sitting on a white chair, was **a nurse**: 24 years old, slim, fair hair cut short, blue eyes, large glasses with silver frames, a short white jacket, pretty legs.

The nurse was reading the magazine *OM.*

Lapin squinted to look at his chest. It was bound in a white elastic bandage. Smooth. You could see a gauze bandage under it.

Lapin took his hand out from under the blanket. He touched the bandage.

The nurse noticed. She placed the magazine on the windowsill, stood up, and walked over to him.

"Good day, Ural."

She was tall. Her blue eyes looked at him attentively through her glasses. Her full lips smiled.

"I'm Kharo," she said.

"What?" Lapin unstuck his cracked lips.

"I'm Kharo." She sat down carefully on the edge of the bed. "How do you feel? Are you dizzy?"

Lapin looked at her hair. He remembered everything.

"I'm, I'm still here?" he asked in a hoarse voice.

"You're in the clinic." She took his hand. She pressed her warm, soft finger to his wrist and took his pulse.

Lapin breathed in cautiously. Breathed out. There was a dull, weak ache in his chest, but no pain. He swallowed some saliva. Frowned. His throat burned. It hurt to swallow.

"Do you want something to drink?"

"Yes, something."

"Juice, water?"

"Orange...juice...Is there orange juice?"

"Of course."

She reached over Lapin. Her snow-white robe rustled and Lapin smelled her perfume. He looked at the open collar of the robe. A smooth, pretty neck. A birthmark just above the collarbone. A thin gold chain.

He turned his eyes to the right. There was a narrow table with drinks. She filled a glass with yellow juice, wrapped it in a napkin, and offered it to Lapin.

He turned over.

With her left hand the nurse helped him to sit up. His head touched the white headboard. He took the glass from her hands and drank.

"You aren't cold, are you?" She smiled. She looked straight at him.

"No. What time is it?"

"Three," the nurse said, glancing at her thin watch.

"I have to call home."

"Of course."

She took a cell phone out of her pocket.

Ice

"Drink up. Then you can call."

Lapin drank half a cup greedily. He exhaled, licked his lips.

"You're thirsty now."

"That's for sure. And you..." he said, using the formal form.

"Use the familiar with me."

"And you...you've been here a long time?"

"In what sense?"

"Well, I mean, working?"

"This is my second year."

"Who are you?"

"Me?" She smiled even more broadly. "I'm a nurse."

"And what is this...a hospital or something?"

"A rehabilitation center."

"Who's it for?" He looked at her birthmark.

"For us."

"Who's...us?"

"The awakened people."

Lapin grew silent. He finished off the juice.

"Some more?"

"A little." He held out the glass.

She filled it up, and he drank half.

"I don't want any more."

She took away the glass and put it on the little table. Lapin nodded at the cell phone.

"May I?"

"Of course." She handed it to him. "Go on and talk. I'll go out."

She stood and left immediately.

Lapin dialed his parent's number, coughed. His father picked up.

"Yes."

"Pop, it's me."

"Where'd you disappear to?"

"Well, um . . ." He touched the bandage on his chest. "You see . . ."

"What do I see? Did something happen?"

"Well . . . um . . ."

"In trouble again? In the slammer?"

"No, not that . . ."

"Where are you?"

"Well, me and Golovastik went to a concert yesterday. At Gorbushka. Well, um, and I ended up staying at his place."

"And you couldn't call?"

"Um, well, we . . . got busy . . . his place is a mess . . ."

"Drinking again?"

"No, no, we just had a little beer."

"Dumbbells. We're about to have dinner. Are you coming?"

"I . . . well, we want to go for a walk."

"Where?"

"In the park . . . near him. He wants to take the dog out."

"Your choice. We've got chicken with garlic. We'll eat it all up."

"I'll try."

"Don't get stuck there."

"I won't . . ."

Lapin turned the cell off. He touched his neck and threw back the blanket. He was naked.

"Shii . . . where's my underwear?" He touched his penis.

He felt a sharp pain in his chest, and gritted his teeth. Pressed his hand against the bandage.

"Goddamn . . ."

The nurse opened the door cautiously.

"Are you finished?"

Ice

"Yes..." He hurriedly pulled the covers back over him.

She entered.

"Where's my clothes?" Lapin frowned. He rubbed the splint.

"Does it hurt?" She sat down on the edge of the bed again.

"I got a twinge..."

"You have a small fracture in your chest bone. You'll have to keep it strapped. You may get a sharp pain from lifting or turning. Until it heals. That's normal. They don't put casts on the chest."

"Why not?" He sniffed.

"Because people need to breathe," she smiled.

"Where're my clothes?" he asked again.

"Are you cold?"

"No...it's just, I...I don't like to sleep naked."

"Really?" She looked at him sincerely. "I'm the opposite. I can't go to sleep if I have something on. Even a chain."

"A chain?"

"Uh-huh. See..." She stuck her hand behind the lapel of her robe and pulled out a chain with a tiny gold comet. "I always take it off at night."

"Interesting." Lapin grinned. "You're so sensitive."

"People should sleep naked."

"Why?"

"Because they're born naked and die naked."

"But they don't end up naked. They're in a suit. And a coffin."

She put the chain back.

"People don't put the suit on themselves. And they don't lie down in the coffin on their own."

Lapin said nothing. He looked to the side.

"Do you want to eat?"

Part I

"I want... I have to... I need my clothes—and to go to the bathroom."

"Urinate?"

"Yeah..."

"There's no problem with that." She leaned over. Pulled a white plastic bedpan out from under the bed.

"No way... I don't..." Lapin gave a crooked smile.

"Relax." She moved the bedpan under the covers with a quick, professional gesture.

The cool plastic touched Lapin's ribs. Her hand took his penis, directed it into the opening.

"Listen..." He pulled his knees up. "I'm not paralyzed or anything..."

Her free hand stopped his knees. Pressed. Pushed them down on the bed.

"There's no problem here," she said softly and emphatically.

Lapin laughed, embarrassed. He looked at the copy of *OM* then at the lily in the vase.

Half a minute passed.

"Ural? Do you want to go or not?" she asked with soft reproach.

Lapin's face grew serious. He blushed slightly. His penis jerked. Urine silently flowed into the bedpan. The nurse held his penis in place.

"There you go. So simple. You've never urinated into a bedpan?"

Lapin shook his head. The urine flowed.

The nurse reached over with her free hand. Took a napkin from the drinks table.

Lapin bit his lip and inhaled carefully.

The stream stopped. The nurse wrapped his penis in the

napkin. She carefully removed the warm bedpan from under the blanket, placed it under the bed, and wiped off his penis.

"Were you born with blue eyes?" she asked.

"Yes." He looked up at her from under his brow.

"Well, I was born with gray eyes. And till the age of six I was gray-eyed. Then my father took me to his factory. To show me some marvelous machine that assembled clocks. And when I saw it, I froze in delight. The way it worked was so amazing! I don't know how long I stood there: an hour, two...I came home, fell sound asleep. And the next morning my eyes had turned blue."

Lapin's penis began to tense.

"Black eyelashes. And eyebrows," she said, examining him. "You probably like gentle things."

"Gentle?"

"Gentle, tender things. Do you?"

"I...well..." He swallowed.

"Have you had women?"

He laughed nervously. "Girls. Have you had women?"

"No. I've only had men," she answered calmly, letting go of his penis. "Before. Before I woke up."

"Before?"

"Yes. Before. Now I don't need men. I need brothers."

"What does that mean?" He pulled his knees up, hiding his hardening penis.

"Sex—is an illness. Fatal. And all humankind is infected with it." She put the napkin in the pocket of her robe.

"Really? That's interesting..." Lapin grinned. "And what about—gentle things? You were just talking about it?"

"You know, Ural, there's tenderness of the body. But that is nothing compared to tenderness of the heart. The awakened heart. And you are going to feel this now."

Part I

The door opened.

A woman came in dressed in a white terry-cloth robe: 38 years old, medium height, plump, light brown hair, blue eyes, her face round, not pretty, smiling, calm.

Lapin pressed his shaking knees to his chest. Reached out for the blanket. But the blanket was down at his feet.

The nurse stood up. Walked over to the woman. They kissed each other on the cheek solicitously.

"I see that you've already met." The woman who had entered looked at Lapin with a smile. "Now it's my turn."

The nurse left. She pulled the door closed silently after her.

The woman looked at Lapin.

"Hello, Ural," she said.

"Hello..." He glanced aside.

"I'm Mair."

"Mayor? Of what?"

"Of nothing." She smiled. "Mair is my name."

She threw off her robe. Naked, she walked over to Lapin and stretched out her plump hand.

"Stand up, please."

"Why?" Lapin looked up at her large, pendulous breasts.

"I beg of you. Don't be embarrassed by me."

"Hey, I could care less. Only... give me my clothes back."

Lapin stood up. He placed his hands on his rickety hips.

She stepped toward him. Carefully embraced him and pressed her chest to his.

Lapin laughed nervously, turning his face away.

"Hey lady, I'm not gonna screw you."

"And I'm not proposing you do," she said. She stood motionless.

Lapin let out a bored sigh.

"Are you gonna give me my clothes back, huh?"

Ice

And suddenly he shuddered. His entire body twitched. He stood stock-still.

They were both transfixed. They stood, embracing. Their eyes were closed.

They stood motionless for forty-two minutes.

Mair shuddered and sobbed. She released her hands. Lapin fell powerlessly out of her embrace onto the floor. He jerked convulsively. Clenched and unclenched his teeth. With a sob he greedily gulped the air. He sat up and opened his eyes. He stared vacantly at the leg of the bed. His cheeks were aflame.

Mair picked up her robe and put it on. She placed her small plump palm on Lapin's head.

"Ural."

She turned and left the room.

The nurse entered holding Lapin's clothes. She squatted down next to Lapin.

"How are you?"

"Okay." He ran a trembling hand down his face. "I really want...um...to...I want..."

"Does your chest hurt?"

"A little...kind of...I...um..."

"Get dressed." The nurse stroked his shoulder.

Lapin reached to pull his jeans over. A pair of underwear was underneath. New. Not his.

He felt them.

"Ma'am...I mean, did you..."

"What?" asked the nurse. "Should I turn around?"

"Did you...what?" He sniffed.

He looked at her, as though seeing her for the first time. His fingers trembled slightly.

The nurse stood up and moved away to the window. She drew back the curtain. She gazed at the bare branches outside.

Lapin stood up with some difficulty. Stumbling and stepping back, he put on the underwear. Then the jeans. He took the black T-shirt. It was new, too. Instead of www.fuck.ru, this one said basic. Also in red.

"But why... this?" His fingers scrunched the new T-shirt.

The nurse looked around.

"Put it on. It's all yours."

He looked at the T-shirt. Then he put it on. He went for the jacket. His things were lying on it: keys, student ID, wallet. The wallet was unusually thick.

Lapin picked it up. He opened it. It was stuffed with money: five-hundred ruble notes, dollars, too.

"But this... isn't mine," he said, looking at the wallet.

"It's yours." The nurse turned around and approached him.

"I had... seventy rubles. Seventy-five."

"This is your money."

"It's someone else's..." He looked at the wallet. Touched his chest.

She took him by the shoulders.

"Listen, Ural. You don't really understand what happened to you yet. I'd say—you don't understand at all. Last night you woke up. But you still haven't shaken off the sleep. Your life will change direction completely now. We will help you."

"Who is—we?"

"People. Who've awoken."

"And... what?"

"Nothing."

"And what will happen to me?"

"Everything that happens to people who've awoken."

Lapin looked at her pretty face with glassy eyes.

"What is—everything?"

"Ural"—her fingers squeezed his bony shoulders—"be

patient. You've only just gotten out of bed. A bed you've been sleeping in for twenty years. You haven't even taken the first step. So put the wallet in your pocket and follow me."

She opened the door. Went out into the hallway.

Lapin put on his jacket and stuck the wallet in the inside pocket. He put the keys and his student card in the side pockets. He went out into the hallway.

The nurse walked briskly. He followed her cautiously. He touched the bandage on his chest.

Near reception, the doctor and Mair were waiting for them. Mair wore a dark purple coat with large buttons. She stood with her hands in her pockets. She looked at Lapin just as warmly and affably as earlier. She smiled.

"So then, young man, we have a little crack in the breastbone," began the doctor.

"I've already been told," muttered Lapin, his eyes glued to Mair.

"Repetition is the mother of instruction," the doctor continued impassively. "Don't take the bandage off for ten days. No lifting cinder blocks. No world records, please. No making love to giants. And take this," he said, holding out two packets of medicine. "Two times a day. And if it hurts—a painkiller. Or seven glasses of vodka. Do I make myself clear?"

"What?" Lapin turned toward the doctor with a heavy gaze.

"It's a joke. Take this," said the doctor, handing over the two packets.

Lapin stared at him. He took the packets and put them into different pockets.

"The young man doesn't understand jokes," the doctor explained to the women with a smile.

"He understands everything perfectly well. Thank you." Mair pressed her cheek against the doctor's cheek.

Part I

"Be happy, Ural," said the nurse in a loud voice.

Lapin turned to her abruptly. He stared at her: pretty, slim, a warm expression. Large glasses. Large lips.

Mair nodded to them. She stepped out into the glass lobby and onto the street. It was overcast. Chilly. Wet bare trees. Leftover snow. Gray grass.

Lapin followed her out. He took careful steps.

Mair walked over to a large dark blue Mercedes. She opened the back door and turned to Lapin. "Take a seat, Ural."

Lapin stepped in. He sat on the springy seat. Blue leather. Soft music. The pleasant aroma of sandalwood. The blond nape of the driver's neck.

Mair sat in the front.

"Let me introduce you, Frop. This is Ural."

The driver turned: 52 years old, a round simple face, small cloudy blue eyes, fleshy hands, and a dark blue suit that matched the car.

"Frop." He smiled at Lapin.

"Yuri... I mean... Ural." Lapin grinned awkwardly. Suddenly he laughed.

The driver turned back. He took the wheel and the car set off smoothly. They drove out onto Luzhnetsky Embankment.

Lapin couldn't stop laughing. He touched his chest with his hand.

"Where do you live?" Mair spoke.

"In Medvedkovo," Lapin managed to say as he licked his lips.

"In Medvedkovo? We'll take you home. What street?"

"Near the Metro... around there. I'll show you.... Near the Metro. I'll get out there."

"Fine. But before that we'll drop in somewhere. There you'll meet three brothers. People your age. They will just say a few words to you. And they'll help you. You need help now."

Ice

"And...where is it?"

"In the center. On Tsvetnoi Boulevard. It won't take more than half an hour at the most. Then we'll drive you home."

Lapin looked out the window.

"The most important thing for you now—is to try not to be surprised by anything," Mair spoke up. "Don't be scared. We aren't a totalitarian sect. We're simply free people."

"Free?" Lapin muttered.

"Free."

"Why?"

"Because we've awoken. And those who have awoken—are free."

Lapin looked at her ear.

"It hurt me."

"Yesterday?"

"Yes."

"That's natural."

"Why?"

Mair turned to him.

"Because you were born anew. And birth—is always painful. For the woman giving birth, and for the newborn. When your mother pushed you out of her uterus, bloody and blue, don't you think it was painful for you? What did you do then? You started crying."

Lapin looked into her blue eyes, which seemed to squint because of slightly puffy eyelids. Around the edges of the pupil a haze of yellow-green was barely observable.

"So that means I...that yesterday I was born again?"

"Yes. We say: you awoke."

Lapin looked at her carefully cut dark blond hair. The ends trembled slightly. In time with the movement of the car.

"I awoke."

Part I

"Yes."

"And...who is sleeping?"

"Ninety-nine percent of humanity."

"Why?"

"It's hard to explain in a few words."

"And who...isn't sleeping?"

"You, me, Frop, Kharo. The brothers who wakened you yesterday."

They turned onto the Garden Ring Road. Ahead of them was a huge traffic jam.

"There you go," sighed the driver. "Soon the only way to get around the center will be on foot..."

A dirty, Russian-made car, a Zero Nine hatchback, was driving next to the Mercedes. There was a fat guy at the wheel, eating a cheeseburger. The paper wrapper grazed his flat nose.

"What about the one...who stayed there?" Lapin asked.

"Where?"

"I mean...yesterday...what about him? Did he wake up too?"

"No. He died."

"Why?"

"Because he was empty. Like a nutshell."

"What...but he wasn't a human being?"

"He was a human being. But empty. Sleeping."

"And I'm....not empty?"

"You are not empty." Mair pulled a pack of gum out of her purse, opened it, and took a piece. She offered some to the driver. He shook his head. She offered it to Lapin.

He took the gum automatically. Unwrapped it. He looked at the pink rectangle. He touched it to his lower lip.

"I...um..."

"What is it, Ural?"

Ice

"I . . . I'll go now."

"As you like." Mair nodded to the driver.

The Mercedes braked. Lapin yawned nervously. He touched the smooth, cool handle of the lock. He pulled on it. He opened the door with difficulty and climbed out. He walked between the cars.

The driver and Mair watched him for a long time.

"Why do they all run away at first?" asked the driver. "I did, too."

"It's a normal reaction," said Mair, chewing again. "I thought he'd try earlier."

"A patient one . . . Where to now?"

"To Zharo."

"At the office?"

"Yes." She glanced back at the backseat.

On the smooth dark blue leather lay the dull pink rectangle of gum, folded in half.

Swiss Cheese

Lapin walked along. Then, with effort, he started to run. He could hardly lift his legs. He grimaced, pressing his hand to his chest. He crossed the street.

All of a sudden.

Pain.

His chest.

Like an electric shock.

He screamed. He felt it in his elbow, the ribs, his temples. He moaned and bent over. He fell on his knees:

"Son of a bitch..."

A well-dressed man stopped.

"What's wrong?"

"Bitch..." Lapin repeated.

"Life, you mean? That's for sure."

Lapin barely managed to stand up. He hobbled toward Patriarch Ponds. There hadn't been any snow here for a long time. Wet sidewalks. The city mud of spring around the pond.

He wandered down Bolshaya Bronnaya Street and turned onto the boulevard. He sat on a bench, leaning on its damp hard back.

"Fuckin'...nonsense..."

Ice

A grimy old woman rambled over. She looked in the trash can and moved on.

Lapin got out his wallet. He extracted the dollars and counted: 900.

He counted the rubles: 4,500. Plus his own seventy. And a five-ruble coin.

He looked around. People walked by at a clip. Others were in no hurry. A guy and a girl drank beer as they walked.

"That's the right idea..." Lapin took out a five-hundred ruble note, put the wallet back.

He stood up carefully. The pain had receded.

He limped over to a kiosk and bought a bottle of Baltic. He asked for it to be opened, drank half straight down, and took a breather. He wiped away the tears that came to his eyes and headed for the Metro. Pushkin Square was crowded. He finished off the beer and placed the bottle carefully on the marble parapet. He started down the stairs, then stopped: "What the fuck?"

He turned back. Standing on Tverskaya Street, he stuck out his hand. Two cars stopped right away: a dirty red one and a green one that was cleaner.

"Chertanovo," Lapin said to the driver of the dirty red car.

"And..."

"And what?"

"A hundred fifty, that's what!"

Lapin nodded. He sat down in the seat next to the driver.

"Where exactly?"

"Sumskoi Passage."

The driver's mustache nodded sullenly. He turned on some music: lousy, but loud.

After an hour of heavy traffic the car pulled up to Lapin's seven-story building. Lapin paid and got out. He rode up to the fifth floor, unlocked the door, and entered a crowded foyer. The apartment smelled like cats and fried onion.

"Ahhhh . . . the appearance of Christ to the people," said his father, glancing out of the kitchen, chewing.

"Goodness!" His mother looked out. "And here we were already hoping that you'd moved in with Golovastik."

"Hi," Lapin barked. He took off his jacket. Touched the bandage: Could you see it through the T-shirt? He looked in the oval mirror: you could see it. He went into his room.

"We already ate everything, don't hurry!" his mother shouted. She and his father laughed.

Lapin kicked open a door with a sign FUCK OFF FOREVER! The room was dark: bookshelves, a table with a computer, a stereo set, a mountain of CDs. There were posters on the wall: *The Matrix*, Lara Croft naked with two pistols, Marilyn Manson as Christ rotting on the cross. An unmade bed. The Siamese cat Nero dozed on a pillow.

Three shirts hung on the back of a chair. Lapin took the black one. He put it on over the T-shirt and lay down gingerly on the bed. He yawned, then cried out, "Aaah—ooooh—shiiiiit!"

Nero rose reluctantly and sauntered over to him. Lapin blew in his ear. Nero turned away. He jumped down onto the old carpet and left the room.

Lapin looked at Lara Croft's large lips. He remembered the nurse.

Khar . . . Khara? Lara. Klara.

He grinned. He shook his head, exhaling sharply through crooked teeth.

Lapin's mother looked in the half-open door: 43 years old, plump, chestnut hair, a young face, tight gray pants, a black-and-white sweater, a cigarette.

Ice

"Are you really full?"

"I'll eat." Lapin buttoned up his shirt.

"Tied one on yesterday?"

"Uh-huh..."

"Too much trouble to make a phone call?"

"Yeah." Lapin nodded seriously.

"Jerk." His mother left.

Lapin lay there looking at the ceiling. He fidgeted with the steel tip of his belt.

"I'm not heating things up twice!" his mother yelled from the kitchen.

"Who cares..." he said, brushing her off. Then he got up. He winced. With difficulty, he pushed himself off the bed, stood up, and shuffled into the kitchen. His mother was washing dishes.

A plate with a piece of fried chicken was on the table. And boiled potatoes. A bowl of sauerkraut stood nearby. A plate of pickles, too.

Lapin gobbled down the chicken. He didn't finish the potatoes. He washed it all down with water.

He went into the living room. He picked up the phone and dialed a number.

"Kela, hi. It's Yurka Lapin. Can I talk to Genka? Gen? It's me. Listen, I need...ummm...to talk to you. No, nothing... Just advice. No, it's not that. It's....uhhh. Something else. Now? Sure. Okay."

He replaced the receiver and went to the foyer. He started to pull on his jacket—and almost screamed with pain.

"Oy...shhhiii..."

"What, you're going out again?" his mother asked, clattering the dishes.

"I'm going over to Genka's, not for long..."

Part I

"Will you buy bread?"

"Uh-huh."

"Need money?"

"I have some."

"You mean you didn't drink everything up?"

"Not everything."

Lapin left the apartment, slamming the door. He walked to the elevator, then stopped. He stood there. He turned around and walked down the stairs to the fourth floor. On the landing, he stopped and squatted. He began to cry. Tears ran down his cheeks. At first he cried silently. His shoulders shook. He pressed his thin hands to his face. Then he began to whine. Grudging sobs broke from his mouth and nose. He began to sob out loud. He wept a long time.

He had a hard time calming down. He rummaged in his jacket pockets. No handkerchief. He blew his nose on the broken, yellowish-brown floor tile. He wiped his hand on the wall next to the words VITYA IS A SHITHEAD.

He started to laugh. He wiped away the tears.

"Mair, Mair, Mair.... Mair, Mair, Mair...."

He began sobbing again. His finger picked at the blue wall. He touched his breastbone.

Gradually he calmed down.

He stood up, walked down the stairs, and went out on the street. He walked past three buildings, entered the fourth. He climbed to the second floor and rang the bell of apartment 47.

The green steel door opened almost immediately.

Kela stood at the threshold: 28 years old, medium height, stocky, muscular, a flat face, reddish mustache, a small shaved head.

"Hey." Kela turned on his heel and left.

Lapin entered the hallway of a two-room apartment: four

tires, a box of audio equipment, a coat stand with clothing, mountain skis, and boots.

The sound of loud music came from Kela's room. Lapin went in to Gena's room: boxes with videotapes, a bed, a chest of drawers with a hutch, photographs.

Gena was sitting at the computer: 21 years old, disheveled, he looked like Kela, but was heavier.

"Greetings." Lapin stood behind him.

"Hi," Gena said without turning around. "Where'd you disappear to?"

"Everywhere."

"Mean you dissolved?"

"Yeah."

"Well, I dug up this cool site yesterday. Take a look..."

He typed in www.stalin.ru. A pale photograph with Stalin's image appeared. Under it was the caption: COLLECT STONE BOUQUET FOR COMRADE STALIN!

Under the caption were seven stone flowers. Gena moved the cursor over one of them. Clicked. A picture came up: a cow, tattooed with Stalin's picture, grazing in a meadow of stone flowers. A slogan floated over the cow: FIGHT THE UNCONSCIOUS, EVERYBODY!

"Cool, huh?" Gena poked him in the thigh with his chubby elbow, directed the cursor to another of the flowers, and clicked.

A picture came up: two Stalins pointing threateningly at each other. The slogan floating over them read: GOT A MAN—GOT A PROBLEM; GET RID OF A MAN, GET RID OF A PROBLEM!

"Way to go, someone's having a blast!" Gena grinned.

"Listen, Gen. You know anything about secret sects?"

"Which ones? Aum Shinrikyo?"

"No, well...others...like an order..."

"Like the Freemasons?"

"Sort of. Can you dig up something on the Web?"

"You can dig up anything you want. What do you need Masons for?"

"I need the ones we have here."

"Kela's up on that stuff. All he does is go on about Freemasons, Masonic lodges..."

"Kela..." said Lapin, touching his chest. "He's obsessed with black asses. And Jews."

"So? He knows about all different kinds. What do you care?"

"Some assholes attacked me. A fuckin' brotherhood. Of 'awakened' people."

"Awakened?"

"Yeah."

"And what do they want?" Gena moved the mouse around quickly, looking at the screen.

"I don't know."

"Then to hell with them....Hey, look! Cool, huh? They're really into that Stalin!"

"I need to talk to someone. Someone who knows who they are."

"So go and ask him. He knows everything."

Lapin went into Kela's room: wood shelving with books, a large stereo with huge speakers, a small television, portraits of Alfred Rosenberg, Pyotr Stolypin, a Russian National Unity poster SUPPORT THE NEW RUSSIAN ORDER!, three sets of nunchaku, laced boots with thick soles, sixty-kilo weights, three-kilo dumbbells, twelve-kilo dumbbells, two baseball bats, a mattress, and a brown bearskin on the floor.

Kela was sitting on the mattress drinking beer and listening to the band Halloween.

Ice

Lapin sat down next to him. He waited until the song was over.

"Kel, I have a problem."

"What?"

"Some kind of sect...or maybe order...sort of...hassled me, got right up in my face."

"How?"

"Well, they go on and on, and talk about, like 'We're—the awakened people. Brothers. Everyone else is asleep.' They promise money. Kinda like Masons."

Kela turned the music off. He placed the remote on the floor.

"Remember, once and for all: there's no such thing as Masons by themselves. There's only kike Masons. You heard about B'nai B'rith?"

"What's that?"

"The official kike Masonic lodge in Moscow."

"Kel, you know, these, the ones that...well, that visited me, they're not Jews. They're all blond, like me. Even got blue eyes. That's right! Hey, listen," he suddenly remembered, "I only just realized! They've all got blue eyes!"

"Doesn't matter. All the Masonic lodges are controlled by the kike oligarchy."

"They said stuff like, everybody is asleep, like hibernating, and we have to wake up, kinda like being born again, and the whole thing started outside, they came up to me near the student union and asked me for—"

Kela interrupted. "Even three hundred years ago all the Masons were either pure kikes or mixed blood. Before that, fuck, I mean the kikes used the Masons like puppets, but now—it's the politicians. All politicians are whores. Man, fuckin' bastards. And our kikes"—Kela locked his sinewy fingers together and cracked his knuckles—"they've all got a Star of David and 666 tattooed on the end of their pricks."

Lapin sighed impatiently.

"Kel, but I..."

"Just fuckin' listen..." Kela stretched out a brawny arm, and took a book off the shelf. He opened it at the bookmark.

"Franz Liszt. A great composer. He writes about the kikes: 'There will come a moment when all Christian nations in which Jews live will raise the question of whether or not to suffer them further, or to deport them. The significance of this question is as important as the question of whether we want life or death, health or sickness, social peace or continual unrest.' Get it!"

The doorbell rang.

"Genka, open it," Kela shouted.

"Why is it..." Gena shuffled angrily toward the door. He opened it.

A huge guy entered Kela's room: 23 years old, shaved head, wide shoulders, leather jacket and pants, big hands, on the side of his palm a tattoo: FOR THE AIRBORNE FORCES.

"Hey! Wazup, my man?" said Kela, getting up from the mattress.

"Wazup, Kel."

They swung their arms back and slapped their right palms together hard.

"They say the iron's rusting over here!" The guy smiled, showing strong teeth.

"Fuckin' rusting away, man. Over there." Kela nodded at the weights.

"Yeah." The guy went over, took hold of them, and lifted. "Got it."

Ice

"But only for a coupla weeks, Vitya, max."

"No prob." The guy took the weights in his right hand. Looked at Lapin. At the beer. "Hittin' the foamy?"

"Nah." Kela flopped on the mattress. "Just shootin' the breeze with the young folks."

"You're a good guy, Kel." The guy nodded and left with the weights.

"You heard about the Union of Satan and the Antichrist?" Kela asked Lapin.

"What's that?"

"How about B'nai Moishe?"

"No."

Kela sighed.

"Jesus fuckin' Christ. I don't know what the fuck makes you guys tick."

"Compooters," said Gena, glancing into the room.

"Fuck compooters." Kela gave a nod. "Do you know who invented the Internet and where? And what he did it for?"

"You already said a million times," said Gena, scratching his cheek. "So what?...So the Jews and Chinese invented everything in the world."

"You read *My Name Is Legion*?" Kela stared at Lapin.

Someone rang the doorbell.

"Open it." Kela nodded at Gena.

The guy in leather came in again. Holding the weights.

"Kel, listen, I forgot: Vovan said to come over on Friday. To have a few. You in?"

"Sure."

"I'll come by."

"Good. Hey, Vityok, these guys ain't read *My Name Is Legion* and they don't do any damn sports."

"Each to his own." The guy smiled, showing his teeth. He held the weights out to Gena. "Hold this a sec, youngster."

"Get outta here!" said Gena, laughing. "I have kidney stones."

"For real?"

"For real!" Kela answered for Gena. "How ya fuckin' like that, Vitya? The kid's only twenty—and he's got kidney stones!"

"Wooow..." The guy leaned against the door jamb, still holding the weights. "I ain't heard of that. So young. Stones. We used to...uhhh. In our battalion the sergeant cured a first lieutenant. He couldn't sleep in the cold."

"How come?"

"Kidney stones. He got him soused, on beer. Four liters. Then he says, 'Let's go take a leak.' So they get up. The first lieutenant's pissing. And the sergeant whacks him on the side of the kidneys—wham-bam! He's like—oooowwww, shit! His piss is all bloody. But all the stones came out. So there you go. Field medicine."

The guy turned around and left.

The phone rang. Kela picked it up.

"Yeah. Hey, my man. Ah! Fucking shit man, what's the story with you? That's fuckin' it! I'm going to pick it up tomorrow. Tell me about it! Today I'm walking down the street thinking— am I really gonna trade in that rotten '04 for a normal fuckin' set of wheels? Uh-huh! Yeah...yeah...That's for fuckin' sure. Uh-huh!"

"Are you buying a new car?" asked Lapin.

"Not new. A '93 Golf." Gena yawned.

"Got rich?"

"The folks laid a coupla thou on us."

Ice

"Great."

"Let's go to a chat and bullshit. There're lots of film buffs."

"I wanted to talk over stuff with Kela."

"That's Voronin. It's gonna be a long one. Come on, let's go."

"All right..."

They returned to Gena's room. They sat down side by side at the computer. Gena quickly entered a chat room under the name **KillaBee :/)**.

Zkhus /:

I bought argento's "Phantom of the Opera" yesterday, too. I was counting on Julian Sands, who's not usually in shitty films. I think he's the coolest actor since Mickey Rourke. Fanfuckintastic flick!!!—

De Scriptor /:

Yeah and "Darkness" is crapola.

Natasha /:

Julian Sands sucks. He was only good in "Black Book 2," but "Phantom of the Opera" is total bullshit.

KillaBee /:

Ur all floppy-dicked cuntsuckers! And Julian Sands is Filipp Kirkorov's nephew :)

Old As A Mammoth /:

Scuzzy! Where the DZTVZ are u coming from?

KillaBee /:

A mammoth's cunt, Fuzzy Wuzzy. How come u r jacking

off on Sands when there's Chuuuuulpan Kamyyyytovaaaaa
and Keanu Reeves!!! Guys, I'm in love with them!

De Scriptor /:
Dumbfuckism is incurable :/(. But it can be used for peaceful
causes.

Mole /:
that wet slit will piss on everything again.

KillaBee /:
Definitely, boys :/—

Zkhus /:
Here's a suggestion—fuck off to your own chain link.

Old As A Mammoth /:
killabeeby, can it, will ya. Check out: www.clas.ru. u can order
rare films. Home delivery. I got my favorite, Cronenberg :)))

Mole /:
anyone seen Argento's "Demons"?

Vino /:
Argento didn't make "Demons." It was either G. Romero or
Lucio Fulci. RenTV showed "Phenomena" by your vapid
Argento—what trash. With a heavy metal soundtrack.

KillaBee /:
Woooow, look who's here! The vin-o-dictive nightingale
is singing sweetly. r u still hard? I'm always ready, motherfucker!!!! :/)

Ice

Vino /:
KillaBee, if you want someone to screw you till you're blue in the clit, then....///!

"Gen, I'm going home." Lapin got up. Touched his chest.

"What's wrong, Lap? Let's write something. Come on, something cool, no kid's stuff."

"Yeah, well . . . to hell with it. I wanted to talk to Kela, but he got onto his kikes again."

"Why'd the fuck you work him up? You shoulda talked about something else. Freemasons, Masonic lodges. . . . That's all he's gonna talk about now. I never bring up ethnic stuff with him anymore. He drives me fucking crazy."

Lapin waved his hand. He stood there a minute.

"Gen."

"What?" said Gena, typing.

"Let's grab a beer."

"Where?" asked Gena, turning around in surprise.

"Anywhere. I have . . . that is . . . I've got tons of money."

"From where?"

"Thin air."

Kela came in with a new bottle of beer.

"And I'll tell you what else, Genka. I'm gonna say it for the last goddamned time: you keep on sucking that hash—I'll send you to the progenitors. Go smoke that fucking shit there, in the can."

"I haven't had a toke for ages, what do you mean?"

"The day before yesterday? Huh? When I brought in the smokes. And your gang of assholes was here? Don't tell me you weren't."

"What're you talking about? Kel? We were listening to the new Air Force CD.

"Don't bullshit the boss. Fuckin' idiots. You don't understand shit." He took a swig from the bottle. "You know what dead Chechens' brains look like? Swiss cheese. With holes. This big. From what? From hashish. Got it?"

"You already told me." Gena popped a piece of gum in his mouth. "Kel, you know beer makes the liver get all covered in fat."

"Just fuckin' think about it. I warned you. For the last time." Kela left.

"Jeez, shit..." Gena sighed. "I'm so sick of this. Christ, why are they so psyched about pumping iron? Vityok, Shpala, Bomber—they're dunces, it figures—they've only got a few gray cells to start, why not pump? But Kela—he's smart. He's read more books than all of them put together. And it's the same thing—a healthy body, shit, a healthy spirit. And every morning he sticks those lousy friggin' dumbbells in my bed! Think about it. I'm sleeping, and he goes and sticks those fuckin' dumbbells under my ass! What a loony bin..."

Lapin looked at the screen. Got up. "I'm off."

"What's wrong?"

"I've still got something to do..."

"Lap, why are you so...today?"

"So what?"

"Well, kind of...beat up?"

Lapin looked at him and laughed out loud. A sudden attack of hysterical laughter forced him to bend over.

"What's with you?" Gena said, confused.

Lapin laughed. Gena looked at him.

Lapin had a hard time calming down. He wiped away the tears that had come to his eyes. Sighed deeply.

"That's it...I'm off."

"What about the beer?"

Ice

"What beer?"

"You were the one who wanted to have a beer, no?"

"I was joking."

"Some kinda joke, leetle boy..."

Lapin left.

It had grown dark outside and was beginning to freeze. The puddles cracked underfoot.

Lapin limped to his door and walked in. He pressed the elevator button, looked at the wall. He saw the familiar graffiti. Two tags—ACID ORTHODOX and DESTRUCTION-97—were Lapin's work. He noticed a new inscription: URAL, DON'T BE AFRAID OF AWAKENING.

Black marker. Neat handwriting.

Diar

07:08
The Kiev Highway
Kilometer 12

A white Volga automobile turned onto a forest road. Drove about three hundred meters. Turned again. Stopped in the glade.

A birch grove. Leftover snow. Morning sun.

Two people got out of the car.

Botvin: 39 years old, heavy, blond, blue eyes, a kind face, a blue-green athletic jacket, blue-green pants with a white stripe, black sneakers.

Neilands: 25, tall, thin, blond, decisively stern, blue eyes, sharp facial features, a brown raincoat.

They opened the trunk.

Nikolaeva lay inside: 22, a cute blond, blue eyes, a short fox-fur coat, high black suede boots, her mouth taped with a white bandage, handcuffs.

They pulled Nikolaeva out of the trunk. She kicked and whined.

Ice

Neilands took out a knife. He sliced through the back of the coat. And the sleeves. The coat fell to the ground. Under the coat was a red dress. Neilands cut it. He cut the bra.

Medium-size breasts. Small nipples.

They led her to a birch tree and began tying her to it.

Nikolaeva let out a muffled wail. She struggled. Her neck and face turned red.

"Not tight. Let her breathe freely." Botvin pressed her writhing shoulders against the birch.

"I don't make it tight." Neilands worked with intense concentration.

They finished. Botvin took a longish white refrigerator case out of the car. He opened it. Inside lay the ice hammer: the neat weighty head, the wooden handle, the rawhide straps.

Neilands pulled a one-ruble coin out of this pocket.

"Heads."

"Tails," said Botvin, trying out the hammer.

Neilands tossed the coin. It landed upright on its edge in the snow.

"Well how do you like that?" Botvin laughed. "So what do we do, try it again?"

"Go ahead and hit," Neilands said with a wave of his hand.

Botvin stood in front of Nikolaeva.

"Now listen, sweetheart. We aren't robbers or sadists. Not even rapists. Relax. There's nothing to be afraid of."

Nikolaeva whimpered. Tears ran from her eyes. So did her mascara.

Botvin swung back.

"Speak!"

The hammer struck her sternum.

Nikolaeva grunted.

"That's not it, hon," said Botvin, shaking his head.

Part I

He drew back. The sun sparkled on the side of the hammer. "Speak!"

Another blow. The half-naked body shuddered.

Botvin and Neilands listened.

Nikolaeva's shoulders and head trembled. She hiccuped rapidly.

"Close, but no cigar." Neilands frowned.

"Let the Light's Will be done, Dor."

"You said it, Ycha."

Two birds called each other in the forest.

Botvin slowly drew the hammer to one side.

"Come on, luv...spea-ea-k!"

The powerful blow shook Nikolaeva. She lost consciousness. Her head hung limp. Her long blond hair covered her breast.

Botvin and Neilands listened.

A sound awoke in the bruised chest. A faint rasp. Once. Twice. A third time.

"Speak with the heart!" Botvin said. He held his breath.

"Speak with the heart!" Neilands whispered.

The sound broke off.

"It was definitely there. . . . Lift her head," said Botvin, raising the hammer.

"One hundred percent..." Neilands moved behind the birch. He lifted Nikolaeva's head, and pressed it to the rough, cold trunk. "Just—take it easy, now..."

"You bet..." Botvin drew back. "Speeeak!"

The hammer smashed into the chest. A spray of ice splinters flew out in all directions.

Botvin pressed his ear to the chest. Neilands looked out from behind the birch.

"Khor, khor, khor..." could be heard from the breastbone.

Ice

"We've got it!" Botvin shouted, tossing the hammer aside. "Speak, little sister, speak with the heart, talk to us!"

"Speak with the heart, speak with the heart, speak with the heart!" muttered Neilands. He began hurriedly searching in his pockets: "Where is it? Where? Where did I...where is it?"

"Wait a sec..." Botvin patted all his pockets.

"Jeez, damn...it's in the car! In the glove compartment!"

"Damnit..."

Botvin lunged toward the Volga. He slipped on the wet snow and fell—onto the dirty, brown grass. He crawled quickly to the car, opened the door, and pulled a stethoscope from the glove compartment.

The sound didn't stop.

"Hurry!" Neilands cried in a falsetto.

"Damnit all..." Botvin ran back. He stretched out a dirty hand holding a stethoscope.

Neilands stuck the ends in his ears. He held the stethoscope to the violet-colored chest.

Both of them froze. An airplane flew by in the distance. Birds called to each other. The sun went behind a cloud.

There was a raspy sputtering sound in Nikolaeva's chest—faint but regular.

"Di...ro...aro...ara..." whispered Neilands.

"Don't be in such a hurry!" said Botvin, exhaling.

"Di...di...ar. Diar. Diar. Diar!" Neilands sighed in relief. He took the stethoscope off and handed it to Botvin.

Botvin put it clumsily in his ears. His plump, dirty hand pressed the black circle to the chest.

"Di...et...di...ero,....Diar. Diar. Diar. Diar."

"Diar!" Neilands nodded his narrow head.

"Diar." Botvin smiled. He wiped his face with his muddied hand. He laughed. "Diar!"

Part I

"Diar!" said Neilands, slapping him on the shoulder.

"Diar!" Botvin replied, tapping on his chest.

They embraced, swayed, pushed away from each other. Neilands began to cut the rope. Botvin tossed the hammer in the case. He took off his jacket.

They freed the unconscious Nikolaeva from the ropes and handcuffs. They wrapped her in the jacket and lifted her. They carried her to the car.

"Don't forget the hammer," wheezed Botvin.

They laid Nikolaeva on the backseat.

Neilands grabbed the case with the hammer. He tossed it in the trunk.

Botvin got in the driver's seat. He started the engine.

"Wait." Neilands strode over to the birch tree. He unzipped his trousers, spread his legs.

Nikolaeva moaned weakly.

"She's coming to. Diar!" Neilands smiled.

A stream of urine hit the birch.

Con

Nikolaeva woke up from a touch.

Someone naked and warm was pressed to her.

She opened her eyes: a white ceiling, an opaque light fixture, the edge of a window behind a semitransparent white curtain, curly blond hair. A smell. "Aftershave lotion." A male ear with an attached earlobe. A male cheek. Well shaven.

Nikolaeva moved. She glanced down: the edge of a sheet. Under the sheet her naked body. An enormous bruise on her chest. Her legs. A dark, muscular male body. Pressing to her. Entwining her in its arms. Turning her on her side. Powerfully pressing her chest to his.

"Listen..." she said hoarsely. "I don't like it that way..."

And suddenly she froze, stupefied. Her body shuddered. Her eyes closed halfway and rolled to the side. The man also froze. He shuddered and his head jerked. Pressed to her, he too was stupefied.

Thirty-seven minutes passed.

The man's mouth opened. A faint, hoarse moan escaped him. The man moved. He flexed his hands. Turned over. Rolled off the bed onto the floor. He stretched feebly and let out a sob. His breathing was heavy.

Part I

Nikolaeva shuddered. She rolled her legs over, sat up, and let out a cry. She held her hands to her chest and opened her eyes. Her face was crimson. Saliva drooled from her open mouth. She whimpered and began to cry. Her shoulders heaved. Her legs trembled restlessly on the sheet.

The man exhaled with a moan. He sat up and looked at Nikolaeva.

She was crying hard, her body shaking helplessly.

"Want some juice?" the man asked quietly.

She didn't answer. She looked at him fearfully.

The man stood up: 34 years old, a slim muscular blond, with big blue eyes and a delicate face, handsome and sensitive.

He walked around the bed. He took a bottle of mineral water from a nightstand and opened it. He poured it into a glass.

Nikolaeva watched: his tanned body, golden hair on the legs and chest.

The man caught her look. He smiled.

"Hello, Diar."

She didn't answer. He drank from the glass. She unstuck her lips, swollen and scarlet with blood.

"I'm thirsty..."

He sat down next to her on the bed and embraced her. He put the glass to her lips. She drank greedily. Her teeth chattered against the glass.

She drank it down. She exhaled with a moan.

"More."

He rose. He filled the glass to the brim and brought it to her. She gulped it down.

"Diar..." he said, stroking her hair.

"I'm...Alya," she said. She wiped her tears away with the sheet.

Ice

"You're Alya for ordinary people. But for the awakened, you are Diar."

"Diar?"

"Diar," he said, looking at her warmly.

Suddenly she coughed. She clutched her chest.

"Careful." He held her sweaty shoulders.

"Ow...it hurts..." She moaned.

The man took a towel from the nightstand. He placed it on her shoulders and began to dry her off carefully.

She examined her bruise, and whimpered.

"Oy...but...why did they..."

"It will pass. It's just a bruise. But the bone is intact."

"Jeezus...and that...what was that you were doing... jeezus...why the fuck were you doing that? Huh? What the fuck was that for?" She shook her head. Held her knees to her chin.

He embraced her shoulders.

"I'm Con."

"What?" she said, looking at him with confusion. "A Con? ...Artist?"

"You didn't understand, Diar. I'm not *a* con, I am Con."

"An ex?...The regular kind?"

"No," he laughed. "C O N—three letters. It's my name. I'm not a con artist, and I've never been a convict of any kind."

"Really?" She looked around, bewildered. "What's this? A hotel?"

"Not exactly." He pressed against her back. "Something like a rest home."

"Who for?"

"For the brothers. And sisters."

"Which ones?"

"Ones like you."

"Like me?" She wiped her lips against her knees. "You mean, I'm a sister?"

"Yes, a sister."

"Whose?"

"Mine."

"Yours?" Her lips trembled and grimaced.

"Mine. And not only mine. Now you have lots of brothers."

"Bro-thers?" She sniffled. She grabbed his hand. Suddenly she screamed at the top of her lungs—hysterically and for some time. The scream turned into sobs.

He embraced her, held her close. Nikolaeva wept, burying her face in his muscular chest. He began to rock her like a baby.

"Everything's okay."

"Why...again...why...oooo!" She sobbed.

"Everything, everything will be all right for you now."

"Ooooo!! How could...oy, what did you do to me.... Christ..."

Gradually she calmed down.

"You need to rest," he said. "How old are you?"

"Twenty-two..." she whimpered.

"All these years you've been sleeping. And now you've awoken. It's a very strong shock. It's not only joyful. It's frightening as well. You need time to get used to it."

She nodded. And sobbed.

"Is there...a...handkerchief?"

He handed her a tissue. She blew her nose loudly, crumpled the tissue, and threw it on the floor.

"Jeezus...I sure cried my eyes out."

"You can take a bath. They'll help you to collect yourself..."

"Uh-huh..." She looked fearfully at the window. "But where..."

"Is the bathroom? They'll take you in a minute."

Ice

Nikolaeva nodded distractedly. She glanced over at the lily in the vase. At the window. At the lily again. She took a deep breath, jumped up off the bed, and ran for the door. Con didn't move. She threw the door open wide and flew out into the hall. Ran. Bumped into a nurse smoking a cigarette next to a tall brass ashtray. She smiled at Nikolaeva with her blue eyes.

"Good morning, Diar."

Nikolaeva ran toward the exit. Her bare feet slapped along the new, wide parquet of the hall. She ran up to the glass doors, pushed the first one, and leaped into the entryway. She pushed the second one. She ran across the wet asphalt.

The doctor looked at her through the glass. He folded his arms on his chest and smiled.

A fair-haired chauffeur in a parked silver BMW gazed after her. He was eating an apple.

Nikolaeva ran naked through Sparrow Hills. Bare trees stood all around. Dirty snow lay on the ground.

She tired quickly. Stopped. Squatted. She sat for a while, breathing heavily. Then she got up. She touched her chest and frowned.

"The bastards..."

She walked on. Her bare feet splashed through puddles.

A big road was visible ahead. Now and then a car drove by. A wet spring wind blew. Nikolaeva stepped out on the road. Immediately she felt the intense cold. She shivered and hugged herself tight.

A car went past. The middle-aged driver smiled at Nikolaeva.

She raised her hand. A Volkswagen passed her. The driver and the passenger opened their windows. They looked out and whistled.

"Assholes," muttered Nikolaeva. Her teeth were chattering.

Part I

A Zhiguli came into view and stopped.

"Are you one of those polar bears or something?"

The driver opened the door: 40 years old, bearded, with glasses, a large silver earring, and a black-and-yellow bandana on his head. "The ice has broken up already!"

"Lis-s-s...sten...t-take...meee...they...s-s-stole..." Nikolaeva's teeth chattered.

"You got mugged?" He noticed the large bruise between her breasts. "They beat you?"

"They b-b-b-eat the sh-sh-shit outta...m-m-m-e...bas-s-s-tards."

"Get in."

She climbed in and sat down. Closed the door.

"Oy, shit...it's sooo cold..."

The driver took off a light white jacket. He threw it over Nikolaeva's shoulders.

"So, where to, the police?"

"No way..." She frowned. She wrapped herself in the jacket. Shaking. "I d-d-don't deal with thos-se j-jerks...take me home. I'll pay you."

"Where?"

"Strogino."

"Strogino...?" he said, in an anxious voice. "I have to get to work."

"Oy, it's so cold..." She trembled. "Turn-n-n the heat up..." He slid the heat up to high.

"Why don't I take you as far as Leninsky Prospect, and you can catch another ride there."

"Come on, how am I gonna...again, I mean...oy...damnit...take me home, I'm begging you," she said, trembling.

"Strogino...that's completely out of my way."

Ice

"How much do you want?"

"Hey... that's not the point, luv."

"That's always the point. A hundred, one fifty? Two? Let's go for two hundred. That's it."

He thought a minute. Changed gears. The car took off.

"Gotta smoke?"

He offered her a pack of Camels. Nikolaeva took one. He held the lighter for her.

"Why did they... they took your clothes and left you in the woods?"

"Uh-huh." She took a deep drag.

"All your clothes?"

"As you can see."

"Wow. That's hard core. Shouldn't you report it?"

"I'll handle it myself."

"What do you mean, you know them?"

"Something like that."

"That's a different story."

He was quiet for a while, then asked, "Are you one of those, um, er, 'butterflies of the Moscow night'?"

"More like... daytime..." She yawned sleepily, exhaling smoke. "A Cabbage White."

He nodded and grinned.

Semisweet

12:17
Strogino
25 Katukova Street

The Zhiguli drove up to a sixteen-story apartment building.

"Come with me," Nikolaeva said, getting out of the car. She walked up to the front door and dialed an apartment number on the intercom: 266.

"Who is it?"

"It's me Natashka."

The door beeped. Nikolaeva and the driver entered. They took the elevator to the twelfth floor.

"Wait here." She handed him his jacket. Rang the doorbell.

Natasha, sleepy, opened the door: 18 years old, a plump face, black hair cut short, a red terry-cloth robe.

"Give me two hundred rubles." Nikolaeva walked past the girl into her room. She got the same kind of red robe out of the closet and put it on.

"Jeezus fucking... What's up?" Natasha followed her.

"Two hundred rubles! To pay the driver."

Ice

"I only have dollars—two one-hundred dollar bills."

"Aren't there any rubles? Do you have any rubles?!" Niko-laeva shouted.

"Hey, no, what are you screaming for...?"

"Or small bills?"

"Two one-hundred dollar bills. What is that, what hap-pened to you?" Natasha noticed the bruise on her chest.

"None of your business. Does Lenka have any?"

"What?"

"Rubles."

"I don't know. She's still asleep."

Nikolaeva went into another room. Two women were sleep-ing on the floor.

"What, Sula came over too?" said Nikolaeva looking at them.

"Uh-huh," said Natasha, looking out from behind her. "They crawled in late last night."

"Then—fuck 'em..." Nikolaeva said, annoyed.

"So, what's up?" The driver stood at the open front door.

"Come in," Nikolaeva said.

He entered. She closed the door behind him.

"Listen, we gotta big problem with rubles. How about I give you a blow job?"

He looked at her, then at Natasha. Natasha grinned. She went back to her room.

"Come on." Nikolaeva took him by the hand.

"Well, actually, um..." He stared straight at her.

"Come on, come on...in the bathroom. What can I do, we're flat out of dough, you can see for yourself. And if I wake those bitches up—I'll never hear the end of their shit..." She tugged at his arm.

"I can go and change money," he said, stopping.

"Don't be ridiculous." She turned on the light in the bathroom. Pulled him by the hand. Locked the door. Squatted. Began unbuttoning his pants.

"Uh . . . how long have you . . . um?" he said, looking up at the ceiling.

"You ask a lot of questions young man . . . Oho! We're quick on the uptake . . ." She touched his stiffening member through his pants.

She unfastened his belt and unzipped the zipper. She pulled his gray trousers and his black underwear down.

The driver had a small, crooked penis.

She sucked him quickly, grasping his lilac testicles in her hand. She began moving rapidly.

The driver stuck his backside out. He leaned over slightly and rested his hands on the washing machine. He snuffled. His earring swung as he moved.

"Wait . . . hon . . ." He put his hand on her head.

"It hurts?" she asked spitting out his penis.

"No . . . It's just that . . . I'll never come that way . . . let's . . . uh . . . the normal way . . ."

"I won't do it without a condom."

"But I. . . . I . . . don't carry them with me . . ." He laughed.

"This is not a problem . . ." She went out and came back with a pack of condoms. She unwrapped one, and slipped it on him quickly and deftly. She threw off her robe, turned her backside to him, and set her elbows on the sink.

"Go ahead . . ."

He entered her quickly, grabbing her with his long arms. He moved back and forth rapidly, wheezing.

"That's good . . . oy, good . . ." she repeated calmly. She examined her bruise in the mirror.

He came.

She winked at him in the mirror.

Ice

"You rascal, you!"

She looked at him attentively. Suddenly her lips began to tremble. She covered her mouth with her palm.

He breathed hard through his nose, his eyes closed. He put his head on her shoulder.

She stretched out her arm and closed the drain on the bathtub. She turned on the water, barely able to restrain her sobs.

"Okay. That's it. I...I...I need to get warm."

He had a hard time turning her around. He opened his eyes. His penis slipped out of her vagina. The driver looked at it.

"In...in the loo," she suggested. She grabbed a half bottle of shampoo off a shelf and dumped it in the bathtub. She sobbed out loud.

He glanced at her glumly.

"What's wrong? You feel bad?"

She shook her head—then grasped his hand. She went down on her knees, pressing his hand to her chest. Her sobs grew stronger, and she squeezed her mouth shut.

"What is it?" he said, looking down at her. "They mistreated you, is that it? How come you're..."

"No, no, no..." She sniffed. "Wait a sec...wait..."

She pressed his hand to her chest. She wept.

He looked sideways at himself in the mirror. He stood there patiently. The sperm-filled condom hung from his shrinking penis. It swayed in time to her sobs.

It took her awhile to calm down.

"It's.... It's all...so...that's all...go..."

The driver pulled up his trousers and left.

Nikolaeva got into the bath and sat down. She hugged her knees and rested her head on them.

The sound of flushing water came from the loo.

The driver glanced into the bathroom.

"Is everything all right?" asked Nikolaeva without raising her head.

He nodded. He looked at her curiously.

"If you want, come by again sometime."

He nodded.

She sat motionless. He wiped his nose.

"What's your name?"

"Alya."

"Mine's Vadim."

She nodded into her knees.

"Are you...in big trouble?"

"No, no." She stubbornly shook her head. "It's just...just ...that's it...bye."

"Well, bye."

The driver took off. The front door slammed.

The bath filled with water. It reached Nikolaeva's armpits. She turned the faucet off and lay down.

"Lord...CON, Con, Con, Con, Con..."

Bubbles fizzled around her tear-stained face.

Nikolaeva dozed off.

Twenty-two minutes later Natasha stuck her head into the bathroom.

"Alya, get up."

"What?" Nikolaeva opened her eyes, annoyed.

"Parvazik's here."

Nikolaeva sat up quickly.

"Fuck! You ratted on me?"

"He just showed up on his own."

"On his own! You viper! Well, just try and ask me for more sheets!"

"Go to—"

Natasha slammed the door.

Ice

Nikolaeva ran her wet hands over her face. She swayed.

"Oh, shit . . . What a little cockroach . . ."

She stood up with difficulty. She took a shower, wrapped her head in a towel, and dried off. She put on a robe and went out into the hallway.

"Have a good soak?" she heard from the kitchen.

Nikolaeva went in.

Two men were sitting there.

Parvaz: 41 years old, small, black hair, swarthy, unshaven, with small facial features, dressed in a gray silk jacket, black shirt, narrow gray trousers, and boots with buckles.

Pasha: 33, heavyset, light-haired, pale skin, a meaty face, dressed in a silvery-lilac colored Puma leisure suit and light blue sneakers.

"Hello there, beautiful," Parvaz said, lighting a cigarette with a match.

Nikolaeva leaned against the door jamb.

"I thought you and me, we made an agreement together." He took a drag on the cigarette. "In, what is it called—good faith? You promised me something. Isn't that right? You said lots of words. Crossed your heart. Isn't that right? Or do I have a problem with my memory?"

"Parvazik, I have a problem."

"What kind of problem?"

"Someone came after me, big-time."

"And who it was?" Parvaz sent a long stream of smoke pouring out of his small, thin lips.

Nikolaeva opened her robe.

"Here, take a look."

The men looked at her bruise silently.

"You see, it's really, I mean . . . I still haven't come to . . . Give me a smoke."

Part I

Parvaz handed her a pack of Dunhills and some matches.

She lit up. She put the cigarettes and the matches on the table.

"So yesterday I did my gig on the pole, and then I went around the club—to rustle up a trick. It wasn't very crowded. There were two guys sitting there, one of them called me over. So I went, did the belly wave, shook my tits. He says, 'Sit down, sit for a while.' I sat. They ordered champagne. We drank and started bullshitting. They were regular johns, they sold some kind of humidifiers or something. One was from the Baltics, gorgeous guy, tall, with a complicated name... Reetus-fetus... I couldn't remember it, and the other guy, Valera, was fat. 'Well,' I said, 'I'm cold, I'll go get dressed,' 'Yeah, yeah, of course. And come back to us.' So I put on a dress and went back to their table. 'What do you want?' I say, 'Something to eat.' They ordered me some grilled sturgeon. 'You been dancing striptease for a long time?' they asked. I say—not long. 'Where are you from?' 'Krasnodar.' Stuff like that. And then the Baltic guy says, 'Let's go to my place?' I said, 'three hundred bucks a night.' 'No problem.' So they pay the bill, and split. With me. They had a Volga, a white one, brand new. I got in with them. We drove away from the club, and then one of them—bam!—sticks this mask on me with some kinda shit. Right on... like this... right on my face. And that's it. Then I came to: it was dark, I'm lying on my side, my hands are cuffed in back, it stinks of gas. I'm in the trunk. I'm lying down. There's some shit near me. The car keeps on driving and driving till it stops. They open the trunk, drag me out. We're in some woods. It's already morning. They rip my clothes off and tie me up to a birch tree. They really did! They taped my mouth before that with some kind of bandage.... So. And then—then the shit really hit the fan! They had this... this kind of case.

Ice

And there was a sort of ax in it, like a stone ax. On a crooked stick. Only it wasn't stone, it was ice. A sort of ice ax. So then, one of these bastards take this ax, swings it back, and wh-a-a-m—he whacks me right in the chest! Right here. And the other one says, 'Tell us everything.' But, I mean, my mouth was taped shut! I'm groaning, but I can't talk, can I? And those shits just stand there waiting. Then they did it again: whacked me right on the chest! And they're still saying, 'Talk.' I got all dizzy, it hurt like hell, jeez, damnit. Then they go and do it a third time. Wham-bam! And I fainted. Yeah. Then I came to in some kind of hospital. And some guy is screwing me. I tried to resist, but he pulls a knife and holds it to my throat. Right. So he gets his rocks off and starts drinking. I'm lying there—didn't have the strength to move a finger. And he says, 'Now you're gonna live here.' I say, 'What the fuck for?' He says, 'We're gonna fuck you.' I say, 'You're gonna have problems, I'm with Parvaz Sloeny.' And he says, 'I don't give a shit about your Parvaz.' So then he gets drunk fast... and I say, 'I need to go to the pot.' He calls some sort of attendant, a strong guy. He took me there. I'm walking down the hall naked, and I see his dick is stiff. I go in the john, and he follows me. 'Turn around and bend over!' So I bent over, what else could I do? He screwed me, and split for the hallway. But in the john there was this window, kinda like a double-glazed one. And no bars, that's the main thing! So I opened the window and crawled out into some woods. I took off for the woods! I ran and ran. Then I realized—it's Sparrow Hills. I went out on the road and flagged a car, and then—well, Natashka saw me come in. I could find that place again easy, that hospital."

Parvaz and Pasha looked at each other.

"And you, brother, you always being surprised—how come we come up with losses..." Parvaz stubbed out his cigarette.

He laughed. "Ice's ax—holy shit! Maybe it's twenty-four-carats gold ax? Huh? Or diamonds? Huh? You made mistake, it wasn't water ice—it was real ice. Diamond. Diamond's ax— right on the chest, on the chest. Huh? It's good. For your healthy. Good for you."

"Parvazik, I swear, it's . . ." Nikolaeva raised her hand.

"An ice's ax . . . fuckin' A!" He laughed. Rocked back and forth.

"Shit, Pash. Ice's ax! I tell you, brother, we gotta get in a different business. *Basta*. Let's go to the markets and sell oranges!"

"Parvazik, Parvazik!" Nikolaeva cried out, crossing herself.

Pasha hooked his powerful hands and twiddled his two short thumbs rapidly. He muttered in a female falsetto, "You shit-sucker, how come you're getting so disrespectful? You don't wanna work like normal people? You tired of normal life? You want things to go bad? Wanna get tough? Get slapped around?"

"I swear, Parvazik, by everything on earth, I swear!" Nikolaeva crossed herself. She kneeled down. "By my mother I swear! I swear on the memory of my dead father! Parvazik! I'm religious! I swear by the Virgin Mary!"

"You're religious? Where's your cruss?" Pasha asked.

"Those bastards tore my cross off too!"

"Your cruss, too? Such bad guys they were?" Parvaz shook his head sadly.

"They almost wasted me! I'm still shaking all over! If you don't believe me—let's go to Sparrow Hills, I'll find the place, the place, my cross will be there!"

"What cruss? What fuckin' cruss? You as bad as they come, that's what you are. Cruss!"

"If you don't believe me—call Natashka! She saw! She saw me limp in naked with the fucking bejeezus beat out of me!"

"Natash!" Pasha shouted.

Ice

Natasha appeared immediately.

"When did she get here?"

"About an hour ago."

"Naked?"

"Naked."

"Alone?"

"With some dick."

"Pash, that was the driver, he brought me back when I..."

"Shut up, cunt. And what kind of dick was he?"

"With an earring, a beard...She owed him money. And she blew him in the bathroom."

"But that was for driving me home! For the fare! I ran off without a stitch on me!"

"Shut up you moldy wad of prick cum. What did they talk about?"

"Nothing special. She blew him real fast and said, 'Come by again if you want.'"

"You little piece of shit!" Nikolaeva stared angrily at Natasha.

"Parvazik, she said she wouldn't give me any more sheets and stuff." Natasha ignored Nikolaeva.

Parvaz and Pasha looked at each other.

"Parvazik..." Nikolaeva shook her head. "Parvazik... she's lying, the bitch, I...she keeps wearing all my dresses! I did everything for her!!"

"Who's at home?" Parvaz asked Natasha.

"Lenka and Sula. They're sleeping."

"Get them in here."

Natasha left.

"Parvazik..."

Nikolaeva was kneeling. Her face was distorted. Tears welled up and splattered.

Part I

"Parvazik...I...I...told you the whole truth....I didn't lie the teensiest bit, I swear...I swear....I swear..."

She shook her head. The towel came unwound. The edge covered her face.

Parvaz stood up. He walked over to the sink. He leaned toward the trash can.

"I believe you that time. I forgive you that time. I was helping you that time."

"Parvazik....Parvazik..."

"I gave you back your passport that time."

"I swear, I swear..."

"I thought to myself that time, I thought, 'Parvaz, Alya, she is a woman.' But now I understood: Alya is not a woman."

"Parvazik...."

"Alya—is a garbage rat."

He pulled an empty champagne bottle out of the trash can. He held it squeamishly with two fingers.

"Semisweet." He pushed the table to one side with a sudden jerk. He placed the bottle on the floor in the middle of the kitchen.

Sula entered the kitchen: 23 years old, small, chestnut hair, olive skin, an unattractive face, large breasts, a slim figure, colorful robe.

Lena followed right behind: 16, tall, a good figure, a pretty face, long blond hair, pink pajamas.

They both stopped at the door. Natasha could be seen in the rear.

"Girls, I got some bad news," said Parvaz. "Very bad news."

He thrust his hand in his slim pockets. Stood up on his toes. Rocked back and forth.

"Last night Alya did something very lowlife, very bad. She behaved herself like a garbage rat. She cut off a piece in a very bad way, very lowlife. She spit on everyone. She shitted on everyone."

He was silent. Nikolaeva kneeled. She sobbed.

"Clothes off," ordered Parvaz.

Nikolaeva untied the belt of her robe. She shrugged her shoulders. The robe slipped off of her naked body. Parvaz yanked the towel off her head.

"Sit on it."

She got up. Stopped crying. She went over to the bottle. Aimed and started to sit down on the bottle with her vagina.

"Not your cunt! Sit on it with your ass! You're gonna work for me with that cunt!"

Everyone watched silently.

Nikolaeva placed her anus over the bottle and sat. She balanced carefully.

"Sit!" Parvaz shouted at her.

She sat down more freely. Cried out. She propped her hands on the floor. "No hands, cunt! No hands!" Parvaz kicked her hand and pushed down sharply on her shoulders.

"Sit!"

Nikolaeva screamed.

Mokho

6 Tverskaya Street

A dark blue Peugeot 607 drove into the courtyard. It stopped.

Borenboim sat in the backseat, reading a newspaper: 44 years old, medium height, thinning blond hair, an intelligent face, blue eyes, thin glasses in gold frames, a dark green three-piece suit. He finished reading, threw the paper on the front seat, and picked up a slender black briefcase.

"Tomorrow at 9:30."

"Okay," nodded **the chauffeur**: 52, a longish head, ash-gray hair, a big nose, fat lips, a brown jacket, a light blue turtleneck.

Borenboim got out. He headed for entrance 2. His cell phone rang in his pocket. He took it out and stopped. He put the phone to his ear.

"Yes. Well? That's what we already agreed on. Nine o'clock. There. No, let's go upstairs, the food's better and it's quieter. What? Why didn't he call me at the office? Huh? Lyosh, what is all this? ... It's like a game of telephone or something! How can

Ice

I consult in absentia? He should just come over like normal. Bonds are in good shape now all around, they've been going up for two months, there's nothing to talk about on that score. What? All right. That's it.... Oh, yeah, Lyosh, have you heard about Volodka? They brought an excavator up at night and dug out two bathhouses. That's right! Savva told me. Ask him, he knows the details. That's the scoop. Okay, that's it."

Borenboim stepped into the entryway.

The door attendant: 66 years old, thin, a wig, glasses, a grayish-pink sweater, brown skirt, and felt boots.

Borenboim gave her a nod.

He entered the elevator, took it to the third floor, and got out. He retrieved his keys and began unlocking the door.

Suddenly he felt something sticking into his back. He started to turn around, but someone grabbed him hard by the left shoulder.

"Don't look around. Straight ahead."

Borenboim looked at his door. It was made of steel. Painted gray.

"Open it," ordered a low, male voice.

Borenboim turned the key twice.

"Go in. Make a move, I beat the shit out of you."

Borenboim didn't move. The butt of a silencer was pressed against his cheek. It smelled of gun oil.

"You didn't get it? I'll count to one."

Borenboim pushed the door with his hand. He entered the dark foyer.

A hand in a brown glove extracted the key from the door. The man followed Borenboim in, immediately closing the door behind them.

"Turn on the light," he ordered.

Borenboim groped for the wide button of the switch. He

pressed it. The lights in the whole five-room apartment lit up at once. Music could be heard: Leonard Cohen's "Suzanne."

"On your knees," said the man, poking the gun between Borenboim's shoulder blades.

Borenboim lowered himself onto the beige area-rug.

"Hands behind you."

He let go of the briefcase and stretched his hands behind him. Handcuffs clicked shut over his wrists. The man began searching Borenboim's pockets.

"There's money in the desk in the study. About two thousand. That's it." Borenboim muttered.

The man went on searching him. Took his wallet out of his pocket, his cell phone, a gold Gucci lighter.

He put everything on the floor.

He opened the briefcase: business papers, two pipes in a leather case, a tin of tobacco, a collection of stories by Borges.

"Get up." The man took Borenboim by the elbow.

Borenboim stood up. He glanced at the man.

The man: 36 years old, short, strongly built, blond, blue eyes, short hair, a heavy face, a thin light-colored mustache, a steel-colored raincoat, a light gray scarf, a black leather backpack on his back.

"Forward," the man said, poking Borenboim with the gun.

Borenboim moved forward. They passed the first living room with the round aquarium and soft furniture. They entered the second. This one had low Japanese furniture. Three scrolls and a flat-screen television hung on the walls. The stereo system stood in a corner—a dark black-and-blue pyramid.

The man walked over to the pyramid. He looked at it.

"How do you turn it off?"

"There's the remote." Borenboim nodded toward a low square table. A black-and-blue remote control lay on the edge.

Ice

The man picked it up. He hit the "power" button and the music stopped.

"Sit." He pushed on Borenboim's shoulder. Sat him down on a narrow chair with a red pillow.

He put the pistol back in his pocket and removed his backpack. He opened it up. Took out a hammer and two steel mountain-climbing spikes.

"What are the walls in the building?"

"What do you mean?" Borenboim, grown pale, blinked tensely.

"Brick, concrete?"

"Brick."

The man yanked two of the scrolls off the wall. He took aim and, level with his shoulders, hammered the spike into the wall with three blows. He moved over a couple of meters, hammered in the second spike. On the same level. Then he took out a cell phone. He punched in a number.

"Everything's okay. All right. It's open."

Dibich soon entered the apartment: 32 years old, a tall, thin, broad-shouldered blond, blue-gray eyes, a cruel bony face, grayish blue coat, dark blue beret, dark blue gloves, a dark blue-and-yellow scarf, an oblong sports bag.

She looked around. Barely glanced at Borenboim.

"Good."

The man took a rope out of his pack. He cut it in half with a knife.

They lifted Borenboim. They removed his handcuffs and began to strip off his jacket.

"Can you tell me what you want—like human beings?" asked Borenboim.

"Not yet." Dibich took his right hand and tied the rope around it.

Part I

"I don't keep money at home."

"We don't want money. We're not robbers."

"Then who are you? Insurance agents?" Borenboim grinned nervously. He licked his dry lips.

"We're not insurance agents," Dibich answered seriously. "But we need you."

"For what?"

"Relax. And don't be afraid of anything."

She tied his hand to the spikes in the wall.

"Are you sadists?" Borenboim stood with his hands out to his sides.

"No." Dibich took off her coat. Under it she wore a dark blue suit with delicate stripes.

"What do you want? What the fuck do you want?" Borenboim's voice cracked.

The man taped his mouth shut. Dibich unfastened the bag. An oblong, mini refrigerator lay in it. She opened it. Took out an ice hammer.

The man unbuttoned Borenboim's vest and shirt, ripped open his undershirt. Suddenly Borenboim kicked him in the groin. The man bent over. Hissed. Fell to his knees.

"Asshole..."

Dibich waited. She leaned on the handle of the hammer.

"Goddamn..." The man frowned.

Dibich waited a bit. She looked at the scroll hanging on the wall.

"The ice is melting, Obu."

The man stood up. They approached Borenboim; he tried to kick Dibich.

"Hold his legs," she said.

The man grabbed Borenboim's knees. Held them tight. Froze.

Ice

"Speak with the heart!" Dibich swung back gracefully. The hammer made a half circle through the air and whistled. It slammed into Borenboim's chest.

Borenboim growled. Dibich placed her ear to his chest.

"Speak, speak, speak..."

Borenboim groaned. He jerked.

Dibich stepped back. Swung back. Hit him—with all her might.

The hammer cracked. Pieces of ice flew all around.

Borenboim moaned. He hung limp on the rope. His head slumped down on his chest.

Dibich pressed close.

"Speak, speak, speak..."

A sound arose in his chest.

Dibich listened carefully.

The man listened, too.

"Mo...kho..." Dibich said.

She straightened up with a satisfied look.

"His name is Mokho."

"Mokho," the man spoke. He frowned—then he smiled.

Brothers and Sisters

Borenboim opened his eyes.

He was sitting in a triangular bathtub. Warm streams of water flowed pleasantly around his body. Two naked women sat opposite him.

Ar: 31 years old, plump, blond, blue eyes, large breasts, round fleshy shoulders, a simple smiling peasant face.

Ekos: 48, small, slender, blond, blue eyes, an attentive intelligent face.

The light in the spacious bathroom was dim. Just three fat blue candles burned on the edges of the tub.

"Hello, Mokho," smiled the plump woman. "I'm Ar, your sister."

Borenboim wiped the moisture from his face. He looked around. He gazed at the candle.

"And I'm Borenboim, Boris Borisovich. My only sister, Anna Borisovna Borenboim-Vikers, died in a car accident in 1992. Near the city of Los Angeles."

"Now you will have many sisters and brothers," said Ekos.

"I doubt it." Borenboim touched the large bruise on his chest. "My mother is in the other world as well. My father is in the hospital following a stroke. The likelihood that he will gladden me with a brother or sister is about zero."

"Blood isn't the only form of brotherhood."

"Of course. There are also brothers in misfortune." Borenboim nodded. "When they put you in a common grave together alive."

"There is a brotherhood of the heart," Ar said softly.

"Is that when a person sells one of his heart valves? And has an artificial one put in its place? I've heard about that. Not a bad business."

"Mokho, your cynicism is boring." Ekos took his left hand in hers. Ar took the right one.

"I'm really a very boring person. That's why I live alone. As for cynicism—it's the only thing that saves me. Rather, that saved me. Up until March 2nd."

"Why only until March 2nd?" Ekos asked, stroking his wrist under the water.

"Because I made a bad decision on March 2nd. I decided to drive only with the driver, and not to take my bodyguard. To loan him to Rita Soloukhina. Who needed a driver. Why? She burned her hand. When? She was making fondue. With soft cheese, with—"

"Do you regret helping her?" asked Ar, stroking his other hand.

"I regret that I betrayed my cynicism for a moment."

"You felt sorry for her?"

"Not exactly... I just like her legs. And she's a good worker."

"Mokho, that's a rather cynical argument."

"No it isn't. If it were truly cynical, I wouldn't have ended up as a chump who gets taken with bare hands."

"Weren't they wearing gloves?" asked Ekos, raising her slender eyebrows. She and Ar laughed.

Part I

"Yes," said Borenboim seriously, biting his lips, "the bastards were wearing gloves. By the way, girls, where are my glasses?"

"Do you take a bath in your glasses?"

"Sometimes."

"They fog up."

"That doesn't get in the way."

"Of seeing?"

"Of thinking. Where are they?"

"Behind you."

He turned around. Next to his head on a marble stand lay his glasses and his watch. On the watch: **23:55**.

He put on his glasses. He began putting on his watch.

A naked girl walked through the open door: 12 years old, a thin angular body, hairless pubis, short strawberry blond hair, large blue eyes, a calm kind face.

"Hi, Mokho."

Borenboim looked at her darkly.

"I'm Ip."

Borenboim was about to say something, but he noticed a large white scar on the girl's chest. He looked at his bruise.

"May I put my hand on your chest?" the girl asked.

Borenboim looked at her scar, then he looked at the women. Each of them had scars in the center of her chest.

"They... you, too?" He straightened his glasses.

The women nodded, smiling.

"They hit me on the chest with the ice ax sixteen times." Ar rose to her knees. "Look."

He saw the scars of healed welts on her chest.

"I lost consciousness three times. Until my heart spoke and pronounced my true name: Ar. After that they carried me to the bathhouse, washed me, and bandaged my wounds. And then one of the brothers pressed his chest to mine. And his heart spoke with my heart. And I cried. For the first time in my life, I cried from happiness."

"I was hit seven times," Ekos spoke up. "Here ... you see ... there's one big scar and two small ones. I was completely covered with blood. They took me at the dacha. Tied me to an oak. And hit me with the ice ax. But my heart was silent. It didn't want to speak. It didn't want to awake. It wanted to sleep until death. To rot in the grave, asleep, like billions of people. . . . My skin is very delicate. The ice broke it right away. There was a lot of blood. The hammer was soaked in blood. But when my heart finally spoke and pronounced my true name—Ekos—the man who wielded the ax kissed me. On the lips. That was my first brotherly kiss."

"Kissed you?"

"Yes."

"The one who struck you?"

"The one who struck me."

"You mean the guy who set you up and knocked you out?" Borenboim laughed nervously, looking into the girl's big eyes.

"Put it that way, if you like," Ekos answered calmly.

"Your cynicism—is a kind of armor. Your only defense against sincerity. Which has always frightened you," said Ar, stroking his hand.

"As soon as that defense crumbles, not only will you be happy. You will understand what genuine freedom is," added Ekos.

The girl was still on her knees. She looked at Borenboim with a childlike, questioning look.

"Hmm, yeah ... probably ..." He had trouble tearing his eyes from the girl. "But the one who knocked me out didn't kiss me. Too bad."

Part I

He straightened his glasses decisively and, without warning, stood up. Water splashed on the women.

"Here's the thing, girls. I'm not in the mood for underwater massage right now. So we're not going to relax. I don't have the time. Call in your muscle. Let them tell me in plain Russian: how much, where, and when."

"There isn't any 'muscle' here," said Ekos, wiping her face with her palm.

"There's only us and a servant." Ar smiled.

"And the cat," said the girl. "But she's asleep in the basket right now. She's going to have kittens soon. May I put my hand on your chest?"

"What for?" asked Borenboim.

"To speak with your heart."

Borenboim got out of the bath. He took a towel and wiped his glasses. He began drying himself. He winced from the pain.

"So the muscle is outside. Got it."

"Outside?" Ekos stroked her shoulder. "There isn't anyone there either. Only birch trees."

"And snow. But it's already dirty," added the girl.

Borenboim glanced at her sullenly. He tied the towel around his thin torso.

"Where are my clothes?"

"In the bedroom."

He left the bathroom. He found himself in a spacious house with many rooms. It was richly decorated: rugs, expensive furniture, crystal chandeliers, old-master paintings. Mozart playing softly somewhere.

He walked over to a window. Pulled back the green velvet drapes. Looked out on the birch forest at night, white patches of leftover snow glowing in the half dark. A dog barked somewhere in the distance.

Ice

"What you like to chink?" It was a woman's voice, heavily accented.

He turned around.

A Thai woman stood a ways off: 42 years old, short, rather ugly, heavy, in a gray leisure suit, blue flip-flops with sequins on swarthy bare feet with lilac toenails.

"Where is the bedroom?" Borenboim looked at her feet squeamishly.

"Heyah it is." She turned around and walked off.

He followed her.

She led him to a room. Pointed with a wrinkled hand.

The bedroom was small, its walls covered in Indian linen in a yellow-green pattern. There was a mirror with a small table under it, an Indian brocade hassock, two large bronze vases in the corners, a double bed covered with an Indian bedspread. On the bed lay Borenboim's clothes in a neat pile.

He went over to them and picked them up. He checked the pockets: his wallet, keys. The cell phone was in his brief-case.

He put on his underwear and trousers. His torn undershirt had been replaced with a new one.

"Efficient..." He grinned.

He put on the undershirt, his shirt, the vest. He began tying his tie.

"May I speak to your heart?" came the sound of the girl's voice.

He looked around: Ip stood naked in the door of the bed-room. Drops of water shone on her child's body.

He knotted his tie, put on his boots and his jacket. He buttoned the two bottom buttons of his jacket.

He glanced at himself in the mirror. He walked out of the room, brushing against Ip's wet shoulder.

Part I

"What you like to chink?" The Thai woman stood in the middle of the living room.

"Chink," he grimaced. "Aspen tree juice?"

"Apsen tea what?" she said, not understanding.

"Aspen juice. Or birch milk, at least?"

"Burr-uch?" she said, her small forehead creasing.

"Forget it," Borenboim said, dismissing her with a wave of his hand. "Where's the exit?"

"Ovah heyah." The woman obediently set off.

She went into the foyer. She opened a white door into a covered entrance. She put on a large pair of felt boots with galoshes, right over her flip-flops. She wrapped a gray wool scarf around her head, opened the front door, and walked down the marble steps.

Borenboim walked out of the house. The yard, and the house itself, were brightly lit. A thick birch forest surrounded the house.

The servant walked down a wide paved road toward steel gates set in a high brick wall. The felt boots shuffled along.

Borenboim looked around. He raised the collar of his jacket and inhaled the raw night air. He followed the servant tensely.

She walked up to the gates, put the key in the lock, and turned it.

The gates slid back.

"May I talk to your heart?" said the voice behind him.

Borenboim looked back at the house. Two stories, white walls, gray roof tiling, two chimneys, decorative grates on the windows, a copper sun over the door. Against the illuminated background of the house stood a barely distinguishable, naked figure. She approached silently. In the gloom Ip's eyes seemed even larger.

Ice

There was no one in the half-dark windows of the house.

"May I?" Ip took his hand in her damp hands.

Borenboim looked through the open gates: beyond them was an empty night street. Puddles. A post. A chipped fence. A normal dacha village.

"You'll catch cold," he said.

"No," Ip answered seriously. "Please, may I? Then you can go home."

"Okay," he said with a businesslike nod. "Only make it quick."

She looked around, looked at the swings near a gazebo, and pulled him by the hand.

"Let's go over there."

Borenboim went. Then he stopped.

"No. We're not going there."

He looked at the gates.

"We'll go over there."

"All right," she said, pulling him toward the gates.

They walked outside the gates. Ip pulled Borenboim to an icy snowbank on the side of the road. He followed her. Ice crunched under his boots. Ip moved silently and easily on her bare feet.

"An angel, damnit..." Borenboim thought. He said, "Only quickly, half a minute. I'm serious."

The small Thai woman in the felt boots stood orphaned at the open gates. The suburban Moscow wind fluttered the ends of her wool scarf.

Ip led Borenboim to the snowbank. She climbed up on him. Her face was on the same level as Borenboim's face. His glasses gleamed in the dark.

The girl carefully embraced him with thin but long arms and pressed her chest to his. He didn't resist. Their cheeks touched.

Part I

"Okay." He turned slightly, moving his face away.

He looked at the illuminated house. He sang out in a low voice in English, "'Darling, stop confusing me with your'..."

Suddenly, his entire body shuddered. He was rooted to the spot.

Ip was, too.

They stood motionless.

The Thai woman watched them.

Twenty-three minutes passed. The girl released her hands. Borenboim fell weakly on the icy road. Ip slid onto the snowbank. She sniffled, pulling air through her clenched teeth, gulping for air. The streetlamp faintly lit her fragile white body.

Borenboim moved. He cried out feebly. He sat up. Moaned. Then fell again, stretching out. He breathed greedily. Opened his eyes. In the black sky, between the flocked clouds, stars twinkled dimly.

The girl got up off the snowbank, barely causing the snow to crack. She walked to the gates and went inside. A faint hum could be heard, and the gates closed.

Borenboim turned over. The snow made a crunching sound. He got up on all fours. Crawled. He pushed his hands against the earth and rose to his feet slowly. Unsteady, he straightened up.

"Ooooo...no."

He looked at the street. At the snowbank.

"Not...oh, my god..." He shook his head.

He went up to the gates. He began banging them with his dirty hands.

"Hey, hey...come on...hey..."

He listened. Everything was quiet on the other side.

Borenboim threw himself at the gates. He beat on them with his hands and feet. His glasses flew off.

Ice

He listened. Silence.

He wailed, pressing himself against the gates. He slipped to the ground and began to cry. Then he got up, took several steps back, and with his legs bent, took a running leap, kicking the gates.

He listened. No answer.

He inhaled more air and cried out as loud as he could.

An echo carried the cry all around.

A dog began to bark somewhere far away. Then another.

"Please, I beg of you.... I'm begging you!" Borenboim shouted, banging on the gates. "I'm begging you! I'm begging you! I'm begging!!! Damnit, I'm begging!!!"

His heartrending cry broke off in a wheeze. He fell silent. He licked his lips.

The moon sailed out from behind the clouds. Two dogs barked reluctantly.

"No...you can't do this..." Borenboim stepped back from the fence, his glasses crunching under his feet. He leaned over and picked them up. The left lens was cracked, but it hadn't fallen out.

He took out a handkerchief and wiped his glasses. Put them on. He threw the handkerchief in a puddle. Sniffling, he sighed. He wandered along the street.

He made it to an intersection, turned, reached another intersection, almost ran into a car. A red Niva jeep braked sharply. The puddle splashed him.

The driver opened the door: 47 years old, a thin wrinkled face, sunken cheeks, steel teeth, a leather cap.

"You outta your fuckin' mind?"

"Sorry, pal." Borenboim leaned his arms against the hood. He exhaled with exhaustion. "Take me to the police. I was attacked."

Part I

"What?" The driver screwed up his eyes nastily.

"Take me there, I'll pay..." Borenboim wiped the drops of water from his face. He dug in his inside pocket. Took out his wallet, and opened it. Held it up to the dirty headlight: all four credit cards were in place. But, as always, not a single ruble. And? Another card: a Visa Electron. In his name. He'd never had one of those. He had a Visa Gold. He turned the new card over.

"What the fuck?" he said in English.

In the corner of the card he made out a handwritten PIN code: 6969.

"Well, are we gonna stand around a long time?" the driver asked.

"Just a minute, just a minute.... Listen...what station are we at?"

"Kratovo."

"Kratovo?" Borenboim looked at the driver's hat. "Novoriazansk Highway...Take me into Moscow, pal. A hundred bucks."

"That's it. Get away from the car," the driver replied angrily.

"Or to the police...I mean, to the highway...to Riazanka!"

The driver slammed the door. The Niva zoomed off. Borenboim jumped back.

The jeep turned the corner.

Borenboim looked at the card.

"Shit...gifts of the magi...with a PIN code, no less! Nonsense, utter nonsense."

He returned the card to his wallet and stuck the wallet in his pocket. He walked down the street past the fences and darkened dachas. He shivered. He put his hands in his trouser pockets.

There was a light on in the window of one dacha.

Ice

Right next to the solid gates in the wall was a little wicket gate. Borenboim went over to it and tugged. The gate was locked.

"Anyone home?" he shouted.

A dog began barking in the house.

Borenboim waited. No one responded. He shouted again. And again. The dog barked.

He dug out a handful of wet snow and made a snowball. He threw it at the window of the porch.

The dog kept on barking. No one came out.

"'And neither wake the prince...nor the dinosaur,' as the poet said...shit." Borenboim spat. He walked along the dark street, which narrowed to a muddy path. Green and gray fences squeezed in on either side.

Borenboim walked along. A thin layer of ice crunched under his feet.

Suddenly the path broke off. Ahead was a steep descent, muddy with melted water and snow. He could dimly make out a small river. Black. Occasional chunks of ice.

"'The ball is over, the candle is out, I'll fuck you slowly'..."

Borenboim stood there for a minute. He shivered and turned around. Walked back. He came to the house with the light in the window and made a snowball. He threw it in the air. He kicked it. Suddenly, he sobbed out loud like a child, defenselessly. He ran down the street, sobbing. He screamed. Then he stopped.

"No...not like that....Oooo. Mama...! You asshole... fucking asshole...oooo! It's just...just...you asshole..."

He blew his nose in his palm. Sniffling, he walked on. Turning right, then left. He came out on a wide street. A truck was driving by.

"Hey, chief! Hey!!" Borenboim cried out hoarsely in desperation. He ran after the truck.

Part I

The truck stopped.

"Chief, give me a ride!" Borenboim yelled as he ran up.

The driver looked out drunkenly through the window: 50 years old, a crude yellowish-brown face, a rabbit-fur hat, a gray padded jacket, a cigarette.

"To Moscow."

"To Moscow," laughed the driver. "Holy shit, man, I'm going home to sleep."

"Then to the station?"

"To the station? It's right here, why drive there?"

"Right here?"

"Sure."

"How far?"

"Ten minutes on foot, for Christ's sake. Go that way..." He waved a dirty hand out the window.

Borenboim turned around. He headed down the road. The truck drove off.

Headlights appeared ahead of him. Borenboim lifted his right hand. He waved it.

The car drove by.

He arrived at the station. A white Zhiguli was parked next to a twenty-four-hour kiosk selling drinks. The driver was buying beer.

"Hey pal, listen," said Borenboim walking over to him. "I have a big problem."

The driver looked at him suspiciously: 42 years old, tall, stout, round-faced, in a brown jacket.

"What is it?"

"I...need to find a house around here...I can't remember the number..."

"Where?"

"Here...right nearby."

Ice

"How much?"

"Fifty bucks."

The driver squinted his puffy, piglike eyes.

"Money up front."

Borenboim automatically took out his wallet, then remembered.

"I don't have any cash...I'll pay, I'll pay later."

"No go," said the driver, shaking his massive head.

"Wait a minute..." Borenboim touched his cheek with a dirty hand. Then he took his watch off his left wrist.

"Here, take my watch...it's Swiss...it's worth a thousand bucks...I was attacked, you understand? Let's go, let's find them."

"I don't play other people's games," said the driver, shaking his head.

"Hey, friend, you won't come out a loser!"

"If you was attacked, go to the cops. They're right here."

"What the fuck do I need the police for?...what's the goddamn problem, it's worth a thousand bucks! Maurice Lacroix!" Borenboim shook the watch in front of him.

The driver thought a moment, then sniffed.

"No. No go."

"Jeez, shit..." Borenboim exhaled tiredly. "Why are you so fucking law abiding all of a sudden?"

He looked around. There weren't any other cars.

"All right, all right. I'll find them later. Can you at least take me into Moscow? I'll give you rubles or dollars when I get home. Whatever you want."

"Where in Moscow?"

"Tverskaya, the center. Or wait...better to Leninsky. Leninsky Prospect."

Part I

The driver squinted.

"Two hundred bucks."

"Okay."

"Money up front."

"Christ! I just told you—I was robbed, mugged! Here's the security deposit—the watch! I can show you my credit cards!"

"Watch?" The driver looked at it, as though he'd never seen it. "How much does it go for?"

"A thousand bucks."

He looked bored, then he sniffed and sighed. Took the watch. Examined it. Stuck it in his pocket.

"All right, get in."

Rat Droppings

35 Leninsky Prospect

The Zhiguli drove into a courtyard.

"Wait just a minute." Borenboim got out of the car. He walked over to the door of entrance 4. Punched in an apartment number on the intercom.

For a long time no one answered. Then a sleepy male voice asked, "Yeah?"

"Savva, it's Boris. I have a problem."

"Borya?"

"Yes, yes, open up, please."

The door beeped.

Borenboim walked in. He ran up the steps to the elevator and took it to the third floor. He approached a big door with a video camera. The door opened slowly.

Savva looked out of it: 47 years old, big, heavyset, balding, a sleepy face, wearing a dark red robe.

"Borka, what's up?" he said, squinting sleepily. "Good lord, you look like something the cat dragged in."

Part I

"Hi." Borenboim straightened his glasses. "Give me two hundred bucks to pay the taxi."

"Are you on a binge? Did someone beat you up?"

"No, no. It's a lot more serious. Come on, come on, hurry up!"

They entered a spacious foyer. Savva slid back the door of a semitransparent wardrobe. He reached in the pocket of a dark blue coat, retrieved his wallet, and took out two hundred-dollar bills. Borenboim grabbed them and rushed downstairs. But the Zhiguli wasn't there.

"Damn!" Borenboim spit on the ground. He went to the corner of the building. The car was nowhere to be seen.

"Sometimes these people are incredibly sharp." He laughed angrily. Crumpled the bills. Stuck them in his pocket. "Fuck you," he said in English.

He went back to Savva's.

"Was it enough?" Savva went into the kitchen. He turned on the light.

"Quite."

"Your glasses are broken. You're all muddy...what happened, were you attacked or something? Come on, why don't you...take this off, put on...you want something else to put on? Or want to go straight into the shower?"

"I want a drink." Borenboim took off his filthy jacket and threw it in a corner.

He sat down at a round glass table with a wide border of stainless steel.

"Maybe take a shower first? Were you beaten?"

"A drink, a drink." Borenboim rested his chin on his fist and closed his eyes. "And something strong to smoke."

"Vodka? Wine? There's...beer, too."

"Whiskey? Or don't you have any?"

Ice

"You insult me, boss." Savva left the room with a sweeping gesture. He returned with a bottle of Tullamore Dew and a pack of Bogatyr cigarettes. "Ain't nothin' stronger."

Borenboim quickly lit up. He took off his glasses. Rubbed his forehead above the eyebrows with his fingertips.

"On the rocks?" Savva took out a glass.

"Straight."

Savva poured the whiskey.

"What happened?"

Borenboim drank silently, emptying the glass.

"Hooooowever, my father in heaven!" Savva sang in a church chant. He poured some more.

Borenboim downed it. He turned the glass back and forth.

"I was attacked."

"Right." Savva sat down opposite him.

"But I don't know who they are or what they want."

"Ich bin ne undershtandt." Savva slapped his palms on his pudgy cheeks.

"Me neither. Nicht undershtandt. Yet."

"And...when?"

"Yesterday evening. I went home. Right by my door some prick stuck a pistol in my side. And then..."

Sabina entered the kitchen sleepily: 38 years old, tall and strapping, athletic.

"Zum Gottes Willen! Borya? Are you having a man's drinking bout already?" she said, speaking with a light German accent.

"Binosh, Borya has a problem."

"Did something happen?" She stroked his messy hair. She leaned over and embraced Borenboim. "Oy, you're all muddy. What's this?"

"Just...men's business." He kissed her on the cheek.

"Serious?"

"So-so. Not very."

"Do you want to eat? We have some salad."

"No, no. I don't need anything."

"Then I'll go to bed." She yawned.

"Schlaf wohl, Schätzchen." Savva embraced her.

"Trink wohl, Schweinchen." She patted him on his bald spot. She left.

Borenboim took another cigarette. He lit it from the butt of the first and continued.

"Then this guy followed me into the apartment. Handcuffed me. A woman came in. They hammered two spike things into the wall. And strung me up with a rope. They crucified me, goddamnit, on the wall, like Christ. So. And then...it was... very strange...they opened a sort of...it was like a safe...and there was this weird hammer in it...an odd, archaic sort of form...with a handle made from a branch...very crude. But the hammerhead wasn't steel or wood, it was ice. Ice. I don't know whether it was artificial or real, but it was ice. And then —picture this—the broad starts slamming my chest with this hammer. She keeps saying, 'Talk to me with your heart, tell me with your heart.' But...it was so strange! They taped my mouth shut! With packing tape. I'm mooing, she's bashing me. With all her fucking strength, man. So, this ice splinters and flies around the room. She's pounding me and talking all this bullshit. It hurt like hell, went straight through me. I've never felt pain like that. Even when my meniscus went out. So. They're banging and banging me. Then I just lost consciousness."

He took a swallow from the glass.

Savva listened.

"Sav, this all sounds like nonsense. Or a dream. But—here, take a look..." He unbuttoned his shirt to show the huge bruise on his chest. "That's not a dream."

Ice

Savva stretched out a pudgy hand. He touched it.

"Does it hurt?"

"A bit...when you press it. My head hurts. And my neck."

"Drink, Borya, relax."

"And you?"

"I...I have to go in early tomorrow, that is, today."

Borenboim emptied the glass of whiskey. Savva poured some more right away.

"But the most interesting part was after. I wake up and I'm sitting in a Jacuzzi. There are two women with me. The water's bubbling. And these women start patting me gently and telling me some nonsense about a brotherhood, that we're all brothers and sisters—talking about sincerity, frankness, and so on. It turns out that they'd been hit in the chest with the same kind of hammer, they showed me the scars. Actual scars. And they were pounded until they spoke with their hearts. They said all of us in this fucking brotherhood have our own names. Their names were Var, Mar, I don't remember. And my name—is Mokho. You get it?"

"What?"

"Mokho!"

"Mokho?" Savva looked at him with small, weak-sighted eyes.

"My name is Mokho!" Borenboim shouted and began laughing. He leaned against the back of the stainless-steel chair. Clutched at his chest. Winced. Swayed.

Savva watched him intently.

Borenboim giggled nervously. He rocked back and forth on the chair. He took a new handkerchief out of his pocket. Wiped his eyes. Blew his nose. Rubbed his chest.

"It hurts when I laugh. So you see, Savochka. But that's not all either. We're sitting there, sitting in that Jacuzzi. And suddenly a girl comes in. Really young ... probably about eleven. Blondish, with huge blue eyes. And with the same sorts of scars on her chest. She comes in and sits down next to me. I'm thinking: Okay, now I get it, they're gonna try and pin rape of a minor on my prick. But she just sits there. And suddenly I notice—they're all blue-eyed blonds. The two who bashed me with the hammer were also blue-eyed and blond. Like I am! You get it?"

Savva nodded.

"And I realized this wasn't the usual kind of attack. I say to them, 'Girls, that's enough splashing, call over your heavies. I'll ask what they want.' And they say, 'We don't have any muscle here.' And you know, I believed them. Uh-huh. And this little girl, this blue-eyed Thumbelina, she kept on saying, kept repeating the same thing over and over like she was a doll: 'Let me talk to your heart, let me ...' So I just got up. My clothes were there. I got dressed. Looked around. Nobody else around. There's no one. It turned out to be a real New Russian house, real fat cats. There's no one there, only the servant. And this naked girl. I walked out into the yard, headed for the gates. And the naked girl followed me. The servant opened the gate, no problem, so I left. There was a street, a normal dacha kind of street, this was all in Kratovo. And the naked girl—followed me out the gate! She started with the 'let me talk to your heart' stuff again. Well, I think, what the hell—go on, talk! She comes up to me, hugs me, and glues herself to my chest like a leech. And you know, Savva"—here Borenboim's voice trembled—"I ... well, you've known me twelve years. . . . I'm a grown-up guy, all business, pragmatic—shit man, I know what's what, it's hard to pull anything over on me, but ... you know ... what happened then was ..." Borenboim's delicate nostrils began to flutter. "I ... it ... I still don't know what it was ... and what the whole thing was ..."

Ice

He fell silent and blew his nose in his handkerchief. He drank a little bit.

Savva poured some more.

"And ... ?"

"Just a minute ..." Borenboim exhaled, licked his lips. He sighed and continued. "You see, she hugged me. So, big deal, she hugged me. But then suddenly I got this funny feeling ... like ... everything in me became ... sort of slower, slower. My thoughts, and everything ... everything. And I could feel my heart really clearly, fucking unbelievably clearly ... very sort of ... acute ... sharp and gentle at the same time. It's hard to explain ... but it's kind of like the body, it's just some kind of senseless meat, and there's a heart in it, and this heart ... it's ... well it's not meat at all, but something else. And it started beating really unevenly, like I had an arrhythmia ... or something. And this little girl ... this ... she froze and didn't move. And suddenly I could feel her with my heart. Just like I could feel someone's hand with my hand. And her heart started talking to mine. But not in words, in ... sort of like ... spurts or waves or something ... and my heart was trying to answer. In the same kind of bursts ..."

He poured himself some more whiskey and drank it. Took a cigarette from the pack and rolled it in his hands. Sighed. Put it back in the box.

"And when it started, everything all around, everything, the whole world, it kind of stopped. And everything was sort of ... so good and clear, right away ... so good ..." He sobbed. "I've ... never, like that ... never, never ever ... felt ... anything like ... that."

Borenboim let out a sob. He pressed his hand against his mouth. A wave of silent sobs rolled over him.

Part I

"Listen, maybe, you..." Savva began to get up.

"No, no...no..." Borenboim shook his head. "Just sit there.... Sit awhile..."

Savva sat back down.

Raising his glasses, Borenboim rubbed his eyes. He sniffed.

"And that's not all. When it was all over, she went back into the house. I...was...I stood there and knocked. Banged on the gates. I really wanted her to be with me again. Not her. But her heart. So. But no one opened them. Those are the rules of the game, damnit. So I left. I walked to the station. Hired some stiff to drive me in. Oh! And when I reached in my pocket, I found this in my wallet..."

Borenboim took out his wallet. He extracted the Visa Electron card. Threw it on the table.

Savva picked it up.

"And now, that's it..." Borenboim drank some whiskey. "I have a premonition that this isn't just a piece of plastic. There's something there. You see, in the corner there?"

"A PIN code?"

"What else could it be?"

"It could be." Savva gave him back the card.

"Yugrabank. Do you know it?"

"I've heard of it. A Gazprom outfit. In Yugorsk. Kind of far away."

"Do you know anyone there?"

"No. But that's not a problem—to find someone. But what exactly do you want to know?"

"Well, like who deposited it? I'm sure there's money in the account."

"Why guess? Wait till the morning. Listen, those...the ones that hammered you?"

"I didn't see them again."

Savva sat there quietly. He chewed on his lip. Touched his small nose.

"Borya, how could they stick a gun in your side if you've got a bodyguard?"

"That's the whole thing! Yesterday I gave my bodyguard to an employee. She burned her hand and can't drive. So I, well... helped a girl out by giving her my guy. Fucking human-loving asshole that I am..."

Savva nodded.

"Well, what do you think?"

"Right now—nothing."

"Why?"

"Listen, Bor. But... just don't get mad. Are you... snorting very much?"

"Not a speck in the last month."

"You sure?"

"I swear."

Savva frowned.

"Well, what should I do?" Borenboim took a cigarette. Lit it.

Savva shrugged his meaty shoulder.

"Call Platov. Or your own guys."

Tipsy by now, Borenboim grinned.

"That's exactly what I'll do! In about three hours. But I want to understand....I want to hear your opinion. What do you think about all this?"

Savva didn't reply. He looked at Borenboim's pointed beard. Beads of sweat appeared on it.

"Sav?"

"Yes."

"What do you think about this?"

Part I

"Well, somehow...nothing."

"Why?"

"I don't know."

"What do you mean, you don't believe me?"

"I believe, I believe," said Savva, nodding his head. "Bor, I believe anything and everything nowadays. Three days ago the health inspectors showed up at the bank. In the basement next door they were spraying for cockroaches. And they did us at the same time, too. They began with the cockroaches, and then found mountains of rat droppings. And you know where? In the ventilation system. Mountains of it, huge deposits. Fucking unbelievable! And the most incredible thing was that no one had ever heard any rats. Not the employees, not the guards, not the cleaning ladies. And there wasn't anything for them to eat in our place. Why would they be shitting so much? Or what— they're eating in one place and crawling into my bank to take a shit? A real mystery! I thought and thought about it. I called a meeting of the directors' council and said, 'Gentlemen, it seems we have a provocation on our hands. There's no goddamn rats anywhere! But there's shit. Therefore, someone put it there on purpose. Is this a hint? About what?' No one said anything. You know that we only recently managed to get Zhorik off our case. And then Grisha Sinaiko, he's a smart guy, he spent four years at Creditanstalt, he looked at me with this intense look and said, 'Savva, this is not a hint. If it was human shit—that would be an obvious hint. Then it'd be time to sweat. But rat droppings—aren't a hint. They're just r-a-t droppings! And if there's rat shit, then that means that rats were shitting. Ordinary Moscow rats. Believe my experience.' You know what, Bor? I thought about it. And I believed him."

Borenboim stood up sharply. He picked up his jacket from the floor. Went into the foyer.

Ice

"Give me some rubles for a taxi."

Savva rose with difficulty. He followed him.

"Listen, Bor," he said, placing a heavy hand on Borenboim's thin shoulder, "I really recommend that you—"

"Give me some rubles for a taxi!" Borenboim interrupted.

"Bor. If you want, I'll call Mishkarik at the FSB, okay? They'll definitely be able to tell you something—"

"Give me some rubles for a taxi!"

Savva sighed. He disappeared into darkened rooms.

Borenboim put on his jacket, and hit the wall with his palm. He clenched his fists and exhaled with a hiss.

Savva returned with a packet of hundred-ruble notes.

"Put my coat on. You'll be cold like that."

Borenboim pulled two hundred-ruble notes out of the pack. He fished the two crumpled hundred-dollar bills out of his pocket and forced them into Savva's hand.

"Thanks a lot, honey child," he said in English.

He opened the door. He left.

Rat Heart

6 Tverskaya Street

Borenboim unlocked the door of his apartment. He entered and turned on the light.

The music started up: Leonard Cohen as usual.

Borenboim stood at the half-open door.

He looked into the apartment. Everything was as it had been.

He closed the door. He walked through the rooms, looked into the bathroom, the kitchen.

No one.

His briefcase, cell phone, and lighter were lying on the low table in the Japanese living room.

He looked at the walls. All three scrolls hung in their previous places. He walked over to them. He moved the left scroll aside. The hole from the spike had been carefully filled. The water-based paint hadn't dried yet. The second hole under the other scroll had also been repaired.

"Holy shit..." Borenboim muttered, shaking his head. "No-waste production. This is a serious outfit."

Ice

He chuckled.

He opened his briefcase and leafed through the papers: everything was in place. He got out his pipe. He filled it with tobacco, lit up, and began to smoke. He walked over to the aquarium shaped like a half circle. He whistled. The fish grew excited. They swam up to the surface.

He retrieved a covered Chinese cup from a niche in the wall. Opened it. The cup contained fish food. He tapped bits of food into the aquarium.

"My poor starving..."

The fish gobbled the food.

Borenboim closed the cup. He put it back in the niche.

He turned off the music. Taking a bottle of Famous Grouse whiskey from the Japanese cabinet, he poured half a glass and drank it. He sat down. He picked up his cell phone, put it back on the table, stood up, and went to the kitchen. He opened the refrigerator.

It was empty except for four identical containers of salad on the second shelf. Wrapped in plastic.

He took out a container of beet salad. He put it on the table, got out a spoon, and sat down. He began to devour the salad.

He ate everything.

He put the empty container in the sink and wiped his lips with a napkin.

Back into the Japanese room: he picked up the telephone and punched in a number. He listened, then changed his mind.

"Shut the fuck up!" he exclaimed in English.

He tossed the phone on the table. Poured some more whiskey. Drank. He knocked the ashes out of the extinguished pipe and started to fill it again. He stopped. Got up. Walked back to the aquarium.

"'Darling, stop confusing me with your wishful thinking...'" he sang. He sighed. His thin lips contorted in a sad grimace. He tapped the thick glass.

The fish swam toward him.

He went into the bathroom and turned on the tap. He placed the glass of whiskey on the edge of the tub. Undressed. Looked at himself in the mirror. Touched the bruise on his chest.

"Speak, heart...speak, mitral valve....Bastards!"

He laughed a worn-out laugh.

He got into the bath.

He drank the rest of the whiskey.

He turned off the water.

He leaned his head back against the cold depression of the headrest.

He sighed in relief.

He slept.

He dreamed a dream: he was a teenager, at his stepfather's dacha in Sosenki, standing at the gate and looking out at the street. Vitka, Karas, and Gera were walking down the street toward him. They were supposed to go together to the Salarevsky dump. The guys were approaching. They held sticks for poking around in the garbage. His stick stood next to the fence. He picked it up and walked toward them. They walked quickly and happily down the street. It was early in the morning, midsummer, the weather dry and cool. He was enjoying himself and his step was light. They came to the dump. It was enormous, stretching to the very horizon.

"We're going to go through and turn it up from south to north," said Karas. "There are turbines in there."

They picked through the garbage. Borenboim sank in to his

waist. Sank even lower. There was an underground vault. An intolerable stench. The heavy, sticky trash quivered like quicksand. Borenboim cried out in fear.

"Don't be chicken," Gera giggled, grabbing him by the feet.

"These are positive catacombs," Vitka explained. "This is where the parent accelerators live."

People walked through the catacombs. Odd, fearsome machines passed by.

"I have to find the computer dough, then at home I'll make traveling boots for super-powered diesel locomotives," Borenboim thought to himself. He kept picking through the trash.

All sorts of objects turned up. Suddenly Karas and Gera broke through a wall with their sticks. A gloomy din emerged from the opening. "It's the turbines," Borenboim realized. He looked into the opening and saw a huge cave with bluish turbines rising in the center. They produced a dismal roar: smoke spread from them, stinging the eyes.

"Let's get out of here before we're squashed!" Vitka advised.

They ran along a twisting path, getting bogged down in sticky, squelching garbage. Borenboim bumped into a piece of computer dough. A silvery-lilac color, it smelled like gasoline and lilac. He pulled the dough from the heaps of trash.

"Mold it in the form, or else it will come unsoldered," said Karas.

Suddenly, a rat jumped out of the computer dough.

"Bastard, he ate the computer program!" Vitka shouted.

Vitka, Gera, and Karas began to beat the rat with their sticks. Its gray body shook with the blows, and it squeaked pitifully. Borenboim looked at the rat. He felt its palpitating heart. It was a tender little bundle which sent waves of the subtlest vibrations across the whole world, sublime waves of love. And the most remarkable thing—they were in no way connected to the death throes and horror of the dying rat, they existed all by themselves. They penetrated Borenboim's body. His heart contracted from a powerful attack of tenderness, joy, and delight. He pushed the guys aside and lifted the bloody rat. He bent over it and sobbed. The rat's moist eyes closed. Its heart quivered, sending its last, farewell waves of love. Borenboim caught them with his heart. He understood the language of hearts. It was untranslatable. Sublime. Borenboim sobbed from happiness and pity. The rat's heart shuddered for the last time. And stopped: FOREVER! The horror of losing this tiny heart seized Borenboim. He pressed the bloody little body to his chest. He sobbed aloud, as he had in childhood. Sobbed helplessly on and on.

Borenboim woke up.

His naked body shuddered in the water. Tears poured down his cheeks. He lifted his head with great difficulty and winced: his chest and neck hurt even more. He sat up in the cold water. Wiped away his tears. Sighed. He looked at his watch: he had slept for one hour and twenty-one minutes.

"Ooo la la ... " He got out of the bath painfully and pulled a towel from the snake-shaped towel hanger. He wiped himself off, hung the towel in place, and turned toward the mirror. He moved closer, studying his blue eyes. The black pupils reminded him of the rat's moist eyes.

"It ate computer dough..." he muttered. A sob escaped him. "It ate ... ate and ate.... The bastards..."

His face was distorted by a spasm. Tears burst from his eyes.

Smithereens

The group Leningrad was wrapping up its concert. The singer, Shnur, sang:

> In the black-black city on black-black nights,
> Doctors and ambulances blackened by the lights,
> Drive merrily along while they sing a song of lies,
> In the black-black city, people die like flies!
> But I don't give a flying...fuck!...

Shnur sent the microphone into the audience. About three hundred young people were standing around and dancing. The audience shouted: "...I'm made—of meat!!!"

Everyone jumped and sang.

Lapin jumped and sang with them.

Ilona, nearby, was doing the same: 17 years old, tall, thin, with a lively laughing face, leather pants, platform shoes, a white top.

Part I

"Farewell, Point!" Shnur shouted. The audience whistled.

"Awesome, right?" Ilona nudged Lapin in the side with her fist.

"Let's get drinks before everyone lines up!" he shouted in her ear.

"Okay."

They went over to the bar.

"A bottle of champagne," said Lapin, handing the barman some money.

The barman opened the bottle and gave him two glasses.

"Let's go over there, in the corner." Ilona tugged on Lapin.

In the corner, the edge of a rough, wooden table was free. They sat down at the table. Lapin poured the champagne into the glasses. Two guys and a girl sat nearby.

"Well, then, master?" Ilona raised her glass. "What should we drink to?"

"Let's drink—to being together." They clinked glasses.

"Maybe to Shnur?"

"Let's drink to Shnur."

They drank.

"Is this the first time you've heard them?" Ilona asked, lighting a cigarette.

"Live—yeah."

"A recording's not the same. You don't get the high. Wow!" she wailed. "Awesome, man, awesome. Aargh...Wish I had a joint."

"You want one?" asked Lapin, emptying his glass.

"Uh-huh. I always want weed when I'm having a blast."

"Well...can't...we get some here?" Lapin looked around.

"It's only the second time I've been here. I don't know anyone."

"It's my first time."

Ice

"Really? So you really came just for Leningrad, right?"

"Uh-huh. I found out by accident that they had a gig here. So I came."

Lapin lit a cigarette.

"Not a bad place, is it?" said Ilona, looking around. She was quickly getting tipsy.

"It's a big space." Lapin rubbed his chest.

"Really cool, huh? Damn, I really want some weed. Listen, you have any dough?"

"Sort of."

"Let's go to this place I know. They've always got it. Lots of things. Only it's not close."

"Where?"

"In Sokolniki."

"What is it?"

"Just a rented crash pad. Some friends live there."

"Well, why not, let's go."

"Fare thee well to our fair... Olympic Teddy Bear."

Ilona stood up and stretched. Lapin took the half-drunk bottle. They headed for the exit through the dancing crowd.

They got their coats at the coat check and stepped out into a dimly lit passageway with walls welded together from sheets of steel. Occasional figures appeared in the distance.

"Whoa! It's cold..." Ilona shivered. Lapin embraced her. He pulled her to him roughly and awkwardly.

"Cuddles?" Ilona asked.

Lapin began to kiss her thin, cold lips. She responded. With his free hand he squeezed her breast. The bottle slipped out of his other hand. It shattered at their feet.

"Damn..." Lapin flinched.

"Ouch!" Ilona looked down.

Lapin laughed.

Part I

"Glass in the plural...not just smashed, but smashed to smithereens—Russian style."

"Out on the town, are we?" some guy asked. He was squatting next to the wall. Smoking.

"Let's get another one, okay?" Lapin breathed into her ear.

"*Basta!*" Ilona smashed the shards with her dark blue platform shoe. The glass crunched.

She took Lapin by the hand. Pulled him toward the exit.

"Champagne is—great. But there'll be stronger stuff there."

Lapin held her back.

"Wait..."

"What is it?" She stopped.

He embraced her. He froze, holding her to him. They stood for a minute.

"It's cold." Ilona giggled quietly.

"Wait..." Lapin's voice trembled.

She grew quiet. Lapin pressed against her and shuddered.

"What's wrong?" She licked a tear from his cheek.

"Just..." he whispered.

"What is it, are you crashing?"

He shook his head. Sniffed.

"It's just...things are fucked up."

"Then let's go." She took his hand decisively.

Liubka

23:59
Andrei's apartment
17 Kutuzov Prospect

A bedroom with pale lilac walls. A wide, low bed. Muted music. Dim lighting.

A naked Nikolaeva was sitting on top of a naked Andrei. She rocked rhythmically. Nikolaeva's upper chest was wrapped in a silk scarf, with both of her breasts left free.

Andrei was smoking: 52 years old, heavy, round-faced, bald spots, a hairy chest, a tattooed shoulder, and short pudgy fingers.

"Don't rush, don't rush..." he murmured.

"The boss is king," said Nikolaeva, slowing down.

"You have fabulous breasts."

"Like them?"

"You didn't do anything to them?"

"They're all mine. Ooooo...what a sweet dick..."

"Does it reach your guts?"

"Oof...and how...oy...Too bad we can't do it in the bottom today..."

Part I

"Why?"

"A boo-boo."

"Hemorrhoids?"

"Uh, not exactly...oy...the, uh, consequences...oy...of an accident..."

"How did you manage to aim like that? To get run over by a car...oy, shit...that was smart...I look both ways four times before I...oy...cross...not so fast..."

"Ohhhh...wow...great...ooo...Andriusha...ooooo... aaahhh!"

"Not so fast, I said."

Nikolaeva held her hips. She lowered her head. Shook her hair. Cautiously moved her rear end. Then some more. And some more.

Andrei frowned.

"Oy, oh, shit...I'm already...Alka, you bitch...I said... don't...rush! It's gonna spray! No! Push, push right there! Damnit! Get off! Come on, why the fuck did you go and ruin it like that?"

Nikolaeva jumped off him immediately. With one hand she grabbed his condom-covered penis. With the other she pushed on the space between his anus and his testicles.

"I'm sorry, Sash...I mean...Andriush..."

"Harder, push harder!"

She pushed harder. He moaned. Jerked his head.

"Now distract me goddamnit..."

"What, how Andriushenka?"

"Come on, tell me something..."

"What?"

"Umm, something funny...come on, come on, come on..."

"Like a joke?"

"Something...oy, shit...come on, come on..."

Ice

"I can't remember jokes..." Nikolaeva scratched her shaved pubis. "Oh, I know! Here's an unfuckingbelievable story Sula told me. When she was fifteen, some guy took her home with him, wanted to screw her, but she wouldn't let him, like—she was a virgin and all that stuff. The guy messes around with her in bed, spends all this time with her, like almost two hours, his dick is smoking, and she still won't spread her legs. Then he says, 'Let me screw you in the butt.' 'Well, okay,' she says. She sticks it up for him. As soon as he gets it in he comes—couldn't wait anymore. And like there was so much fucking sperm! It just poured inside like they were giving her an enema. He rolls off her. And Sula, can you believe it? She gets up, squats, and takes a dump right on his Persian rug! While he's sitting there with his mouth open, can't believe his eyes, she gets dressed and off she goes!"

"Oy, shit...Alya, come on...I can't stand it anymore anyway..."

"Right away, hon," she said, and sat on him. She directed his penis into her vagina. Began moving quickly. Took his balls in her hand.

"Yeah...yeah...that's it..." Andrei murmured. He froze. Squeezed his fists. Cried out. Began pounding Nikolaeva's sides with his fists. "Yes, yes, yes!"

She covered herself with her arms. Moved up and down. Squealed.

Andrei stopped hitting. His arms fell helplessly on the bed.

"Oh, shit..." He reached for the ashtray. Picked up a stubbed-out cigarette.

"How was it?" Nikolaeva licked his pink, hairy nipple.

"Oy..." He stretched. "Like sparks were coming out of my eyes..."

"You're so great..." She stroked his shoulder. "So round...

like Winnie the Pooh. And your penis is awesome. I come right away."

He grinned. "Cut the bullshit. Pour some wine."

"Seel vous play." She reached over. Pulled a bottle of white wine, Pinot Grigio, out of a bucket of ice. Poured two glasses.

Andrei took his wine, lifted his sweaty head, and drained the glass. He lay back on the bed.

"Jeez... you're one cool babe."

"Pleased to hear it."

He looked at the empty pack of cigarettes.

"Run into the kitchen, there's some cigarettes on the shelf."

"Where?"

"Next to the vent. There's a glass shelf."

"Andriush, can I take a shower first?"

"Sure. I'll go and get them."

Nikolaeva got up. She held her vagina with her palm. She ran into the bathroom. In the bath she stood under the shower. Turned on the water. Rinsed her whole body quickly. Washed her vagina for a long time. Turned off the water. Shouted: "Petya! Sheesh, I mean... Andriush! May I take a bath?"

"You may..." came the reply from the bedroom.

Nikolaeva sat down in the cold tub. She turned on the faucet, took some shampoo from the shelf, and squirted it into the stream of water. Bubbles spread across the bath. She started singing. The water rose to her armpits. Nikolaeva turned off the water. She drew her knees up and slept.

She dreamed about Liubka Kobzeva, who'd had her throat cut in the Solnechny Motel. They were in the kitchen of that very apartment on Sretenka in Moscow that Liubka rented and shared with Billy-Goat-Gruff. Nikolaeva was sitting at the window, smoking. Outside the window it was winter, snow was falling. It was cold in the kitchen. Nikolaeva was dressed lightly, for summer, though she wore high gray felt boots. But Liubka was barefoot and wearing a blue robe. She was fussing about the stove and making her favorite dish, Uzbek meat pies.

"What a stupid idiot I am, really," she muttered, kneading the dough. "I went and let myself be stabbed! I mean, really..."

"Did it hurt?" Nikolaeva asked.

"No, not too much. It was just scary when that SOB came at me with a knife. I completely froze. I should have jumped out the window, but me, idiot that I am, I just stared at him. He goes and gives it to me, first in the stomach, I didn't even notice, and then in the neck... and then it was like, there's blood all over everything, tons of it....Hey, Al, where did I put the pepper?"

Nikolaeva looks at the table. All the objects can be seen quite clearly: two plates, two forks, a knife with a cracked handle, a grater, a salt cellar, a rolling pin, a packet of flour, nine round medallions of dough. But no pepper shaker.

"That's always the way it goes when you need something— it disappears into thin air," said Liubka, continuing to look around. She bent down. Looked under the table.

Through the open collar of her robe Nikolaeva saw the crudely sewn incision reaching from her neck to her pubis.

"There it is..." Liubka said.

Nikolaeva saw the pepper shaker under the table. She leaned over, picked it up, and handed it to Liubka. Suddenly, she felt quite intensely that Liubka's HEART WASN'T BEAT-ING in her chest. Liubka was talking, muttering, moving around, but her heart was motionless. It was standing still, like a broken alarm clock. Nikolaeva was seized by a terrible

Part I

sorrow. Not because of Liubka being dead but from this stopped heart. She felt an overwhelming pity that Liubka's heart was dead and would NEVER beat again. She realized that she was about to cry.

"Liub...do you...put onion in the stuffing?" she asked with incredible difficulty, standing up.

"Why the hell do you need it when there's garlic?" Liubka looked at her attentively with dead eyes.

Nikolaeva began to cry.

"What's wrong?" Liubka asked.

"I need to piss," Nikolaeva's disobedient lips babbled.

"Piss here," said Liubka with a smile.

Sobs overwhelmed Nikolaeva. She cried for the GREAT LOSS.

"Liub...ka...Liub...ka..." escaped her lips.

She grabbed Liubka, pressed her to her breast. Liubka moved her aside with her cold hands, covered in flour and dough.

"What's wrong with you?"

Liubka's icy chest was HEARTLESS. Nikolaeva sobbed. She understood that this could NEVER be fixed. She heard the beat of her own heart. It was alive, warm, and TERRIBLY dear to her. This feeling only made things even more painful and bitter. She suddenly understood how SIMPLE it was to be dead. Horror and grief filled her. Warm urine flowed down her legs.

Nikolaeva woke up.

Her face was covered in tears. Her mascara was running.

Andrei stood next to the bath in a red-and-white terry-cloth robe.

"What's wrong?" he asked impatiently.

Ice

"Huh?" She sniffled. She began to sob again.

"What happened?" he asked, frowning sleepily.

"I...ummm..." She cried. "I dreamed about my girl-friend...her...she...was murdered six months ago..."

"Who did it?"

"Oh...some guys from the market...some Azeris..."

"Ah..." he said, scratching his chest. "Listen, I want to get some sleep. I have an important meeting tomorrow. The money is on the kitchen table..."

He left.

Nikolaeva wiped away her tears. She got out of the bath. She glanced at the mirror.

"Jesus..."

She spent a long time washing her face. She dried off, wrapped herself in a big towel, and left the bathroom.

The apartment was dark. The sound of Andrei snoring came from the bedroom.

Nikolaeva crossed the bedroom on tiptoe. She found her things and went into the kitchen. The light on the vent above the stove was the only one on. Two hundred dollars lay on the table.

Nikolaeva got dressed. She put the money away in her wallet. She drank a glass of apple juice. She went into the foyer, put on her overcoat, and left the apartment, carefully closing the door behind her.

Upper Lip

02:02
Komar and Vika's Rented Apartment
1 Olenii Bank

"Work your fist a little." Komar tied a tourniquet around Lapin's forearm.

"There's nothing to work—you can see everything," laughed Vika. "Wish I had veins like that!"

"Komar, you fucker, you could do me first!" said Ilona, watching angrily.

"Guests first, jeezus fucking Christ. Specially 'cause he's bankrolling. . . ." Komar inserted the needle into the vein. "Shit, I ain't seen such spotless ropes in a blue moon."

"So Ilona, did you really see Leningrad?" asked Vika.

"Uh-huh . . ." Ilona looked at Lapin's arm.

"Was it hot?"

"Uh-huh."

"What did they play? Old stuff?"

"Old stuff! Old! Old!" said Ilona, shaking her wrists crossly.

Komar pulled the plunger toward himself: 27 years old,

shaved head, big ears, skinny, stooped, long arms, sharp facial features, wearing a torn blue T-shirt and wide black pants.

Blood appeared in the hypodermic. Komar tugged on the end of the tourniquet. He smoothly injected the contents of the hypodermic into Lapin's vein.

"There we go."

Vika held out a piece of cotton: 18 years old, small, dark, plump, long-haired, purple polyester pants, a light blue top.

Lapin pressed the cotton to his vein. He bent his elbow. Flopped back on a filthy pillow.

"Oh, shit . . ."

"Well?" said Komar, smiling.

"Yeah . . ." said Lapin and smiled, parting his lips with difficulty. He looked at the rusty water stains on the ceiling.

"You fucker, are you gonna hit me or not for heaven's sake, Komar?" Ilona shouted.

"No problem, Madam." Komar unwrapped a new hypodermic.

Vika poured the white powder from the packet into a tablespoon, added water, and boiled the spoon over a candle. Komar sucked the semitransparent liquid in the spoon into the hypodermic.

Ilona tied the tourniquet around her upper arm herself. She sat down opposite Komar. Stretched out her arm. In the bend a few tracks could be seen.

"Ilon, I didn't get it, did they just play old stuff?" asked Vika, lighting up a cigarette.

"No, not only," Ilona answered irritably, pumping her fist.

" 'When summertime comes, we'll go to the dacha and leave the town / A shovel in hand, we'll mess around, mess around. . . .' They did that one?"

"Yeah, yeah, yeah," Ilona muttered crossly.

Part I

"I really like the one they do: 'Ta-ta-ta...some people shoot up / me, I do booze / but I could speed up, after a snooze...'"

Komar took his time and found a place for the needle.

"Hmm, it's good you don't overdo things, sweetheart."

"You think I'm an idiot or something?" Ilona laughed nervously.

"Women! Go figure!" The needle entered her vein.

Lapin smiled. Stretched. Rolled his shoulders around. "Yeah...now...this is...totally different..."

"What's different?" asked Vika. "Speedball? Of course it is. It's heavier than plain old smack."

"Heavier. But I don't like all this bullshitting: speedball, speedball, and they haven't really tried a fuckin' thing.... There are so...so many...ummm...mediocre people around here...hacks...no talent..."

"Why?" asked Vika with a happy smile.

"Because every asshole wants to be smarter than he really is. Smarter and more authoritative. Everybody's all buzzed about their authority, that's all they think about. As if a human being's main purpose on earth were to achieve a position in society at any price, even at the price of other people's suffering."

Vika and Komar exchanged glances.

"Yeah. Well, one thing's for sure, if we got a lot of anything, it's suffering...leaking right outta our assholes..." Smiling, Komar injected the dose into Ilona's vein.

"Oy..." She closed her eyes. Bent her arm at the elbow. Coughed.

Vika stretched her arm out for Komar. It was riddled with needle tracks. "There's still another little place here."

"Just don't breathe on my forehead."

"Sorry, Kom."

Ilona stretched.

Ice

"Awesome!"

She kissed Lapin. He embraced her awkwardly.

"Only don't go too fast, Kom." Vika looked at the needle.

"Are my pupils big?" Ilona leaned over Lapin.

"Yes," he replied seriously.

"Are they pretty? What color?"

"Something...like...you know...." Sweating, Lapin looked at them carefully, straight on. "Here's the thing...it's those balls...you know, those Chinese equilibrium balls...you have to roll them around in one hand, they're made of different precious stones, like, maybe jasper or something, and when a ball like that...the yin or the yang, I think it's the yin...so...and one ball lies there, that is, there's this energy, this bioenergy that flows from it, and there's also all these electrical accumulations, and all this stuff together...the energy of the stones, too, we hardly know anything about the energy of stones, I mean stones are so fucking ancient...but you know they used to be soft like sponges, and then over time they petrified and became real stones and there's all this...this unfuckingbelievable information stored up in them, so it's kind of like a super memory chip, there's all this stuff written down there, so mucking fuch that....I mean, so fucking much of everything, about everything, different events, people, everything that happened.... It's all in stones, man.... And who needs computers, you just have to know how to use the stones, find the right approach... a normal, competent approach...and then the shit'll hit the fan, I mean, human beings will become the fucking lords of the world."

"Your upper lip is really incredible," said Ilona happily, touching his lip with her finger.

Sand

Warehouse of the Cargo Trading Company
2 Novoyasenevsky Prospect

A large semi-circular hangar, a multitude of boxes and pack-ages containing food products. A one-meter-square sheet of thick plywood lay on top of four cases of canned vegetables. Around the plywood several people sat and smoked.

Volodya Straw: 32 years old, medium height, a thickset body, brown hair, a sullen disposition, a motionless face with a small broken nose, a short sheepskin jacket.

Dato: 52, pudgy, small, bald, with a round face in a perma-nent grin, an unbuttoned white raincoat, delicately knit white sweater, beige silk shirt with a high collar, white leather trousers, a gold Tissot watch, a gold bracelet, and a gold ring with a ruby.

Khmelev: 42, medium height, thin, dark brown hair, a thin narrow calmly worried face, steel-gray jacket, a dark blue three-piece suit, white shirt, and a light-blue-and-red tie.

Khmelev's cell phone rang.

Ice

"Yes," he said, putting it to his ear.

"They're here," a voice informed him.

"How many?"

"Six . . . seven guys in two cars."

"Okay, just let Blindeye and a couple of bodyguards through."

"Got it."

Dato tossed a cigarette butt on the cement floor. Crushed it with his black patent-leather boot.

"Two of them won't be able to carry it in."

"That's their problem," muttered Khmelev.

"So, like usual?" said Straw, sniffing as he stood up.

"Like usual, Vova," said Dato, slapping his fleshy knees.

The door opened.

Gasan Blindeye entered the hangar: 43 years old, short, puny, swarthy, balding, hook-nosed, wearing a black leather coat. Two strongmen carrying a heavy metal coffer followed him in with some difficulty.

Dato stood up. He stepped forward to greet Gasan. They embraced, touched cheeks twice.

"Hello, Dato."

"Hello, my friend."

The two guys set the coffer on the floor.

"Put it here," Dato pointed to the plywood with his small, pudgy hand.

The two lifted the coffer. They carried it over and set it down. The plywood cracked, but held.

"Sit down, my friend." Dato nodded.

Straw moved a case of macaroni toward Blindeye.

"Dato, let everyone leave us alone." Blindeye unbuttoned his coat.

"Why?"

"We need to talk."

"These are my people, Gasan. You know them."

"I know them, Dato. But let them leave."

Dato glanced at Khmelev. Khmelev nodded.

"All right then, my friend. We'll do it the way you say. Go on, go out for some air."

Khmelev, Straw, and the other two went out. Gasan sat down on the box. He rubbed his cheeks in exhaustion. Dato waited silently.

"I've changed my mind, Dato," Gasan said.

"I don't understand. What did you change your mind about?"

"I'm not selling."

"Why?"

Gasan clenched his hands. He touched the tip of his sharp, crooked nose with his thumbs.

"Just because . . . I'm not selling. That's all."

Dato chuckled louder than usual.

"I don't understand you, Gasan. Why aren't you selling? The price doesn't suit you? You want more?"

"No. The price is the old one. It always suited me."

"So then what's the deal?"

"No deal. Just—I don't want to."

Dato looked at him attentively.

"What's with you, brother. Are you sick or something? You got problems?"

"I'm not sick, brother. And I don't have problems. But I'm not selling the product."

Dato didn't say anything. He took out a gold cigarette case, removed a cigarette, and took his time lighting it. He walked around, then turned to Gasan.

"But why did you bring the product if you don't want to sell?"

"To show you, brother."

Ice

"I saw it before. More than once."

"You take another look at it. Look carefully."

Gasan stood up. He opened the locks on the coffer and pushed back the metal lid. Under it was a white plastic lid. Gasan pulled it. It opened. Under it was a refrigerator—completely filled with sand.

Dato froze for a minute with the cigarette in his lips.

"Now you understand, Dato, why Gasan does not want to sell you the product."

"Now I understand."

Gasan went up close to him.

"We have rats, brother. Fat goddamn rats."

"Does Tractor know?" asked Dato.

"Not yet. Why the hell should he know?"

Dato stuck his hand in the sand, felt around, scooped up a handful. He threw it forcefully on the floor:

"Crooks!"

"But it's definitely not the ice cutters."

"Then who? Your guys?"

"I know my own. And they know me. I would cut off my hand, that's how I trust them."

"Hand . . . foot . . ." Dato spat angrily. "Your own guys could also turn into rats. Fuckers! Crooks! Gasan, look for them yourself. I'm not going to those blonds. I'll give the money back. And that's it."

"Just wait a minute, brother."

"What's to wait? One of your people skimmed some off the top, it's your problem. You go talk to them."

"Don't get all overheated, my friend. It's not my problem. It's our problem."

"No fucking way! They pinched it from your place, what've I got to do with it? I'm not involved."

"You're involved because the rat lives in your house."

"What? What fucking rat?"

"A fat one. And it sleeps in your house. It eats your bread."

Dato stared hard at him.

Gasan rummaged in his pockets. He took out a round wooden tobacco box, opened it. It contained cocaine. He shook a little onto the lid. He took out an ivory straw and a plastic card.

"Let's have a snort, brother. I haven't slept for three days."

"And what about...the rat? In my place? You ready to answer for what you're saying?"

"I'll answer."

"So who is it?"

"Don't rush."

"What the fuck do you mean, don't rush? Who is it?"

Gasan quickly cut the powder with the card. He split it into two thick lines. Handed Dato the straw.

"Come on, brother."

Dato took the tube. He leaned over and quickly snorted his line. He returned the tube to Gasan, who placed it in his hooked nose. Slowly he drew half of the line into one nostril, then he drew the rest into the other.

"But how did you find out?" Dato sniffed. "You never talked to my people. How did you find out? What is it, I have a stool pigeon in the house?"

"Your boys are all right, Dato."

"Well then, who, goddamnit?!"

"Just wait a minute." Gasan made two more lines. "Let's finish it off. And I will tell you how to handle this."

"Handle...handle...There you go!" Dato kicked the box. Buckwheat spilled out of the hole.

Gasan snorted his line. Dato brushed him away.

Ice

"I don't want any more."

Gasan snorted the second line. He put away the tobacco box and the straw. He wiped his nose with a handkerchief.

"All right, let's do it this way. We'll close this. And you'll take it to your place."

"What the fuckin' hell I want sand for?"

"Let your people think that everything's okay"

"And the dough?"

"You give me the briefcase. But you'll take the dough out."

"And?"

"You take the trunk to your place. And then we start hunting rats."

"So you know who it is—or not?"

Gasan came closer, whispering in his ear.

"And does he have the ice?"

"No."

"But where's the ice? The blonds got it already?"

"No. No, Dato. The ice is at your house."

Dato looked straight at him.

"What? Where?"

"In the freezer."

"At my place?"

"At your place, at your place, Dato."

"And who did this?"

"Your Natasha."

Bosch

A spacious kitchen. White furniture. Expensive utensils. A gold-plated saucepan full of water on the lit burner.

Orange lay on the marble floor, tied up: 29 years old, red hair, with the massive body of a former athlete.

Natasha sat in the corner: 26 years old, pretty, long-legged, in a torn red dress. Her hand was handcuffed to the radiator.

Dato and Gasan Blindeye sat at the table.

Crowbar and **Boiler** stood nearby: broad-shouldered, muscular, with small shaved heads and thick necks.

A half-drunk bottle of Yury Dolgoruky vodka stood on the table in front of Dato. Gasan was cutting cocaine on a plate.

Dato poured himself some vodka. Drank it. Took his time lighting a cigarette. Looked at Natasha.

"There's one fucking thing I can't understand. Not for the life of me. What was it you didn't have?"

Natasha didn't say anything. She looked at the leg of the chair.

Ice

"I picked you up out of the shit pile, I helped your brother, I helped your mother. I took you to the Caribbean, dressed you like goddamned Princess Diana. Fucked you every day. What else did you need?"

Natasha said nothing.

"Yeah. Women—they're a mystery." Dato blew smoke out. "Huh, Gasan? Third time I run into a rat. What's going on?! Shit. Is it fate?"

"I don't know, brother." Gasan snorted his line. "Might be fate."

"And then I can't get my head around the fucking thing: so, say you skimmed some ice on the sly, I dunno, knocked off fifty thou. Then what? What're you gonna do then? Where would you go? Dig a hole underground or somethin'? Or what, fifty thou is such big bucks for you?"

Natasha didn't answer.

"Dato, leave her alone," said Gasan, wiping his nose. "Women's roles are always secondary."

"Live and learn, live and learn...." Dato knocked the ash off his cigarette. He looked at the pan. "Well, is it boiling?"

Boiler glanced in the saucepan.

"It's about to boil."

Orange tossed and turned on the floor. Crowbar pushed him down with his foot.

"Lie down."

"Dato, I swear to God or I'm a skunk, it wasn't my idea. I swear, I swear," Orange muttered.

"You're already a fuckin' skunk." Dato glanced at his sweaty red head. "A stinking rat."

"Shakro put a piece to my head two times. In Dagomys that time, and after the wedding. He heard about the blonds from Avera."

"From Avera?" Gasan grinned. "Avera is in the ground."

"He hit on Shakro, Shakro owed him from the Tibet pyramid," said Orange, raising his head a bit. "And then he sold him this stuff about the blonds and the ice. He said, 'Here's a nice piece of action, take it. If you get yourself a slice, you'll pay me back.'"

"And what, Shakro ordered you to pinch it from Gasan?" Gasan asked.

"Shakro wants to take over the ice..."

"What?" Dato grinned. "What kinda bullshit're you shoveling, asshole? Avera was taken down. What fucking debt, what Tibet?"

"Even without Avera he wants to. I swear to God, Dato. His boys are saying he's totally naked now, he and Ryba are on the outs, and they'll jump you."

"And take over the deal?" Dato smiled.

"They want to."

"So rough and rude? No parlay?"

"He told me, 'Go on, grab a piece of it, I'll see. If you don't —we'll take him down.' "

"And just what does he wanna see?"

"Well, he wants to watch you stew."

Dato stubbed out the butt, got up, and walked over to Orange. He thrust his hands in his pockets. He rocked on his feet.

"Hmm. Yeah. You fuckin' mutt. You're a mad dog, stark raving mad. Strayed from the code."

He nodded to Boiler. Boiler took the pan off the stove. Crowbar held Orange's head down to the light blue marble floor with his boot.

"I swear, Dato...Gasan...I swear..." Orange mumbled.

Boiler sat on Orange's legs. He started pouring boiling water on his back.

Ice

Orange howled and jerked.

Crowbar and Boiler flattened him.

"The truth, dog, give us the truth," said Dato, rocking on his feet.

"I swear! I swear!" bellowed Orange.

Boiler splashed water on his back. Orange thrashed.

"The truth, the truth."

"Dato! Don't!" Natasha shouted.

"The truth, dog."

"I swear, I swear!"

"Splash some on his face," Gasan suggested.

Boiler splashed water on Orange's head. He moaned.

"Don't, Dato! Leave him alone!" Natasha cried.

"You'll get your turn, rat!" said Dato, kicking her.

"Talk, otherwise we'll boil you like a crab," said Gasan, calmly watching Orange's shuddering body.

"Shakro wants to take over the ice!" Orange roared.

"Don't bullshit me, you little crook! Don't bullshit me! Don't bullshit! Don't bullshit!" Dato began to kick him in the face.

"A little rat..." Gasan spat. "Pour some on his balls!"

Boiler and Crowbar began to pull down Orange's pants.

"Dato! Dato! Dato!" Natasha cried.

"Quiet, rat!"

"Dato, don't, don't! I'll tell you everything!" Natasha screamed.

"Shut up, rat!"

"Let her tell, Dato." Gasan went over to Natasha. "Tell us the truth."

"I'll tell you everything, just don't!"

Dato made a sign to Boiler. He stopped splashing boiling water on Orange.

Part I

"Go on bitch: talk."

Natasha wiped her nose with her free hand. She sobbed.

"He's lying about everything. It wasn't Shakro. It was me."

Dato looked at her.

"What the fuck for?"

"You'll dump me at some point. Like Zhenka. I know about your...that...ballerina. And I...I'm...I don't really have anything. My mother's about to die."

"And so?"

"Well...I wanted to skim off some dough...just..."

"And you put him up to it?"

She nodded.

"For how much?"

"Fifty-fifty."

Dato turned his gaze to Gasan. Gasan remained silent. Natasha let out a sob. Orange moaned on the floor.

Dato looked at Orange.

"Turn him over."

Boiler and Crowbar turned him over on his back. Dato squatted down. He looked into Orange's gray eyes.

"It's true."

He stood up. Gasan proffered his hand. Dato slapped his palm. He exhaled in relief.

"Let's go talk."

They went into the next room: dim light, a lot of expensive furniture.

"That's what I thought, that it wasn't Shakro." Gasan stretched and then shivered, as though chilled. He locked his thin fingers together. Cracked his knuckles.

"Take over...shit!" Dato grinned nervously. He opened the bar, took out a bottle of cognac, and poured some. He drained his glass.

Ice

"Every fucking punk crook is just waiting to set me on Shakro. Fucking jackals, alla'them!"

"He just heard about it...maybe from Avera, from his boys...maybe from Dyriavy..."

"But why does everyone know, Gasan? Why does every god-damn cockroach know about the fucking ice?"

"You're asking me?"

"Who should I ask? Avera? Zhorik? They're fucking worm food. But you're alive."

"You're alive, too, my brother," Gasan looked at him seri-ously. "We're both alive. So far."

"So far as what?"

"So far as we understand that there's no pockets six feet under."

Dato turned away. He walked to the window. He rocked on his toes. Gasan went up to him. He placed a hand on his shoulder.

"You know me, my friend. I don't need anybody's share. Mine is plenty for my powder."

Dato look out the window at nighttime Moscow.

"Little shits!"

"We have to do something about them, friend."

"Something..." Dato repeated, rocking on his stocking feet. "Somefuckingthing."

He turned abruptly. Went into the kitchen. Gasan followed him slowly.

In the corner of the kitchen stood a massive white Bosch refrigerator. Dato opened the freezer section. It was filled with frozen food. He began to throw the packages on the floor. They hit the marble floor with dry clunks. Under the food lay a large cube of ice. Dato looked at it angrily.

"Because I never eat anything frozen...right, bitch?"

He approached Natasha.

She whimpered and turned away.

"A safe place, right?" Gasan stared glumly.

"Why're all these fucking broads so smart all of a sudden?" Dato slapped himself on his thighs. "I don't get what's going on."

"Liberation," Boiler spoke out unexpectedly.

"Huh?" Dato turned to him.

"Yeah...that's when chicks got equal rights with guys," Boiler muttered.

Dato looked at him attentively. Turned to Gasan. "Let's have the box."

Gasan took out his cell phone. He dialed. "Drive on over."

A few minutes later two guys entered the apartment with the coffer. They put on rubber gloves. They took the cube of ice out of the freezer, put it in the coffer, and carefully took the coffer away.

Dato poured himself some vodka, downing it in a gulp.

"Okay. Orange—goes in the garbage."

Orange jerked as hard as he could. He shouted something inarticulate. Boiler and Crowbar fell on him. Crowbar threw a noose around Orange's thick, freckled neck.

Natasha vomited. Her head hung down impotently.

Orange wheezed and tossed a long time. He passed gas.

Finally he was still.

Boiler rolled in a large blue plastic suitcase from the coat closet. He put Orange's corpse in it. They wheeled it out of the kitchen. Out of the apartment.

The door closed behind them.

Gasan sat down at the table. He took out his tobacco box and sprinkled some cocaine on a plate. He began cutting it with a plastic card.

Dato took a key out of his pocket. He un-handcuffed

Ice

Natasha from the radiator. She slumped weakly to the floor. Her breathing was shallow. She was shaking.

Dato opened the door of the freezer.

"Get in."

Natasha lifted her head.

"Get in, rat!"

She obediently crawled into the freezer. Dato slammed the door. Leaned his back against it.

"I'll fuckin' freeze her. That's it."

Gasan grinned. Snorted a line of cocaine. Then some more.

Dato took out a cigarette. Lit it.

Natasha could barely be heard whimpering in the freezer.

Dato smoked. Gasan rubbed cocaine on his gums.

"I'll get myself a new whore," Dato mumbled.

Gasan stood up. Went over to him.

"Send her to Turkey. To Rustam."

"What fucking Rustam?!" Dato shook his head angrily. "She going to the fucking morgue. Turkey!"

"Friend, don't do this."

"Go fuck yourself. She's my broad."

"The woman is yours. The business is ours."

Natasha whined and banged on the door.

"I'll fuckin' waste her." Dato shook his head stubbornly. "Shameless cunt."

"Don't do this, Dato."

"Get outta here!"

"Don't do this, brother."

"Back off, Gasan, don't bug me goddamnit."

"Don't do this! You'll bring us all down, you pig head!" Gasan grabbed Dato.

"What the hell . . . get your paws off . . ." Dato struggled.

"Pig head . . ."

Part I

"Get...your...paws off...asshole..."

They fought next to the huge white refrigerator.

"I'm pregnant!" could suddenly be heard out of the freezer.

The struggle stopped.

Dato pushed Gasan away. He opened the door.

"What?"

Natasha sat there, bent over.

"What did you say?"

"I'm pregnant," she said quietly.

"By who?" growled Dato.

"By you."

Dato looked at her vacantly. At her bare knees. Then at her toes with their dark blue nail polish. A frost-covered dumpling lay next to her feet.

Dato stared at the dumpling.

Natasha fell out of the freezer onto the floor. She crawled across the marble.

"When...how long?" asked Dato.

"Second month..." She crawled out of the kitchen. Crawled into the bathroom.

Dato rubbed the bridge of his nose in exhaustion. Gasan slapped him on the back.

"So there, you see, brother...and you wanted to freeze her!"

Blockade

Komar and Vika's Rented Apartment

A dilapidated bathroom, light blue tile cracked and chipped off in places, rust stains in the bathtub and sink, the dim light of an old lightbulb, dirty underwear soaking in a basin.

Lapin and Ilona lay naked in the overfilled tub. Ilona was sitting on Lapin and smoking. His penis was in her vagina. She moved slowly. In a state of semi-oblivion, Lapin opened and closed his eyes.

"But the main thing...is, I mean....He doesn't understand anything about craft...the actor's craft..." Ilona mumbled rapidly through dry lips. "Keanu Reeves is fabulous, too, I get off on him because he can do a love scene honestly, but he seems so hot and cool and all...and I really, you know...well I just don't believe him...not even a smidgen...and I mean what the fuck should I pay money for if I don't believe the actor, I mean, if there's no belief....Oy, your balls are so hard!"

She moved sharply. Water splashed over the edge of the bathtub.

136

Part I

The peeling door opened. Komar entered, naked. His penis was erect.

"Let's switch, you cool Texas Ranger dudes."

"Okay." Ilona climbed out of the bath.

"Oh, shit man, you've flooded the place..." Komar looked at the floor. "The neighbors are gonna be banging on the door again..."

"You two are just about the same." Ilona grabbed Komar by the penis.

"Size makes a difference?" he asked hoarsely, grinning.

"You bet."

"Then let's go."

"What about shooting up?"

"As soon as I come—we'll do it."

They went out. Lapin took his hand out of the water. Looked at his nails: they were blue—like the tile.

Vika walked in, naked.

"So, then, right in the water?"

Lapin opened his eyes. Vika crawled in with him. Took his penis and placed it in her vagina.

"It's cold..." said Lapin, unsticking his lips.

"We can let this out and run a new bath," said Vika, beginning to move.

"Okay, let's..."

She reach over to the drain and pulled the plug. The water began to flow out.

"I had this boyfriend, he was a junkie too, he like to stick his balls in that hole when the water was draining, that is, when he was a little boy."

"What?"

"We used to tell each other how we got off when we were kids...I...umm...Oy, what a great penis you've got...I...

liked to sit on the corner of the table and cross my legs like this . . . and he would squat in the bathtub, fill it, and then pull out the plug and stick his balls in there. Then he'd jack off. And think about Communism."

"What for?"

"Well, I mean, not exactly about Communism itself, who the fuck needs Communism . . . It's not too hot?" She turned on the hot water.

"It's fine."

"But, you know, about how in Communism there would be communal women . . . and . . . he . . . Oy, oy, oy . . . he . . . ummm. Oy, oy, oy . . . I mean . . . Oy, oy . . . oy . . . "

"Fucked all of them." Lapin held Vika's breasts.

"Oy, oy, oy . . . " She frowned. "Oy, I'm coming . . . O-o-o-o-oy . . . "

"For some reason, ummm, I mean, I can't seem to come . . . "

"Oy . . . oy . . . " She stopped moving. "Koma will give us a hit—and you'll come."

"I want to now," said Lapin, moving.

"If you want, stick it in my ass. Koma does that sometimes too, when he can't come, he sticks it in my ass—and it spurts out right away. Want to?"

"I don't know . . . I've never tried . . . umm . . . there's shit in there."

"You jerk-off. There's no shit in there! So are you going to or not . . . Then let me masturbate you."

"You?"

"I'm really good at it. Come on, turn on your side . . . and I'll lie down behind you. It's hot already."

She turned the faucet off. Put the plug in.

Lapin turned on his side. Vika laid down behind him. Her

right hand took his penis. She stuck the left one between his legs and squeezed his balls.

"Oh, poor guy, we're so tense here."

She began masturbating his member.

Lapin let his eyes shut. He dropped off into a dream.

He was an old man. Eighty-two years old, thin and dried up. He was descending the dark, cold staircase of a large apartment building. Pieces of plaster and broken glass lay on the stairs. He was wearing a heavy winter coat, felt boots, and heavy mittens. It was very cold. He shivered down to his very bone marrow. A slight steam escaped from his dried lips. His right arm was half bent. He held the handle of a copper teakettle in the bend of his elbow. The empty kettle knocked against his hip. Descending, he held on to a wooden banister. Each step was difficult. The cold air burned his throat. His head trembled slightly, and as a result, everything he saw also trembled and swayed. He stopped on the landing of the second floor and fell back against the gray, cracked wall. He held the kettle with his left hand. He stood there, breathing heavily. He looked at the space between two doors. The words THE KUZOLEVS ARE KULAKS! *and* SLONIK IS A TICK *had been scratched on the wall. One of the doors had been pulled out. The black space of a burned apartment yawned beyond it. The insignia of the Zenith soccer team was drawn in ink on the door of the other. He stood there, his eyes half open. He breathed. Below, someone was climbing the stairs. He opened his eyes. A hunched figure in a gray padded jacket appeared before him. The man placed an icy bucket of water on the dirty cement floor. He straightened up with a faint moan. He* wore a black navy-issue winter hat with earflaps, tied with a torn gray scarf, and huge mittens; his soiled padded pants were tucked into felt boots. A thin, yellowish-gray, ageless face with an overgrown beard arose in front of him. The whitish eyes looked at him.

"Building 2 has been completely cordoned off. Half of it collapsed."

"And... this one?" he asked.

"Now you have to go through 12."

The bearded man glanced through the door of the burned-out apartment.

"While we were standing around with our mouths open, the stoker and Yanko took everything out. I dropped in yesterday—not a splinter left. The SOBs. They could've at least shared. Shut themselves up in the boiler room—and that's it. Can't get through to them. That's who should be shot. They're worse than the Fascists.

The bearded man picked up his bucket, and moaned as he lifted it. He suddenly really wanted to ask the bearded man something important. But then he immediately forgot what, exactly. Worried, he pushed himself away from the wall.

"Umm and... Andrei Samoilovich... I'm, you know... not a Party member. You don't have any plywood, do you?"

But the bearded man was already lugging the bucket upstairs, holding out his left arm for balance.

His eyes followed the man for a long time. Then he continued down. Exiting the half-dark entryway, he was immediately blinded: everything around was bathed in bright sunlight. Standing for a bit, he opened his eyes. The courtyard was still the same: enormous snowdrifts, the stumps of two poplars that were cut down, the carcass of a burned-out truck. A narrow path led through the snowdrifts to the street. He moved *cautiously along it. A black arch swam over his head. This is the gateway. Dangerous. Very dangerous! He moved along the wall, leaning on it with his left hand. But there's light ahead: the street. He took longer steps—and he was suddenly on the avenue. In this place it was wide open. The middle of the avenue had been cleared, but near the houses there were still mountainous snowdrifts. People moved along the avenue. There weren't many of them. He moved slowly. Someone was pulling something on a sled. A sled! He had had one. But the Borisovs stole it. They burned the wooden seat in their makeshift stove; they hauled water on the iron frame. But he carries it in his teakettle. It's a long way to the Neva. You can melt snow, of course. But you need a lot of it. And it's heavy too...*

He readied himself to go out into the middle of the avenue. A ways away, the groundskeeper was talking to Lidia Konstantinovna from building 8. They stood next to a corpse lying facedown in the snow. The corpse's buttocks had been cut off.

"Just look, all the dead have their asses sliced off!" croaked the groundskeeper, who was wrapped up in some kind of rags. "And why is that, I wonder? A gang! They make croquettes and meatballs from corpses and fry them up in axle grease! Then they barter them for bread at the market!"

Lidia Konstantinovna crossed herself. "We should show the patrols."

He walked over to them. "You wouldn't have a splinter or two?"

They turn away and plod off.

"How does the earth stand these goddamned White Guard bastards?" he hears.

Chewing his lips, he walks out onto the prospect. What were they talking about? Croquettes! He remembered the pork

Ice

croquettes at the Vienna restaurant on Bolshoi Morskoi, and at Testova's Moscow pub. And at the Yar restaurant. At the Yar! They were served with potato croutons, red cabbage, and green peas. The Yar had truffles, too, a divine six-layered kulebiaka pasty, sterlet soup, crème brûlée, and Lizanka made a fuss, she wanted to go visit those... that... oh... the one with the mustache who couldn't say his r's.... poems, poems, lord, how the frost goes right through you... croquettes.... Meatballs.

A truck suddenly passed him, almost hitting him. Red Army soldiers with rifles sat in it, wrapped in overcoats. The chains on the truck's wheels clanked. He stopped. His eyes teared as they followed the truck. What's this? On the side of the truck instead of a number there was a large white sign: CROQUETTES. Croquettes!! There were croquettes in there! He suddenly understood this keenly and clearly, with every cell of his weak body.

Throwing down the kettle and waving his hands, he began to run after the truck. His large kneecaps jolted forward, the mittens flew off of his bony black hands and hung on their elastic. He ran after the truck. It was crawling along slowly. He could catch up with it. There are croquettes in there! He could see them, skewered on Red Army bayonets. Hundreds, thousands of them!

"Let me have a croquette, too!" he screeched like a rooster.
"Cr... cro... quette... too!"
"And... let me... croque... too!"
"Cr... cro... croque... ettooo...!"

His heart was beating, beating, beating. Broad and wide. Like building 6. Like the Irtysh River in May 1918. Like Big Bertha. Like the siege itself. Like God.

His feet became tangled. He careened. Creaked. Cracked.

Part I

And split in pieces like a rotten tree, on the snow the truck had tamped down. A whitish haze swallowed up the truck. His heart beat.

Pdum.

P-dum.

Pa-dum.

And stopped. Forever.

Lapin opened his eyes. He was crying. Clots of sperm spurted from his penis into the water. Vika's hand helped. Lapin's legs jerked convulsively.

"Like thick sour cream." Vika's huge, wet lips moved near Lapin's ear. "Don't get laid much, huh?"

A Girl Is Crying

14:11
The Balaganchik
10 Tryokhprudny Lane

A half-empty restaurant. Nikolaeva came out of the restroom, approached a table.

Lida was sitting at it and smoking: 23 years old, a slender model's figure in a tight leather outfit, mid-size breasts, a long neck, a small head with a very short haircut, a pretty face.

"The john is downstairs." Nikolaeva sat down opposite Lida. "It's not very convenient."

"But the food is fabulous," said Lida, chewing.

"The cook is French," said Nikolaeva, pouring red wine into their wineglasses. "So, where did I stop?"

"Cheers," said Lida, raising her glass. "At the naked blond with blue eyes."

"Cheers," said Nikolaeva, clinking glasses with her.

They drank. Nikolaeva took an olive, chewed it, spit out the pit.

Part I

"It didn't even matter, naked—or not. You know, the thing is that I've never felt anything like it, nothing has ever gotten to me that way. I just...sort of like fell into it...and my heart felt so...sweet...sort of...as if...I don't know...it was like...I don't know. Like being with Mama in childhood. I cried my eyes out later. You get it?"

"And you're sure he didn't screw you?"

"Absolutely."

Lida shook her head.

"Hmmm. One of two things: it's either some kind of druggies, or Satanists."

"They didn't shoot me up with anything."

"But you lost consciousness. You said you fainted."

"Yeah, but there's no tracks! My veins are intact."

"Well, maybe it wasn't in a vein. I had one client and he stuck cocaine up his ass. Got high. He said that that way his septum wouldn't get ruined."

Nikolaeva shook her head in disagreement.

"No, Lidka, they definitely weren't druggies. There's something else going on there. You know what kind of assets they have? This is a serious company. You can tell."

"So that means Satanists. Talk to Birutia. The Satanists fucked her once."

"And? Was it hard core?"

"Nah, but they smeared so much chicken blood on her that she kept on washing and washing—"

"Yeah but this was my blood, not chicken blood."

Lida stubbed out her cigarette.

"Well, I just don't get it."

"Me neither."

"Alya, you weren't soused, were you?"

Ice

"Come on!"

"Yeah, well...And your heart, you said...well...it was really intense? Like if you fall in love with someone?"

"Stronger...it...how the hell to explain it...well...like when you really really feel sorry for someone and it's someone really really close to you. So close, so close that you're ready to give him everything, everything...I mean...well, it's..."

Nikolaeva sniffled. Her lips trembled. And suddenly she began sobbing, readily and intensely, as though she'd vomited. The sobs overwhelmed her.

Lida grabbed her by the shoulders.

"Alya, sweetie, calm down..."

But Nikolaeva sobbed harder and harder.

The few customers in the restaurant looked at her. Her head was shaking. Her fingers clutched her mouth and she began to slide off the chair.

"Alechka, Alya!" said Lida, holding her up.

Nikolaeva's body writhed and shuddered. Her face turned red. The waiter came over.

Sobs burst from Nikolaeva's mouth along with saliva, her head shook and tears spurted on all sides. Powerless, she sank to the floor. Lida leaned over and began to slap her on the cheeks. Then she took a swallow from a bottle of mineral water, and sprayed it on the ugly red face and distorted features.

Nikolaeva sobbed. Until she was hoarse. Until she began hiccuping. She arched on the floor, twitching like an epileptic.

"Oh my God, what's wrong with her?" Frightened, Lida tried to help her.

"Give her ammonia salts!" a portly man advised loudly. "It's a typical case of hysteria."

The waiter leaned over and stroked Nikolaeva. She passed a violent stream of gas and began sobbing with renewed force.

A woman came up.

"Did something happen to her?"

"She was mistreated," said Lida, looking at her in fright. "Oh my God, this is awful! I've never seen her like this.... Alya, sweetie, come on, Alya! Oy, call a doctor!"

The woman got out her cell phone and dialed 03.

"What should I say?"

"It doesn't matter!" said Lida, brushing her aside. "I can't stand this!"

"Well...I have to say something..."

"Just say..." The waiter chewed on his small lips worriedly. "Say that a girl is crying."

Suite of Diamonds

Empty Lot near Karamzin Passage

A silver Audi-A8 stood with dimmed headlights. Inside were Dato, Volodya Straw, and Crowbar. A dark blue Lincoln Navigator turned off from the road and approached them. It stopped twenty meters away. Uranov and Frop got out. Uranov held a briefcase in his hand.

Dato, Straw, and Crowbar got out of the car. Dato raised his hand. Uranov raised his in response. Uranov and Frop approached Dato.

"Hey, man." Dato proffered his stubby fingers.

"Hello, Dato." Uranov offered his long, slender hand.

They shook hands.

"Why the delay?" asked Uranov. "Are there problems?"

"There was one problem. But we disposed of it. Now everything's in order."

"Something having to do with delivery?"

"No, no. Internal affairs."

Part I

Uranov nodded. He looked around. "Well, then, shall we touch it?"

"Touch it, my friend."

Uranov raised his hand. Frop opened the back door of the vehicle. Mair got out and walked over to Dato's car.

Crowbar opened the trunk. A refrigerated coffer lay in it. Crowbar opened it. Ice shone in the coffer.

Mair took her blue leather gloves off and put them in her pocket. She stood, looking at the ice. Then she put her hands on it. Her eyes closed.

Everyone froze.

Two minutes and sixteen seconds passed.

Mair's lips opened. A moan escaped her mouth when she exhaled. She took her hands off the ice and pressed them to her red cheeks. "Fine."

The men began moving around with relief. Uranov gave Dato the briefcase. Dato opened it, looked at the packets of dollars. He nodded and closed it. Mair turned and went back to her car. Crowbar closed the coffer, removed it from the trunk, and gave it to Frop. Frop carried it to the car. Crowbar slammed the trunk.

"When's the next?" Dato asked.

"In about two weeks. I'll call you." Uranov stuck his hands in the pockets of his beige overcoat.

"All right, pal."

Uranov quickly shook his hand, turned, and strode over to the automobile.

Dato, Crowbar, and Straw got into their car.

"Count it." Dato handed the briefcase to Straw. He opened it and began counting the money.

The off-road vehicle turned around sharply and took off.

Ice

Crowbar gazed at it as it disappeared.

"I swear, I just don't get it, Dato."

"What?" said Dato, lighting a cigarette.

"I mean, those blonds... what sort of ice is it?"

"What do you care? You hand over the goods—and that's it. Let's go."

Crowbar started the car and turned onto the highway.

"Yeah, sure, of course. But what, can't we pass off some other ice? I mean, it's a waste. Just some piece of ice and so much bullshit around it: the ice, the ice, the ice. What kind of ice is it? No one knows. And it costs a hundred thou. What's the big fucking deal, man?"

"I don't even want to know," said Dato, blowing smoke out. "Everybody gets their rocks off how they want. The main thing is it's not radioactive. And not toxic."

"You checked?"

"Damn straight."

"Then all the more reason to slip them a phony. Hey, we can freeze a couple of buckets of water. And fuck it!" chuckled Crowbar.

"You're green. Even though you done time." Dato yawned.

"They've already been double-crossed," murmured Straw, counting the dollars.

"Who?" asked Crowbar.

"Vovik Shatursky. He was found later. In the fuckin' garbage. With his throat slit."

"Shit, man," Crowbar exclaimed in surprise. "But that's... wait a minute! You mean he ran the ice too?"

"Yeah, he did. Before Gasan and us. He and Zhorik shipped it together."

"And now they're in the underground business together." Straw slammed the briefcase shut, and handed it to Dato.

Part I

"In the shareholder's society Mother Earth-Worm. Heard about it?" Dato smiled. "It's a business with a lotta prospects. Want the phone number?"

Dato and Straw laughed.

"Shit." Crowbar shook his head in surprise, without taking his eyes off the road. "And here I thought the Chechens or somebody offed him."

"No, brother." Dato placed the briefcase on his knees and drummed on it with his short fingers. "It wasn't the spades. It was the diamonds."

"But how? And this . . . Dato, tell me, this ice here, is it—" Crowbar continued.

Dato interrupted. "What fucking ice! What are you talking to me about, boy? Ice! Spades! Zhorik! I got more serious things on my mind!"

"What?" asked Crowbar quietly. "The mayor's office again?"

"What fucking mayor's office!"

"Shishka pull some kinda shit again?"

"What goddamned Shishka!"

"Taras making trouble, then?"

"Whaaaat fucking Taras?!" said Dato, rolling his eyes angrily. "Baby food, you fuckin' asshole! That's the most god-damn important thing in the world!"

For a moment they all rode in silence.

Then Straw began to laugh. Crowbar stared at Dato in the rearview mirror, not understanding.

Dato leaned back and was overcome by a high-pitched, Asiatic giggle.

They passed the Teply Stan metro station.

Then the Konkovo station.

Crowbar started laughing too.

Peace

The long, narrow space of the office, gray-brown walls, Italian furniture.

Matvei Vinogradov sat behind a Spanish cherrywood table bent like a wave: 50 years old, small, black-haired, narrow-shouldered, sharp-nosed, thin, a well-tailored suit of lilac-gray silk.

Borenboim sat opposite.

"Mot, for heavens' sake, forgive me for pestering you so early in the morning." Borenboim stretched. "But you can understand."

"Don't worry about it," said Vinogradov, sipping his coffee. He picked up that very same Visa Electron card.

"69,000, is that right?"

"69," Borenboim nodded.

"And the PIN code is written down. Heavy. This is serious business, Borya. Presents like this smell bad."

152

Part I

"Very."

"Listen…and no one's done anything, called you, threatened you, right?"

"Absolutely."

Vinogradov nodded.

Sokolova entered with a piece of paper: 24 years old, slim, in a light green suit, unremarkable face. She handed over the piece of paper. Vinogradov took it and began reading.

"That's what I thought. You're free, Natashenka."

She left.

"And…?" Borenboim frowned.

"They did it the simple way. Completely legal, in accordance with the Central Bank and the Civil Code. Here's how it goes: the donor applies for the main card using the passport of some front guy, and in the application form indicates he wants to have an additional card issued. In your name. When the cards are received, the primary card in the name of the front guy is confiscated and destroyed. Only yours remains. Finding the front, in your case—Kurbashakh, Radii Avtandilovich, born August 7, 1953, in the town of Tuimaz—would be almost impossible. Only Allah knows where this Kurbashakh abides at present. All in all, it's smart. Although…"

"What?"

"I would have made it even simpler. There's a completely anonymous product: Visa Travel Money. There's no owner's name at all. Have you used them?"

"No…" said Borenboim grumpily, averting his eyes.

"Any Petrov can get one of these cards and give it to Sidorov. I've seen it done. One woman sold six apartments in Kiev, and in order to avoid taking the money through Ukrainian customs, she asked for this Visa Travel Money. But there's one problem: the limit on individual operations in Russian ATMs is three hundred and forty bucks a day. In a nutshell, this woman milked the ATMs like goats for almost five months, and then it all ended when one of them swallowed her card, and she—"

"Motya, what should I do?" Borenboim interrupted, impatiently.

"You know what, Borya"—Vinogradov scratched his forehead with an ivory knife—"you need to talk to Tolyan."

"Is he at home?" asked Borenboim, rocking nervously in the armchair.

"No. He's swimming right now."

"Where?"

"At the Olympic."

"Early morning? Good for him."

"Unlike you and me, Tolya does everything right." Vinogradov laughed. "He swims in the morning, works during the day, snorts and screws in the evening, and sleeps at night. And I do everything the other way around! Go on over there. You won't be able to find him during the day. No way."

"I don't know...whether it's okay. I've met him a couple of times. But we aren't very well acquainted."

"It doesn't matter. He's a businesslike guy. Mention my name if you want, or Savka."

"You think?"

"Go on, go right this minute. Don't lose any time. Your FSB agents don't know shit. And he'll explain the whole thing."

Borenboim got up suddenly, frowned, and clutched his chest.

"What's wrong?" Vinogradov's handsome eyebrows knit in a frown.

"Oh...it's just something...like arthritis," said Borenboim, straightening his thin shoulders.

"You need to swim, Borya," Vinogradov advised seriously.

Part I

"At least two times a week. I used to be falling apart. And now I've even stopped smoking."

"You're strong."

"Not stronger than you." Vinogradov stood up, stretched out his hand. "Give me a call afterward, okay?"

"Of course." Borenboim shook Vinogradov's thin, firm fingers.

"And anyway, Bor, how come we hardly ever see each other? It's like we're some kind of hard-hearted workaholics."

"What?" Borenboim asked cautiously.

"We never drink together, Bor. You and I've become totally heartless!"

Borenboim paled abruptly. His lips began to tremble. He clutched at his chest.

"No. I...have...a heart," he enunciated firmly. And burst out sobbing.

"Borya, Bor..." Vinogradov rose halfway.

"I...h-have...a...a...a...h-h-heart!" Sobbing, Borenboim got the words out and then collapsed on his knees. "I haaaave...I haa...aaa...aaaa...veee...aaaa!!"

Sobs wracked his body, tears sprang from his eyes. He bent over. Fell on the rug. Thrashed about in hysterics.

Vinogradov pressed a button on his phone.

"Tanya, quick, come here! Quick!"

Walking around the ornate table, Vinogradov leaned over Borenboim.

"Borka, hey pal, what's going on...come on, we'll find these assholes, don't be afraid..."

Borenboim sobbed. Intermittent sobs merged into a hoarse wail. His face turned crimson. His legs jerked.

The secretary entered.

"Give me some water!" Vinogradov shouted at her.

Ice

She ran out. She returned with a bottle of mineral water. Vinogradov swigged a mouthful and sprayed it on the wailing Borenboim, who continued to wail.

"Do we have any tranquilizers?" Vinogradov held Borenboim's head.

"Just aspirin," muttered the secretary.

"No valerian drops?"

"No, Matvei Anatolich."

"You don't have anything..." Vinogradov wet a handkerchief, and tried to place it on Borenboim's forehead.

Borenboim howled and writhed.

"Jesus fucking...what the hell is this...?" Bewildered, Vinogradov smacked his lips, got down on his knees.

He began to pour the water from the bottle onto Borenboim's red face.

It didn't help. Convulsions shook the thin body.

"Something's wrong here," said Vinogradov, shaking his head.

"Did something bad happen to him?"

"Yeah, something real bad. He got sixty-nine thousand dollars transferred to him, and he doesn't know who did it! A big disaster, shit!" said Vinogradov, smiling bitterly, losing his patience. "Borka! Come on, that's enough, really! Enough!! Borya!! Stop! Quiet!!"

He began to slap Borenboim on the cheeks. Borenboim wailed even louder.

"Jeez, what the hell's going on here?" Vinogradov stood up and stuck his hands in his pockets.

"Maybe some cognac?" the secretary proposed.

"Damn, everyone's gonna come running now! Tanya, call an ambulance right now. They'll give him a shot of something in the ass...I can't stand this. I can't listen anymore!"

Part I

He sat on the edge of the desk. He looked around, searching for a cigarette. Then remembered that he quit. He shook his hands in the air.

"What a way to begin the fuckin' day..."

The secretary picked up the receiver. "What should I say, Matvei Anatolich?"

"Say that...the man has lost..."

"What?"

"His peace of mind!" Vinogradov shouted irritably.

Boy Is Crying

Lapin strolled from the Lenin Library metro station to the old Moscow University building. A backpack hung on his shoulder. Fine-grained snow sifted down from an overcast sky.

Lapin entered the cast-iron gates, looked in the direction of the "psychodrome"—a small square near the monument to Lomonosov. A group of students with bottles of beer stood there.

Skinny, stooping Tvorogov and **small, long-haired Filshtein** noticed Lapin.

"Lapa, come over here!" Filshtein waved.

Lapin walked over.

"How come you're so early?" asked Tvorogov.

Filshtein laughed. "Lapa lives on New York time! Mr. Radlov was asking about you."

"Yeah. Like: Where does my pet hang out?" Tvorogov butted in.

Part I

"What?" Lapin asked in a gloomy voice.

"Got a hangover, Lap? Bring your paper? Gonna hand it in?"

"No."

"We didn't either!"

Filshtein and Tvorogov laughed.

"Gimme a swig." Lapin took Tvorogov's bottle and drank. "Is Rudik here?"

"Don't know," said Tvorogov, lighting a cigarette.

"Take a look in 'Santa Barbara.'"*

"Listen, is it true that his ancestors were in some kind of sect?"

"Hari Krishnas, I think," said Tvorogov, blowing out smoke.

"No, not Hari Krishnas." Filshtein shook his curly head. "Brahma Kumaris."

"What's that?" Lapin returned the bottle to Tvorogov.

"Brahma is one of the gods of the Hindu pantheon," Filshtein explained. "You can ask Rudik what Kumaris is. They go to the Himalayas every year."

"Him too?"

"Are you nuts?! He's not into that stuff. He gets off on heavy metal. Hangs out with Spider. Why? You interested?"

"Just a little."

"What were you up to yesterday, Lap, you get drunk or get laid?"

"I shot up too." Lapin headed for the entrance.

He entered. Went up to the second floor. Walked through the empty smoking room. Walked through the open door of the men's toilet. It was empty except for a hunchbacked cleaning

---

* Bathroom on the second floor of the university building.

woman of uncertain age. An overturned urn lay on the dirty floor in a puddle of urine. Cigarette butts, cans of beer, and other garbage were piled up nearby. The cleaning woman was moving the trash toward the trash bin with her mop. Lapin clucked in dissatisfaction. Noticing him, the hunchbacked woman shook her head accusingly.

"A lot of pigs. Trash and trash. No heart in you."

Lapin winced. The hand that held the strap of the backpack unclenched. The backpack slipped from his shoulder and fell on the floor. Lapin let out a sob. His eyes quickly filled with tears.

"No!" he hissed.

He opened his mouth and let out a long, plaintive cry that rang in the empty toilet and burst into the hallway. Lapin's legs gave way. He clutched his chest and fell backward.

"Ooooo! Oooo! Oooooo!" He gave a drawn-out wail.

The cleaning woman stared at him angrily. She set her mop in the corner. She walked around Lapin and limped into the hallway. Three students were heading for the bathroom, drawn by the cries.

"Granny, what's going on?" asked one.

"Another drug addict!" The cleaning woman looked at them indignantly. "Who studies here these days? Fairies and drug addicts!"

The students stepped over Lapin. He moaned and sobbed, and every so often let out a lengthy scream.

"Shit, man. Typical withdrawal," one of the students concluded. "Vova, call 03."

"Forgot my cell." Another was chewing gum. "Hey, who has a cell around here?"

"Oy, what's wrong with him?" squealed a girl who had just come out of the women's room and looked in.

Part I

"You got a cell phone?"

"Yes."

"Dial 03, he's in withdrawal."

"Zhenia, maybe we shouldn't?" one of the students began to doubt.

"Call, you idiot, he'll croak here!" the cleaning lady screamed.

"Go fuck yourself...." The girl dialed 03. "What should I say?"

The student spit out his gum.

"Like in the song. Say: 'Boy is Crying'..."

Eight Days Later

12:00
Private Clinic
7 Novoluzhnetsky Prospect

A spacious white ward with a wide white bed. White venetian blinds on the windows. A bouquet of white lilies on a low white table. A white television. White chairs.

Lapin, Nikolaeva, and Borenboim were asleep in the bed. Their faces were haggard and gaunt: there were circles under their eyes, their sunken cheeks had a yellowish tinge.

The door opened silently. The same plump, stooped doctor entered. He began to open the blinds. Mair and Uranov followed him in. They stood near the bed.

Daylight flooded the ward.

"But they're still sleeping soundly," said Mair.

"They'll wake up soon," the doctor said with certainty. "The cycle, the cycle. Tears, sleep. Sleep and tears."

"There was a problem with the kid?" asked Uranov.

"Yes." The doctor stuck his hands in the pockets of his blue robe. "The other two were sent to hospital 15, as usual. But

Part I

they initially thought he was a drug addict. So we had a bit of a hassle with the transfer."

"Did he really shoot up?"

"There's a needle track on his left arm. But no, he's not a drug addict."

They stood silently.

"Tears..." said Mair.

"So what—tears?" The doctor straightened the blanket over Borenboim's chest.

"They change faces."

"Well, if you cry for an entire week!" chuckled the doctor.

"I still don't understand why people always call the ambulance when someone starts sobbing uncontrollably. Why don't they try to calm them down themselves..." said Uranov thoughtfully.

"It's frightening," the doctor explained.

"How...wonderful it is." Mair smiled. "The first weeping of the heart. It's like...the first spring."

"You remember yourself?" The doctor shook his massive head. "Yes, you blubbered like a Beluga whale."

"You remember?"

"Now, now, my dear, it was only some nine years ago. I remember your graybeard, too. And the girl with the dried-up hand. And the twins from Noginsky. Doctors have a good memory. Don't we?" He winked and laughed.

Mair embraced him.

Borenboim stirred. He moaned.

Lapin's pale hand flinched. His fingers closed. And opened.

"Perfect." The doctor glanced at the white clock. "When they're together, the cycle evens out. All right, then! Hurry up ladies and gentlemen!"

Mair and Uranov left quickly.

Ice

The doctor stood for a minute, turned, and followed after them.

The nurse, Kharo, silently pushed a wheelchair into the room.

A skinny old lady sat in the wheelchair.

She wore an old-fashioned, light blue dress. Her head was covered by a pillbox hat with a blue veil. Blue stockings stretched over unbelievably thin legs ending in blue patent-leather boots.

The old woman unclasped the wrinkled, dried-up hands on her knees and lifted her veil.

Her narrow, thin, wrinkled face was filled with extraordinary bliss. Her large blue eyes shone young, smart, and strong.

Kharo left the room.

The old woman looked at the three, who were awakening.

When all three had awoken and noticed her, she spoke in a quiet, even, calm voice.

"Ural, Diar, Mokho. I am Khram. I welcome you."

Ural, Diar, and Mokho looked at her.

"Your hearts wept for seven days. This weeping is in grief and shame for your previous, dead life. Now your hearts are cleansed. They will no longer sob. They are ready to love and speak. Now my heart will speak the first word of the most important language to your hearts. The language of the heart."

She stopped speaking. Her large eyes closed half way. Her sunken cheeks turned slightly rosy.

The three in the bed shuddered. Their eyes also closed halfway. A slight convulsion crossed their haggard faces. The features of these faces came to life, blurred, and shifted, abandoning their usual expressions, which had been conditioned by the experience of their former life.

In agony, their faces began to be revealed.

Part I

Just like the buds of wild plants, dormant for decades in cold and timelessness.
Several moments of transformation passed.
Ural, Diar, and Mokho opened their eyes.
Their faces shone with a rapturous peace.
Their eyes sparkled with understanding.
Their lips smiled.
They were born.

Part II

I had just turned twelve when the war began.

Mama and I lived in Koliubakino, a small village with only forty-six houses.

Our family wasn't very big: Mama, Grandma, Gerka, and me. My father left for the war right away on June 24. No one knew where he went, where he ended up, or whether he was even alive. There were no letters from him.

The war went on and on somewhere. Sometimes at night it thundered and boomed.

But we lived in the country.

Our house was on the outskirts. Our family name was Samsikov, but in the village manner we were called the Outskirts, because we had lived forever at the edge of town, my great-grandfather and grandfather, everyone had always lived at the edge of the village; that's where they built their huts.

I grew up a sensible girl, I did everything around the house, helped my elders if something had to be cleaned or made. Back then, everyone in the village worked, from the tiniest to the oldest. That's the way things were done, there weren't any shirkers.

I understood that it was hard for Mama with Father gone.

Ice

Although things had been even harder with him: he drank a lot. Before the war began, he worked in timber for a while. He and the forest warden sold timber on the sly, and drank up the proceeds. He was a binger. And he had a mistress in the next village. She was fat, with a large mouth. Polina.

The Germans arrived in our village in September '41, and they set themselves up. They stayed there until October of '43. They stayed for two years.

The soldiers were rear-line forces, not battle troops. The fighting ones went farther on—to capture Moscow. But they never did.

Our Germans were mostly about forty years old; they seemed like old men to me, since I was just a girl. They stayed in the peasant houses, all over the village. Their officers lived in the village council building. Things were all right with these Germans around, in two years they didn't kill anyone, but when they retreated they did burn our village. Well that was the order they were given, it wasn't their own idea.

They were intelligent men, and practical.

The day after they came they started building a privy. Our village had never ever had any privies before this. Everyone went "out in the yard"—you'd squat somewhere and that was it. Grandma would go in the cowshed, where the cow stood. Mama—in the garden. Us kids—wherever we needed to. You'd squat by a bush—and that was that! No one in the village had any privies, it never occurred to anyone to build one special. The Germans kept on building, and Grandma laughed: Why waste all that hard work, the shit ends up in the ground anyway!

But Germans are Germans: they like order.

As soon as they arrived they started building privies and benches. Next to the houses, like they were planning on living with us for a long time.

Part II

They would throw some food our way—that helped. They had corn, flour, and tins of meat. They even baked their own bread—they didn't trust us. Were they afraid we'd poison them?

They had schnapps. I didn't try it, I was just a girl. But I did try beer for the first time in my life that winter.

They had their own Christmas; they all gathered in the village council. Mama and some of the other women cooked pork, chickens for them; they fried potatoes in lard, and baked white rolls from their flour. They put everything on the table. The other girls and I crawled up on the stove and watched. Then the Germans rolled out a small barrel, stuck a sort of copper faucet in it, and began pouring beer into mugs and glasses. It was yellowish and foamy. They drank, then they sang and swayed back and forth. It went on and on till nighttime. They drank schnapps too. I watched from above. One German gave me a mug: Drink! I tried the beer. It had a strange taste. But I remembered it. So there you go.

All in all, life was cheery with the Germans. It was kind of interesting: Germans! They were completely different, and they were funny. Three of them lived with us: Erich, Otto, and Peter. The settled in the house and we moved into the bathhouse. The bathhouse was brand new; father had built it of thick logs, it would warm up good and hot.

The Germans occupied the house. They were an odd bunch! They were all about forty. Otto was fat, Erich was small and had a hook nose, and Peter was a beanpole, wore glasses, and had flaxen hair. Erich was the shittiest: he was always displeased. Do this for him, bring that. He'd say nothing or mumble something. He loved to fart. He'd fart, mumble, and head off into the village.

Otto was the kindest and funniest. Mama and I would make

them breakfast in the morning, and he'd wake up, stretch, look at me and say, "Nun, was gibt's neues, Varka?"

At first I just smiled. But then Peter-with-the-glasses taught me some words, and I always answered, "Überhaupt nichts!"

Otto would roar with laughter and go take a leak.

Peter was always lost in thought, he had "his head under a pillow," as Grandma would say. He'd go out, sit on the new bench, and smoke his long pipe. He'd sit, smoke, and swing his leg. He'd stare at something, just sitting there like a bump on a log, and then suddenly sigh and say, "Scheiss der Hund drauf!"

He also loved to shoot crows. He'd go out into the orchard with a gun—and bang away, until the glass shuddered.

The Germans made three things in our village: ropes, sleigh runners, and wooden plows.

That is, our village people did all the work, and the Germans kept an eye on things and sent the stuff off somewhere. Mama and the other women went out to collect the bast, weave the ropes, and the old men and young fellows bent the sleigh runners and cut the plows. Iliukha Kuznetsov, an armless deserter, explained: This is so the bombs in the boxes don't bump around and blow up.

Our three Germans really loved milk. They went crazy over it: as soon as Mother or Grandma milked the cow, before it was even strained, the Germans would be pushing into the cowshed.

"Ein Schluk, Masha!"

They called Mama Gasha. They called me Varka. But they called all our other girls Mashas. They were just crazy about their milk...! They'd almost get up under the cow with their cups. There wasn't any hurry—they drank all the milk anyway! But they were in a rush so the fresh milk wouldn't cool down, they liked to drink it warm. They'd make a big fuss. We laughed.

Part II

So that year passed, and then the Red Army began to attack. The Germans ran off.

They had two orders: burn all the villages, and take all the young people with them to work in Germany. They only gathered up twenty-three people from the whole village. The rest ran off or hid. I didn't bother for some reason. I don't know why, but somehow I just didn't want to run anywhere. And where could you run to anyway? There were Germans everywhere. We didn't have any partisans. And it was scary in the forest.

Mama didn't say anything to me, either. She didn't even cry: she was used to everything. She wailed when they burned our house. But she wasn't very afraid for the children. And we were sort of numb, too, we didn't know what was happening, where they'd take us and why. No one cried. Grandma kept on praying and praying that we wouldn't be killed. They let me go. But Gerka stayed with them, he wasn't even seven yet.

They quickly gathered us in a column. Mother handed me father's padded coat, and managed to slip me a chunk of lard. But I lost the lard on the road! What a laugh!

I can't figure out how it fell out of my pocket! That piece weighed about three pounds...

Later I dreamed about that lard. Dreamed I grabbed hold of it, but it was like the oat pudding they boil up for wakes—it slipped between my fingers!

We walked on foot with the Germans to Lompadi, where the railroad was. There they put us in this big farm building where they used to keep the collective farm cattle, but the Germans had also taken the cattle back to Germany. There were about three hundred of us from the entire region crowded in that place, all young guys and girls. They stationed guards so we wouldn't run off. Took us out only when we had to go. We stayed there for three whole days.

Ice

The Germans were waiting for a train to load us up and send us off. This train was coming from Yukhnov and collecting all the others like us. It was a special train, just for young people.

It was pretty cold at that farm—it was late autumn, there was already a ton of snow, the roof had holes in it, and the windows were covered with boards. There wasn't any stove. They fed us baked potatoes. They'd bring in a tub, set it in the middle; we'd grab the potatoes, laugh and eat, all of us grimy! And somehow everyone was happy: we were all young! We weren't afraid of anything, we never even thought about death.

The front wasn't far away. At night when we lay down, we could hear the guns firing: boom, boom, boom!

Then the train came. It was huge, with thirty-two cars. It had been going for a long time and was already full. So they started pushing us into the cars: girls separate, boys separate. There were already plenty of our people there. Then it finally hit us. Everyone was suddenly afraid, and the girls started crying: What will happen to us? Maybe they'll murder us all!

I began to cry too, though I rarely cried.

They shoved us in, and slid the doors shut. The train headed west. There were about fifty of us girls in the car, but no benches, no bunks. The straw on the floor was soaked in piss; the corner was piled with shit. There was one tiny little window with a grate. It stank. Thank god, at least it was freezing cold; the shit in the corner froze solid. In the summer we'd have all suffocated from the stench.

The train crawled along slowly, stopping often. Some of us sat, some stood, like herrings in a barrel.

We began to talk. That made things easier. Some older girls nearby told me about their lives. They were from Medyn, city folk. Their fathers had died in the war; one had deserted, then worked as a *polizei* and blown himself up with a grenade: he touched the wrong part of it and that was that. He took out a couple of people's eyes along with him.

One girl, she was eighteen, had lived with a German. Her mother lived with a German too, so they lived all right. This Tanya fell in love with the German, and when his division was moved and went on to Belorussia, she ran six versts alongside and kept howling: Martin! Martin! Then some officer got tired of her, took out his pistol, and shot at her feet. Three times. Then she left them alone.

Two women in our village also lived with Germans. They liked it fine. One of them always had tins and corn flour. She got pregnant after a while.

The girls in the car said that we'd be taken to work in Poland or Germany. Half the girls wanted to go to Germany, and half to Poland. The ones who wanted to go to Germany thought that there was no front there and a lot of food. And the ones who wanted to go to Poland said that the Germans would be defeated anyway and there would be war everywhere, so it was better to go to Poland, it would be easier to escape. They had big arguments.

There were four girls from Maloyaroslavets, committed Komsomol members; they had wanted to join the partisans, but didn't make it in time. Now all they could think of was how to get out of here, away from the train. But the Germans didn't take us out for nature's calls, and they didn't feed us at all: How could you feed such a crowd?

We pissed right on the floor, on the straw. It all ran out through the cracks. And we made our way to the corner, to the pile, to take a shit. Everyone stood with their back to it, crowding away from it. They threw straw on the shit. One girl, a halfwit, sat nearby. She sang all kinds of songs. She was a village idiot, but the Germans took her, too, since she was young. She wasn't afraid of the smell of shit. She sat next to that pile, picking lice out of her hair and singing.

The worst part was when the train stood still for a long time at substations, or in the middle of a field. We're moving, moving, and then—screech! We stop. And stand there—for an hour, then maybe another. Then we'd creep on along.

We crawled across all of Belorussia that way.

We slept sitting up. We'd lean against one another and fall asleep...

Then the girls woke us up and said: We've entered Poland. It was early, early in the morning. I made my way to the little window and looked out: it was kind of cleaner there, prettier. There were fewer troops. Neat little houses. Very few burned ones.

Everyone started talking about how near Katowice there was a big camp for workers. There were only Russians and from there they sent everyone all over Europe. Europe was very big, and in every corner there were Germans, in all the countries. At the time I didn't know anything about Europe: I had only managed to finish four years of school. I just knew that Berlin was the capital of Germany.

But the girls from Medyn knew everything about Europe and talked about different cities, though they'd never been to them, either. That Tanya, the one who ran after Martin, said that Paris was the best of all. Her Martin had fought there. He told her how beautiful it was and what delicious wine they had. He gave her schnapps to drink. And he gave her a scarf. But she left him, it was all so stupid.

One girl said that we would all be herded into an underground factory where they sewed clothes for the Germans. Right now all across Germany there was an emergency secret order to sew a million padded jackets for the eastern front. Because they were getting ready to attack Moscow, and the Germans' overcoats weren't very warm. That's why they were retreating. As soon as there were a million padded coats they would put them on the best divisions and those troops would jump into new tanks and make for Moscow. A *polizei* she knew had told her all about it.

Then the Komsomol girls started screaming that she was a rat and a traitor; that the Germans hadn't been able to take Moscow in '41, they'd frozen in their overcoats—and rightly so. And when the Red Army finally smashed the Germans, they'd bring Hitler to Moscow, straight to Red Square, and they'd hang him by his feet across from the Mausoleum; they'd hang traitors like her right next to him. They said Comrade Stalin would demand an account from everyone: people who had surrendered, people who'd licked the Germans boots, and women who'd laid down under Germans.

Tanya shouted at them to shut up with their Stalin. Because two of her uncles had been attacked as kulaks, and her father had rotted who knows where, and she and her mother had to live from hand to mouth, and with the Germans they could at least eat normally for the first time, and she'd even fallen so deep in love that she'd almost gone mad.

The Komsomol girls shouted: "Fascist whore!"

She shouted at them: "Stalinist dogs!"

They jumped on one another and started fighting. Then other girls got involved: some for Tanya, some for the Komsomols.

What a scene! Everyone all around was fighting, I wanted to get through to the wall, but I didn't have the strength. They all began fighting in bunches, then the train started suddenly and tossed us around. Gracious! Where did all that strength come from—we hadn't eaten in two days!

Ice

A couple of times I got slugged in the kisser, and sparks filled my eyes. People rarely fought in our village. Only in the spring, during the planting. Or at a wedding. In springtime—it was over fields. Someone would always get their head cracked open with a coupling bolt. At weddings—it was because of moonshine. They'd distill it from potatoes, set it on the table, drink—and start fighting.

My late grandpa told us stories: once there was a wedding, the guests sat down, drank, everything was calm, people were eating, the young people were kissing. But everyone was bored. One guy sat and sat, then sighed and said, "Well, someone has to start!"

He hauled back and slugged the guy sitting across from him right in the face. The guy fell head over heels, and the fight started.

Well, I don't know what would have happened if not for that half-wit idiot. She was sitting there near her pile and dozing, but as soon as the girls started fighting—she woke up. And oh did she howl! She was probably scared out of her wits, being half asleep. She scooped up some shit from the pile—and flung it straight at one of the girls! Again! And again!

They all squealed bloody murder! But they stopped fighting.

Then we came to a halt somewhere before Kraców. We stood and stood and stood. We stood there almost the whole night. It was stifling. Some cried, while others slept. Some laughed.

The four of us made it over to a corner and sat down. It was dark, and somewhere far away outside we could hear someone playing on a harmonica. Right away I began remembering home, Mama, Grandma, and Gerka. The tears came all by themselves. But I didn't cry out loud.

Our life hadn't been bad: Father earned money from selling timber, and not from a workday salary like on the collective farms. Not because he wasn't from the village—he just got lucky. One time he pulled Matvei Fedotovich, the forest warden, out of the bog. When he worked as a ranger he learned to hunt. What would you expect? After all, he spent all his time on a horse with a gun. When something jumped out—bang! Our forest warden loved to hunt, too. So they would go out and hunt together. Once, when they were duck hunting in the Butchinsky swamp, the forest warden stepped into quicksand and was pulled down. Father pulled him out. The old forester, Kuzma Kuzmich, had been murdered by Gypsies, so there was a job open. And the forest warden just up and appointed father! He became a forester. He got paid 620 rubles salary every month.

When you have money you can get by. Other men, as soon as winter hit—they'd be off to the city to earn money and buy something. You can't buy anything with workday credits. They'll give you potatoes or maybe rye. Sometimes it was oats. They'd boil and boil the oats in a cauldron all winter and eat them. Like horses.

But we ate well. We kept a horse, a cow, two pigs, geese, and chickens. We always had lard. Once in a while Mama would fry eggs in the morning on the big frying pan—they swam in lard! You'd take a piece of bread and dunk it—glorious! And afterward—buckwheat blini with cottage cheese.... You'd dunk them, and wash them down with baked milk—oh it was delicious! We had honey too, we bought it at the market. Father bought me boots at the market, too, and a princess doll, and four books so I could learn to read.

The other girls only had alphabet books, but I had real books with pictures: *The Magic Horse*, *Soviet Moscow*, *The Gingerbread Man*, and *The Wolf and the Seven Kids*.

The market was amazing, wonderful! Some mornings father

Ice

would say: "So, then, Varyusha, what about going to the market today?"

I would fly out ahead of mother to harness the horses! Oh how I loved to harness horses! Father taught me when I was a small child: there weren't any grown boys in the family! And I rode horses well—what else do you expect? I was always around horses: first there was Frisky, then Zoya, who was stolen, and then Boy.

I'd take them out, brush them down, and hitch them to the cart with the painted backboard. Father would put on his calf boots, fill a new powder bag, and sit down in front. Mama and I always sat in the back. The whip went "Crack!" and off we'd go. It was thirty-six versts from our place to the market. It's in Zhizdra. What didn't they have there! All kinds of dishes, and rugs, and yokes. I loved the toys. One man sold little painted whistles. Another one sold toys: a peasant and a bear working in the forge. And there were all kinds of dolls. Good ones.

Everything would have been fine if father hadn't been a drinker. Mama said that's why there weren't any more children...

On the other hand—why remember the past? The Germans burned the village anyway.

So I bawled quietly.

That's right. We stood there and stood there. Then in the morning the train jerked. We moved along awhile and stopped: Krac ów. Girls started standing up—we're here! Then someone slid the door back—and there were the Germans. They were looking at us, saying something. One of them held his nose and turned away. They started laughing: the stench in our car was strong. Then a Pole came over with a bucket of water. The Germans said, "Trinken!"

The Pole handed us the bucket. We began drinking one at a

time. We drank up one bucket, and he brought another. We drank up the second as well. He gave us a third! I wasn't really very thirsty, but when my turn came, I started and couldn't stop, like I was in a trance. They barely got it away from me.

Altogether, our car drank four whole buckets of water.

Then two Poles drove a cart over. It had chopped up pieces of raw horse meat on it. And one of them began shoveling the pieces into our car. He tossed them. The German shouted: "Essen!"

And they closed the door again. We stood there, and then—what else could we do? We all tried to sort it out: if they're feeding us, then that means that we're going on farther, to Germany itself. And how far is it? No one knew. Maybe two weeks or more? Maybe a month? Europe is big. Maybe even bigger than Russia.

We were hungry. We tore that raw horse meat into smaller pieces and chewed on it.

The train kept on going. We didn't stop for long anymore. Probably the railroads were better in Poland, so our train moved at a clip.

I chewed on the horse meat and fell asleep for a long time. I slept and slept, like a corpse. I was exhausted, of course. And it was scary. Whenever I was scared—I got sleepy. As soon as Father started beating Mother—I'd start yawning from fear. My head would hurt, I felt like lying down on the floor and not getting up, like sleeping until it was all over.

One time, Avdotia Kupriyanova and I got lost in the forest. We were sent to gather mushrooms, and she said: "Var, I know a secret mushroom glade, there are only white mushrooms growing—let's go." So she took me to that field. She walked on and on, and led me into such a thicket that I got scared: the trees were huge, you couldn't see the sun, it was dark as night.

Ice

We were lost. It was terrifying! There were wolves in our parts, and in '30 a bear ripped two cows to shreds. As soon as Avdotia saw that we were lost she began howling like a total idiot! What could I do? We went on, and I pulled her by the hand. Then I got so scared that I lay down under a bush and fell asleep. She fell asleep next to me. When I woke up—we'd been found. The road was nearby, some peasants were heading for the fields, we heard them. We shouted. They came over. Mother said it was a miracle...

I woke up when they slid the door back and shouted: "Stehen auf! Aussteigen! Schnell! Schnell!"

We got up little by little and crawled out of the car.

We crawled out onto an enormous public square. Not exactly a train station, but the sort of place where trains park, drive up, and drive off. I'd never seen anything like it: lots and lots of tracks, and freight trains standing idle. Whole trains with timber, and empty cars. And cisterns. There were soldiers everywhere.

They made us line up next to the train. Four people had died along the way, who knows from what. They were immediately taken away.

A German stood on a box and began speaking in Russian. He said that now we were in the great country of Germany. This was a huge honor for us. For that reason we should all work hard for the good of Greater Germany. He told us that we would go to a filtration camp where we would be given good, good clothes, and our documents for living in Germany would be processed. And then we would go to different factories and plants where we would live and work. All of us would be fine. And the most important thing for us to understand was that

Part II

Germany was a cultured country, and that everyone in it lived happily. And that young people were even happier than others.

Then we were formed into columns and led off.

We walked from that place. We walked about seven versts. We arrived at a large camp with a barbed-wire fence and guard towers. Germans walked around with German shepherd dogs, and there were cars.

We were divided into barracks: girls separately, boys separately. There were bunks in our barracks. And there were other girls too—from Poland, Belorussia, and the Ukraine. But there weren't very many of them. They told us that no one stayed here more than three days: they put us through the camp and then took us to our workplace.

We asked them—where will you send us? They said, "Different places." No one could know for sure. And if someone got sick—they'd go to the work camp. That was the worst of all. They beat you with bricks there.

We stayed put awhile and then we were taken to the hygiene processing center.

It was an enormous bathhouse—gracious! I'd never seen anything like it. It was a huge sort of barracks—all brand new, and smelling like fresh boards. As soon as I entered, and smelled that smell, I remembered our saw mill at Kordon. How I would ride behind the board when Uncle Misha's place was being built. We built him such a beautiful house, father got the best lumber. Then Uncle Misha went and hung himself. These things happen.

First thing they did in the barracks was line us up. Then they began taking us off three at a time.

I went with two other girls. There were tables, and German women in army uniform were sitting there writing something.

Ice

But one stood holding a kind of crop. And she talked in Russian: "Take your clothes off."

We undressed. Stark naked. She looked at us front and back. Then she looked at our hair. Everybody had lice. I had lice too, what do you expect? She pointed her crop at two of the girls, and gestured toward a pile of hair: "Haircut!"

One girl began sobbing. The German lady snapped the crop across her bottom. She laughed. The girls sat down on the chairs, and women with clipping machines descended on them. She didn't tell me to cut my hair. She pointed the crop at the door of the bath: "Go in there."

I went in. It was sort of like a steam room. But there weren't any basins, just iron pipes with holes in them up above. Lukewarm water sprayed out of the holes. I looked at those pipes—what was I supposed to do? I stood there awhile, then I went on. Then there was a kind of dressing room. Again there were German army ladies. And tables with different kinds of clothes. The German lady gave me a clean undershirt and a blue scarf. She nodded at the exit. I went out and found another dressing room. Our clothes were there. But they smelled funny. It turned out that this was the place where we'd undressed. The barracks were built in a kind of circle, like the carousel at the fair. The same German lady with the crop said, "Get dressed."

I pulled on the new underclothes, then the wool stockings, and my green dress. Then a sweater. Then my padded coat. My old head scarf wasn't there. They took it. My old undershirt wasn't there either. I tied the new scarf around my head. And the other girls, their hair already cut, went to wash.

The German lady said, "Sit down at the table."

I sat down. There was another German woman across from me too. She also spoke Russian: "What's your name?"

Part II

I said, "Samsikova, Varya."

"How old?"

"Fourteen."

She wrote everything down. Then she said, "Stretch out your arm."

I didn't understand at first. She repeated, "Give me your arm!"

I stretched it out. She put a stamp on my arm—bam! It was a number in ink: 32-126.

Then she said, "Go over there."

There was a door. I opened it. I was in the yard. A soldier with a machine gun pointed me to another barracks. As I approached it I started to smell food. Lord, I thought, are they really going to feed us? I thought I was walking, but my legs ran all by themselves. Behind me some more girls came out. They ran, too.

We went inside. It wasn't a barracks, but a lean-to made of planks. Under it there were these huge cauldrons, about ten of them, and there was food cooking. There were Germans with bowls and ladles, and some of our people, who'd already come out. The Germans gave everyone an empty bowl. They gave me one, too—and we got in line. I waited my turn, and a German put a ladleful in my bowl—plash! It was pea soup. Thick, like porridge. But nobody had a spoon. Everyone sucked it over the rim.

I sipped it up quickly, wiped up the bowl with my hand, and licked the soup off.

A German was watching me. "Willst du noch?"

And I said, "Ja, ja. Bitte!"

And he gave me some more—plop! I sipped the second bowl more slowly. I looked around me: our people were chatting, there were Germans everywhere. Everything was different; a totally different life had begun.

Ice

I ate the second portion—and felt drunk. I rested next to the cauldron. It was warm and shiny. The German laughed. "Also, noch einmal, Mädl?"

I remembered what Otto said when he'd drunk enough milk. So I answered, "Ich bin satt, ich markt kein Blatt."

The German roared with laughter, and asked me something. But I didn't understand.

I went back to the barracks.

By evening, everyone on our train had been processed and fed. But for some reason they didn't cut everyone's hair. Me and three other girls from our barracks hadn't had their hair cut. Tanya explained: "It's because you don't have lice."

I said, "What do you mean? Just take a look!"

She parted my hair.

"You do have them! Well, then they forgot. Hide your hair under a head scarf, or else they'll remember and lop it off till you're bald."

That's what I did: I tied the scarf tighter, to hide my hair.

When it got dark, that same German lady with the crop came in and said, "Now you all go to sleep. In the morning you'll be taken to your workplaces. You'll live and work there."

And they locked the barracks doors with a chain.

Some fell asleep right away, some didn't. I settled down close to Tanya and Natasha from Briansk and we kept on talking about what would happen. They were older than me, they'd heard a lot about Europe, and about Germans.

Natashka told us that in Briansk the Germans had showed films for their people. And two times a German invited her and a girlfriend. And she saw a film of Hitler and a naked woman who sang and danced and laughed. There were Germans dressed in white wandering around the woman. They looked at her and smiled. Hitler, she said, looked like he was so nice, with his lit-

Part II

tle mustache. He was cultured, you could tell right away. And he talked very loud.

I'd been to the movies six times in all. Our closest club was in Kirov, twenty-five versts away. My father took me two times on Boy. Then Stepan Sotnikov took me with their children. I saw *Chapaev* twice, then *Volga-Volga*, *We Are from Kronshtadt*, *Seven Brave Hearts*, and one other picture, I forgot what it was called. It was about Lenin, how a woman took a shot at him. And he ran away in his cap. Then he fell. But he didn't die.

Down below on the bunks girls kept on trying to figure out who would win the war, us or the Germans.

Tanya and Natashka didn't care who, as long as they didn't bomb anything.

We'd been bombed three times. But all the bombs hit the orchards, not the village. But they did break the glass and slash the cows. One village woman stepped on a mine and it blew up. They brought her to the village. They brought her in on a mat, no leg, her guts spilling out. And she kept saying over and over, "Mamochka my beloved, my sweet mama. My sweet mama, Mama, Mama, Mama." Then she died.

Then I fell asleep.

When I woke up—everyone had already risen. The girls and I ran to piss. There was a big privy, nice and clean. We pissed, and some even took a shit. Then we went to eat, to those cauldrons. Again there was pea soup. But watery, not like yesterday. And they didn't give seconds. I sipped the soup. I'd just finished licking the bowl when they shouted: "Line up!"

And we all went out to the big square.

They lined us up—fellows separate, us girls separate. The

Ice

Germans stood around watching. They were silent. One kept looking at his watch. So, we stood there, the Germans not saying anything. We stood there for an hour, until our legs went numb. Natashka said, "They're waiting for trucks, to take us."

Suddenly we heard cars coming. And they drove straight into the camp. But not trucks, light passenger cars. Three cars. Shiny black, beautiful. They drove up and Germans got out of them. Just like the cars, all dressed in black. One of them, the most important—was very tall; he wore a black leather coat and gloves. All the other Germans saluted him.

He saluted too, walked over to us, crossed his arms on his stomach, and looked. He was handsome, fair-haired. He looked and said, "Gut. Sehr gut."

Then he said something to the Germans. The lady who spoke Russian said, "Remove all headgear."

I didn't understand at first. I understood when the fellows took off their caps and hats and the girls started untying their scarves.

I thought: Here we go, now they're going to shave my head. And sure enough, the German lady said, "Whoever has hair—step forward."

There was nothing to be done—I took a step. Another fifteen or so people stepped forward: boys and girls. All of us they hadn't shaved. The strange thing was that everyone was towheaded, like me! It was even funny.

The German lady said, "Line up!"

So everyone stood side by side.

That German, the important one, walked over and looked at us. His look was sort of...I don't know how to say it. Long and slow. And then he came up to each of us. He'd come close, lift our chins with two fingers, and stare. Then he'd move on. He didn't speak.

Part II

He came up to me. He lifted my chin and stared at my eyes. He had a face that was...well, I'd never seen anything like it. Like Christ on an icon. Skinny, tow-headed, with blue blue eyes. Very clean, not a speck of dust or dirt. He wore a black peaked cap, and on the top of it—was a skull.

He looked at me, then at the rest. And he pointed to three of us.

"Dieses, dieses, dieses."

Then he touched his nose with his glove, as if he was thinking. He pointed at me.

"Und dieses."

He turned and went back to the cars.

And the German lady said, "Those who were chosen by his honor the Oberfürher—follow him immediately!"

So we went, the four of us.

The German went to the first car; the door was opened for him and he got in. Another German nodded for us to go to the second car. He opened the door. We walked over, and climbed in. He closed the door and sat down in the front with the driver.

We took off.

I had never ridden in a passenger car. Only in trucks, when we transported the grain. And when we had the cattle plague in Koliubakino, they brought us calves in two cars for breeding. The Party *raikom* provided the cars. And Mamanya and I rode after those calves with the cattle worker Pyotr Abramych, all the way to Lompadi. I saw a passenger car in Kirov once. When we went to the movies. That car just stood there, because it had driven into the mud and gotten stuck. And everyone was standing around thinking how to get it out. The fat man who arrived in the car swore at the other one, from the *raikom*. The fat man yelled real loud: "Up your ass, Borisov, you have to go and drive in the ice."

Ice

Borisov stood there, silent, staring at the car.

Well, then. I looked around the Germans' car. It was all so beautiful! The driver sat in front with the German, we sat in the back. Everything was shiny and clean, the seats were made from leather, there were all sorts of handles. And it smelled like airplanes—the way it does in the city.

That car ran real easy. You didn't feel it driving, it just rocked over the potholes, you coulda thought you're in a cradle. That's when I understood why they call those cars "light" passenger cars.

There were two other girls with me and one young fellow. We drove and drove. Who knows where.

We drove about two versts, then turned into the forest and stopped. The German jumped up, opened the door and said, "Aussteigen!"

We got out. We looked and saw the two other cars nearby. There was new forest all around.

The important German stepped out of his car. He said something to the other Germans. They tied our hands behind our backs. So quick and crafty that I didn't understand what was happening, and—poof—they'd already got me! They pulled us along with a rope, and led us over to four trees. They tied us to the trees.

The girls began to whimper. So did I. It was clear as day—we wouldn't get out of this forest. We're wailing, one girl started praying, and the boy, who was older than us, he shouted: "Sir, sir, I'm not a lousy Yid! Please, sir!"

But they just tied us up to the trees. And then they gagged us so we couldn't shout. Then they waited. The important one looked at us—and pointed to the boy. Two of the Germans went to the car.

I realized that they were going to kill us here and now. For what—I didn't know. Lord almighty, could it really be because we hadn't had our heads shaved?! Was that really our fault? It was those horrible Germans who forgot to shave our heads, not me who refused! I didn't care! Was I really going to end up underground because of my hair?! Mama, Mama mine. So this is how everything would end! I was going into the wet earth here, and no one would ever know where the grave of Varka Samsikova was!

I stood there thinking. Tears filled my eyes.

The Germans were getting something out of the car. They carried an iron trunk toward us. They set it down, opened it, and took out a sort of ax or sledgehammer—I couldn't tell at first. So, they weren't going to shoot us, just chop us to bits alive. Oh, how evil!

They went over to the young man. He struggled against his ropes, poor dear guy, like a little bird. The German pulled open the fellow's coat—whap! Then his shirt—rrrip! He tore it open. His undershirt, too—rip! They bared his chest.

The important one nodded. "Gut."

He reached out his gloved hand. The other German handed him the sledgehammer. I looked at it—it wasn't exactly a sledgehammer, it wasn't clear what it was. It looked as though it was made of ice. Or salt, like the kind they give cows to lick on the farm. No metal. The important German swung the sledgehammer back and hit the young fellow in the chest with all his might—bam! His whole body shuddered.

Another German put a kind of pipe to the fellow's chest, like a doctor, and listened. The important one stood by with the sledgehammer. The German shook his head. "Nichts."

Again, the important one swung back, and—bam! The other German listened again. Once again he said, "Nichts."

The important one smashed the fellow's chest again. They

Ice

had beaten him to death. He just hung there on the rope. The Germans tossed the sledgehammer, took a new one from the box—and went over to the girl who was tied to a birch tree, next to me. She sobbed wordlessly, and trembled all over. They unbuttoned her plush jacket, slashed her sweater with a knife, and tore her undershirt. I looked—she had a little cross around her neck. My grandma put one on me, too, but the schoolteacher Nina Sergeevna took it off. "You are Pioneers," she said, "and there's no God. So we're going to tear up religious prejudice by the roots." She pulled the crosses off every student who had one and threw them into the weeds. Grandma said: "Unbelievers never die." I think that's the truth.

The important German again picked up the sledgehammer that wasn't made of metal, swung back easily, and slammed the girl on the chest—crack! Her bones seemed to crunch. The fiend stood back, while the other one put the tube on her and listened. He listened to the girl dying. After the first blow, she just hung unconscious on the ropes, her head all floppy. Then the third German lifted her head and held it, so it wasn't in the way. Again—crack! crack! crack! They beat her so hard that her blood splattered on my cheek.

The beasts.

Then they beat the other girl. She was only about fifteen, I think, like me. And the same height as me. But her breasts were already big, nothing like what I had. They beat her, beat her until blood spurted from her nose. She had a gag in her mouth.

I was the only one left.

When they'd finished beating the busty girl they threw down the sledgehammer. They took out cigarettes, stood in a circle, and lit up to take a break. They talked. The most important German wasn't happy. He said nothing. Then he shook his head and said, "Schon wieder taube Nuss..."

Part II

The other Germans nodded.

I stood there, I could see them smoking. I was thinking: any minute now, any minute, these fiends will finish their smoke— and that'll be it. I didn't feel afraid or sad, deep down. It was more like everything was as clear as the blue sky when there aren't any clouds. Like in a dream and I wasn't alive at all. Like everything had been a dream: Mama, the village, and the war. And these Germans.

They finished smoking and tossed their butts. They crowded around me.

They unbuttoned my jacket, and took a knife to my sweater, the one that Grandma knit out of goat's wool. They pulled it back. I had my green dress on under my sweater. Father bought it for me at the county store in Lompadi. They slashed my dress with the knife, and then the German undershirt I'd been given at the camp. One German rolled the ripped edges of my dress and sweater back, sticking them under the rope, so that my chest was bared.

The important man stood with the sledgehammer and looked at me. He mumbled something, and handed the sledge-hammer to another German. Then he took his cap off his head and gave it to the one behind him. He stood just to my right.

The other German hauled back, grunted like he was splitting firewood, and bashed me right in the chest! I saw sparks. It took my breath away.

The important man suddenly dropped to his knees in front of me and put his ear to my chest.

His ear was cold, but his cheek was warm. His head was very, very close, fair and smooth, like it had been rubbed with cooking oil. His hair laid straight and flat, and stank of perfume.

I looked at his head from above, looked, and looked, and

looked. Like it was a dream. Here I was dying, and I felt so calm. I even stopped bellowing.

He called to the German with the sledgehammer. "Noch einmal, Willi!"

Willi heaved once more—wham!

The important German pressed his ear to me again, listening. "Noch einmal!"

Oof! He hit me so hard that chips flew off of the sledgehammer. I realized that it really was made of ice.

Everything swam before my eyes.

The important guy pressed his ear to me again. His ear was already covered with my blood. And suddenly he shouted, "Ja! Ja! Herr Laube, sofort!"

And the German with the doctor's tube rushed over to me. He stuck the tube to my chest and listened. He mumbled something, squinching his sour face.

The important German pushed him away.

"Noch einmal!"

And they slammed me again. I felt as though I was falling asleep: my lips filled with lead, and my mouth grew numb and heavy, like it was someone else's; it felt fuzzy like the inside of a stove. Then I was so, so light, like a cloud, and the only thing in my chest was my heart and that was all. No stomach—I wasn't breathing, or swallowing. This heart in me seemed to *move*. That is, it was just...I couldn't tell what. Like some little creature. It stirred, fluttered. It muttered something sweet as honey: khrr, khrr, khrr. Not the way it used to—from fear, you know, or joy. This was completely different, as though it had just awoken and before it was really deep, deep asleep. Here they were, killing me, and my heart woke up. There wasn't any fear in it, not the tiniest smidgen. There was only this sweet muttering. Just everything good, honest, and so tender that I felt petrified. The hair on my head moved: that's how good I felt. All the fear drained away: *What is there to be afraid of, if my heart is with me!*

Nothing of the sort had ever happened to me.

I froze stiff and didn't breathe.

The German with the tube started listening to me again. He spoke very loud, "Khra...Khra...Khram!"

The important one grabbed the tube from him and put it on my chest himself.

"Khram! Genau! Khram!"

And he began to shake with joy.

"Herrschaften, Khram! Khram! Sie ist Khram! Hören Sie! Hören Sie! Hören Sie!"

They all started blabbering and fussing around me. They cut the ropes off. But suddenly everything about them was disgusting to me—their horrible nasty voices, and hands, and faces, and their vehicles, and this drooling forest, everything all around. I stiffened so as not to scare off my heart, so that it would keep on muttering so sweet, so that the heart sweetness would take all of me in through my guts. But they started pulling me out of the ropes like a doll, grabbing me. My heart suddenly fell quiet.

I fainted dead away.

I don't know how much time passed.

I came to.

I hadn't even opened my eyelids, and I could feel—everything was rocking. They were taking me somewhere.

I opened my eyes: I saw that the room was small. It swayed slightly. I looked around—there was a window next to me, with a curtain on it. There was a little gap in the curtain and I could see the forest going by.

Ice

I realized I was on a train.

As soon as I realized this, my head became sort of empty. As though it wasn't a head, but a hay barn in spring—not a stick of straw, not a blade of grass. The cattle had gobbled everything up over the winter.

Emptiness. Enormous, no end to it. In all directions. But this emptiness didn't scare me or anything, it was sort of good. It was—whoosh! Like racing down an icy hill on a sled—whoosh! You start and you're already at the bottom. This emptiness was the same—whoosh! It rode into my head. And my head was empty, completely empty, though I understood everything and acted the right way.

I freed my hand from under the blanket. I looked at it—my left hand. I'd seen it thousands of times. But I looked at it—as though seeing it for the first time. Even though I knew everything about it! I remembered all the little scars, the one where I cut myself on the sickle, and where I hit a nail. I remembered so well, like someone was showing me a movie. That blue spot on my pinkie over there: Where did it come from? Well, it was from the time that Uncle Semyon returned from the army, he'd made himself a badge he pinned on his chest: a heart with an arrow. And he was teaching the boys how to make them: you had to nail a picture to a bit of wood, then burn a boot heel, take the soot, and rub it on the nails. That was it! You pinned the wood on your chest. Our neighbor Kolka made one, but father scolded him and threw the wood out, and then I pricked my pinkie on that wood with the nails. On one nail.

That's what.

The little room I was in was so lovely, all wood. And the screws in the wall were shiny. Two beds, a little table in the middle, a yellow ceiling. Warm. And it smelled clean, like in the hospital.

Part II

Someone was lying on the other bed. In a uniform. Turned toward the wall.

I freed my hand from under the blanket and sat up. I saw that I was only wearing my underclothes. And my chest was bandaged.

Then I suddenly remembered everything. At first, it was like my memory was lost: who I was, where I was—I couldn't understand anything: I was just riding and riding.

I looked around: there was an iron box on the table. A book.

I lifted the curtain: woods, woods, and more woods. Trees were the only things flashing by.

I sat up and hung my legs over the edge of the bed. I looked down—my cowhide boots weren't there. There were no clothes to be seen. I hung my head down, looking in the corners. Then my throat got scratchy and I started coughing. It made my chest hurt terribly.

I moaned and grabbed my chest.

The guy who was dozing jumped up and rushed to me. It was the same German who had brought the ice sledgehammers. He fussed about, embraced me by the shoulders and mumbled, "Ruhe, ganz Ruhe, Schwesterchen . . ."

He laid me down on the bed and covered me with the blanket. He leaped up, buttoned his collar, straightened his tunic, unlocked the door, and ran out, closing the door. I had barely managed to think a thought when the important German came in.

He was still the same—tall and fair. But not wearing black anymore. He wore a blue robe.

He sat on my bed and smiled. He took my hand, lifted it to his lips, and kissed it.

Then he took off his robe. Under the robe he had on a shirt and pants. He took off the shirt. His skin was so white. Then he started taking off his pants. I turned away.

Ice

Now he's going to go and make a woman of me, I thought. I lay there, listening to his trousers rustling, and wasn't even afraid. I lay there senseless. What did I care? I'd just lived through so much in that grove that nothing mattered anymore.

He got undressed. He threw the blanket off me and started taking off my underclothes.

I looked at the wall, at the new screws.

He undressed me all the way. And then he lay down next to me. He patted my head. And turned me toward him. I closed my eyes.

He turned me to him carefully, wrapping his long arms around me. He pressed his whole body to mine, pressed his chest to mine.

And that was it! He lay there, that's all. I thought, that's the way the Germans do it, they're careful with girls, first they calm them down, and then—bam! In our village they do it right off, I'd been told.

I lay there. Suddenly I felt a shock, a jolt through my whole body, as though I'd been hit by lightning. My heart stirred once again. Like some little creature. At first I felt strange, anxious, as if I'd been hung upside down like a piece of meat in the cellar. Then it felt good. I felt I was floating down a stream, riding a wave that carried me, faster and faster. Suddenly I could feel his heart as if it were my own. His heart began to tug at my heart. It was so incredibly sweet. So dear and familiar.

It burned clear through me.

Even my mama hadn't ever been so close to me. No one had.

I stopped breathing, and plunged into the feeling as into a well.

He kept on plucking and pulling at my heart with his heart. Like it was a hand. He'd squeeze it, or open it up. I grew numb.

Part II

I completely stopped thinking. I wanted only one thing—for it to never stop.

Lord, how sweet it was. He'd start plucking at my heart, I'd just go numb, go numb like I was dying. My heart would flutter and stop. It would just stand there, like a horse sleeping. Then—bing! It would come alive again, quiver, and he'd start plucking at it again.

But everything on earth comes to an end eventually.

He stopped. We both sort of died. We lay there in two big lumps. Neither of us could lift a finger.

The train kept on going—chug-a-chug, chug-a-chug.

Then he loosened his hands. And collapsed on the floor.

I lay there and lay there. Then I sat up and I looked around. He was on the floor, as still as a corpse. Then he moved, suddenly embracing my legs. It was so dear and sweet!

I didn't even have the strength to cry.

He got up and dressed. Laid me down in bed and covered me with a blanket. Then he left.

I couldn't lie still. I got up. I pulled back the curtains from the window and looked out. I saw forest, fields, and villages. I looked at them as though I was seeing all this for the first time. I felt no fear. There was such joyous peace in my chest. Everything was clear!

Then he returned. This time he was dressed in his black uniform. He brought me some clothes: a pretty dress, all sorts of underclothes, boots, a coat, scarf, and beret. And he started dressing me. I watched him. On the one hand, I was embarrassed, but on the other, my soul was singing!

He dressed me and sat down next to me. He looked at me with his blue eyes. And I looked at him.

I felt so good!

Ice

It wasn't that I'd fallen in love with him. It was good in a totally different way. You can't say it in words. I felt I'd been given in marriage. To something great and good. Something that was forever and eternity my own, very dear, very beloved.

It wasn't love, the thing you have between girls and fellows. I knew about love.

I'd fallen in love twice before. First with Goshka the shepherd. Then with Kolya Malakhov, an already married man. Goshka and me kissed, and he squeezed my breasts. We'd go up in the hayloft to do it. He wanted to paw me lower down—but I didn't let him.

I fell in love with Kolya Malakhov myself. He didn't know anything and still doesn't, if he's alive. Like Father, he was sent to the war on June 24.

Before the war he was married off to Nastenka Pluyanova. He was seventeen and she was sixteen. We worked at the haymaking together. He cut, I dried and raked. I got stuck on him. He had curly hair, he was handsome and merry. When I caught sight of him—my heart would freeze. I'd be soaked to the bone in embarrassment. I'd go beet red. I even stopped eating for two days. Then it would pass somehow. Later—it happened again. I could think only of him. I cried and cried: dumb old Nastenka was so lucky! Then it sort of let go of me. Just as well. Why should I pine after someone else's fellow? That's love for you.

But this—was something else.

We rode the whole day in silence. We sat side by side.

Then the train stopped. The German got up, put the coat on me. And took me by the hand through the entire car. It was full of German officers. We got off the train at the station. I looked around—what a station, I'd never seen anything of the sort! It was all iron and so high, no beginning or end to it. There were trains everywhere! People everywhere! And they all had things with them, and were well dressed. Everything was clean. Like in the movies.

He took me across the station. The other Germans followed him. Behind them a peasant with a mustache wheeled the suitcases on a cart.

I walked behind him. Everything was different. It all smelled different. A city smell.

Suddenly the station came to an end. We walked straight out into the city. It was so beautiful! All the houses were beautiful. There wasn't any war here at all—all the buildings were whole, people strolled down the streets calmly. Some even had dogs. They sat on benches and read newspapers.

We came to some automobiles. Just as black as the other one I'd ridden in, and just as shiny. Everyone got in. The important German and I got in the first car, and it drove off. Through the whole city.

I looked out the window and suddenly said, "Was ist das?"

He laughed. "Oh, du sprichst deutsch, Khram! Das ist schöne Wien."

Then he started talking fast, but I didn't understand anything. Over the two years that the Germans stayed with us, I learned some German words. I even knew swear words. But I never studied German in school.

I just smiled. Then he made a sign to the German who sat in front. He had met us at the station. And he was fair and blue-eyed, too. But he wasn't wearing a black uniform, he was in regular clothes. And a hat.

He spoke to me in Russian, and I thought he must be Polish. He said, "This city is called Vienna. It's one of the most beautiful cities in the world."

Ice

He told me all about the city: when it was built and what marvelous things there were to see. But I didn't remember anything.

Suddenly the important German ordered the chauffeur, "Stop!"

We stopped. The important one said something. And the Germans nodded.

"Eine gute Idee!"

The important one got out, opened the door, and signaled to me. I got out. I looked around: just a street. And a store with a pretty sign was right in front of us. Such a wonderful aroma came from that store! I felt faint!

The important German and I went inside. There were mirrors all around, and thousands of candies, cakes, pies, and other sweets. Very pretty girls in white aprons stood around. Behind me the Pole said, "What do you want?"

I said, "I don't even know."

The important man pointed to something behind the glass. The girl began to do something like mixing dough, and then— whoop! She handed me a little funnel with a pink ball on it. I took it. The ball smelled sweet. I tried it—but it was cold. It made my teeth ache. I looked at the German.

He nodded as if to say, go ahead and eat it.

And I ate it. It resembled sweet snow, but thicker. Delicious, but strange.

I ate and ate. And stopped.

Really, after everything that had happened, I didn't much want to eat. But the smells were good. I said, "It's cold. You can't eat much. May I wait for it to thaw?"

The Germans laughed. And that Pole said, "It's ice cream. You have to eat it cold. A little at a time. You don't have to hurry, you can finish it in the car."

Part II

I nodded. And we got back in and drove off down those beautiful streets. I looked out the window and ate slowly.

But honestly, I didn't really like the ice cream. The caramel roosters that Papa brought from the market were tastier. I could have sucked on them day and night.

We left the city and drove into the hills. The hills got higher and higher, till they were as high as the sky! I'd never seen anything like it in my life. We had two hills between Koliubakino and Pospelovka. When the girls and I walked to the Pospelovka village store we walked across the hills. You'd climb up to the tippy-top, stand there—oh, you could see so far! You could see our house like it was on the palm of your hand. Sometimes I could even see our rooster.

These hills took your breath away. The road became a narrow, twisty snake, and when you looked down you saw enormous pits! There were fir trees growing everywhere.

I asked, "What is this?"

"These are the mountains called the Alps," the Pole answered.

We drove through those Alps. Higher and higher.

We were so high that we reached the clouds, and drove on into them!

I kept looking down, but I couldn't see anything—that's how high it was!

We kept on driving and driving, there was no end to it. I was rocked from side to side, and my chest began to smart. I dozed off.

I woke up.

It was already dusk and I was being carried in someone's arms! The important German was carrying me. It was so embarrassing! No one had carried me for a long time.

Ice

I didn't say anything. He carried me along a road. The woods all around were covered in snow. The stars shone in the sky. The other Germans walked behind us. I looked to the right: Where was he taking me? And there was a large house! All made of stone, with light in the windows, and towers and everything, how beautiful!

He walked up the steps to a sort of porch. They were expecting him—the doors clanked open. The doors were incredibly heavy, all strapped with iron.

He walked in carrying me; everything was made of stone, the ceiling swam before my eyes. The lamps were lit. His boots made a sound—clok, clok, clok.

He walked and walked.

Suddenly some other doors flew open and there was a lot of light all at once.

The German stopped. He set me down carefully, like a doll. But not on the floor. He put me on a white stone, as big as a trunk. In Zhizdra an iron Lenin stood on that kind of stone before the war. Then the Germans knocked him down.

I lay on that stone. I looked around—there were lots of people, maybe forty. Men, women. And they were all looking at me silently.

The German said something to them in German. And they approached me from all sides. They came, like sheep, smiling. And they all came over to me! I was kind of dumbstruck. They walked up to that stone and suddenly all of them got down on their knees and bowed to me.

I looked around for my German—what should I do? But he had also bowed down to the floor in his black uniform. So did all the Germans who came with us. And the Polish man.

Everyone was bowing to me!

Part II

Then they lifted their heads and looked at me.

I saw that they were all blond. And they all had blue eyes.

They got up from their knees one by one. An old man came over to me and stretched out his hands. He spoke in plain Russian.

"Come down and be with us, Sister."

And so I got off the stone.

He said, "Khram! We are happy to have found you among the dead. You are our sister forever. We are your brothers and sisters. Each one of us will now greet you heartily.

He hugged me and said, "I am Bro."

A jolt passed to me from his heart. As though his heart was saying good day to my heart. Once again I felt the sweetness I'd felt in the train. But he soon unclasped his hands and moved aside.

All the others began to approach me. They took turns. Spoke their names and hugged me. Each time something pulsed and tugged at my heart. In all different ways: from one person it was like this, from another—like that.

It was all so sweet, it went right through me. Like glasses of wine were being poured onto my heart. One! Two! Three!

I stood there in a dream. My eyes closed. I wanted only one thing—for it continue an eternity.

Finally the last one walked up, said his name, hugged me, tugged at my heart—and stepped back. Suddenly it was empty around me—they all stood a ways off, warm and friendly, smiling at me.

The old man took me by the hand and led me off through room after room filled with expensive things. Then up a staircase. He brought me to a big room, entirely done in wood. In the middle was a bed. White, clean, fluffy, airy. He led me over to the bed and began to undress me. He shone all over. He had such an amazing smile, like his whole life he'd only seen kind things and had dealings with kind people.

He undressed me naked and put me in bed. He covered me with a blanket and sat down next to me.

He sat there and looked at me, holding my hand. His eyes were blue, oh so blue, like water.

He held my hand, then he put it under the covers and said, "Khram, my sister. You must rest."

But I felt so good. My whole body was singing. I said, "What do you mean? I slept the whole way, like a broody hen! I'm not the least bit sleepy now."

He said, "You have used a good deal of energy. You have a new life ahead of you. You must prepare for it."

I wanted to argue with him, to say, I'm not at all tired. But then exhaustion suddenly overwhelmed me, as though I'd been hauling sacks or something. I fell into a deep sleep straight-away.

I came to: Where was I?

It was the same room, the same bed. The sun was blazing in through a crack in the curtains.

I slid off the bed and went to the window. I pulled back the curtain: oh my goodness gracious, what a beautiful sight! There were mountains all around. They didn't have any forest covering them, they were naked, covered only in snow. And they reached to the sky. They were all blue. And the sky, it was right up close.

And there wasn't a soul in these mountains.

I suddenly needed to piss bad. Then I remembered what woke me up! I dreamed that I was a baby wrapped in diapers.

Part II

And some strange person was holding me on his knees. I want to piss so bad. I have to ask, so I don't wet him. But I don't know any words yet! And there I am in my diapers, squirming and thinking, how do you say, "I want to piss?" That's when I woke up.

And I needed to go so bad it was as if I'd done nothing but drink water for days. But I didn't know where to go. I went and opened the door. There was a hallway. I walked out and along it, thinking maybe there's a bucket around somewhere. Then I saw a staircase going down, a pretty, wood one with carved pinecones. I walked a few steps down and looked around—there were all sorts of doors. I pushed against one of them—it wasn't locked. I entered.

There were three couples on their knees, embracing. Naked. And silent.

No one even glanced at me.

As soon as I saw them I remembered everything that had happened in the train. I suddenly felt so good, that I couldn't hold it anymore and pissed all over myself. It flooded out of me onto the floor. There was so much—it poured and poured! I just stood there and watched them, and everything went kind of blurry. And the puddle reached all the way over to them! I wasn't ashamed at all—I froze there as if I was made of stone, it was good, no energy to move. I stared at them like they were sweets in a candy shop, that was all. They were standing in my urine! And they didn't budge!

Then someone called out behind me.

"Khram!"

I came to my senses—it was a woman. She spoke to me, but the language was strange—I sort of understood the words separately, but together it was hard. It wasn't Ukrainian or Belarusian. And it wasn't Polish. In the camps I understood Polish.

Ice

The woman took me by the hand and led me somewhere. Naked, I walked behind her, the wet soles of my feet slip-slapping along.

She brought me to a huge room that was covered with sparkling stones. In the middle of the room was a tub—all white—filled with water. The woman unwound the bandage from my chest, and took the cotton off the wound. Then she pulled me toward the tub. I got in and lay down. The water was warm and pleasant.

Then another woman came in. They began to wash me as they would an infant. They washed me all over, then told me to stand up. I stood up. There was this metal plate above my head. And this plate suddenly began to pour water on me, like a little rain shower. It was so wonderful! I just stood there laughing.

Then they dried me off. They put a new bandage on my wound. They sat me down on a stool with a cushion and rubbed sweet-smelling stuff all over me. When I was rubbed down, they combed my hair and wrapped me up in a soft robe. They picked me up like a sack and carried me off.

They brought me to an enormous room. There were all kinds of wardrobes and cabinets, and in the middle there were three mirrors, and a little table right next to them that was covered with little bottles. It smelled of perfume. They sat me down at that table, and I could see myself in three mirrors at once. Good lord! Was that really me? I'd turned into someone completely different over the last weeks. I don't know what happened—either I'd gotten older, or smarter, but the only thing left of the old me was my hair and eyes. It was even kind of scary. . . . But what could I do about it? At times like these my late grandfather used to say, "Live and don't be afraid of anything."

First they cut my hair. They gave me a pretty hairdo, and put some smelly stuff on it. Then they trimmed the nails on my hands and feet. Then they evened my nails out with this little file. Just like you do with horses' hooves, when you shoe them! I could barely keep from laughing, but I realized: this is Germany!

Afterward the women began dressing me: they slipped off the robe, and started pulling all kinds of clothes out of the wardrobes and chests of drawers: dresses, underclothes, and brassieres. They laid them out. Everything was so pretty, clean, white!

First they measured me for the brassiere. My titties were still little. They chose the smallest bra and put it on me. Lord almighty! In our village even the grown women never wore brassieres, never mind the girls! I'd only seen these brassiere things in Zhizdra and in Khliupin in the village store where they sell dresses and bolts of dress fabric.

Then they put white drawers on me. Short, pretty ones, like on a doll. Then they hooked stockings onto the drawers. And right over it all—a short white slip. Oh, what a slip. Covered in lace and smelling of sweet perfumes! Everything was beautiful—no doubt about it. Over that they put on a blue dress with a white collar. Then they started picking out shoes. When they opened the boxes I took a look. Oh my goodness! Not ankle boots, not boots at all, but honest-to-god shoes, all patent-leather shiny! They brought me three boxes to choose from. My head almost began spinning. I pointed with my finger—and they put the shoes on my feet. Shoes with heels!

They painted my lips, and powdered my cheeks. They hung a string of pearls around my neck. I stood up and looked at myself in the mirror—I even squeezed my eyes shut! A real beauty stood there in front of me, not Varka Samsikova!

They took me by the hand and led me on. We went downstairs.

Ice

Downstairs there was another enormous room, made of stone. It had a huge table. The people who met me the night before were sitting around it. Only they weren't in uniform, they were in regular clothes. Everyone was eating. The food was pretty, all kinds.

They sat me down at my place. Everyone smiled at me, like family. That old man, Bro, said, "Khram, you are our sister, share our repast with us. The rules of our family are to eat nothing living, neither boil nor fry food, neither cut nor pierce it. For all of these things violate its Cosmos."

He took a pear and handed it to me. I took it and began eating. So did everyone at the table.

I looked at the table: there was no meat, no fish, no eggs, no milk. No bread. But there were different fruits—tons of them. Not only pears—watermelon, cantaloupes and other melons, tomatoes, different kinds of cucumbers, apples, even cherries! And many, many more fruits that I had never seen.

Everyone ate with their hands. No knives, forks, or spoons were to be seen.

I looked at the cantaloupe—I'd never eaten it, only seen it at the market. One man noticed me looking at it, so he took the largest melon. He pulled over a sort of sharp rock. He swung back and—crack went the stone against the cantaloupe! It spurted all over and pieces went flying all around! Everyone smiled. He picked a piece out and handed it to me. Then he gave the rest to the others. I tasted cantaloupe for the first time. It was scrumptious!

Then I ate strawberries, sweet peppers, and three other kinds of fruits. I stuffed myself with cherries.

They all ate, rose, and each went his own way.

The old man Bro came over to me. He took me by the elbow and led me to a little room. It was full of books. He sat me down at a small table and took a seat across from me. He said, "Khram, what are you feeling?"

I said, "My chest aches a little bit."

"And what else?"

"Well," I said, "I don't know… it's hard to say…"

"Do you feel good with us?"

"Yes," I said.

"Has your heart felt good?"

"Very," I answered. "I have never felt this good."

He looked at me with a smile and said, "There are very few people like us. Only one hundred fifty-three on earth."

I said, "Why is that?"

"Because," he said, "we aren't like everyone else. We know how to speak not only with our mouths but with our hearts. Other humans speak only with the mouth. Their hearts will never speak."

"Why?"

"Because they are living corpses. The absolute majority of people on this earth are walking dead. They are born dead, they marry the dead, they give birth to the dead, and die; their dead children give birth to new dead—and so on, from century to century. That is the circle of their dead lives. There is no way out. But we are alive, we are the chosen. We know what the language of the heart is, the language we have already spoken to you. And we know what love is. Genuine Divine Love."

"What is love?"

"For hundreds of millions of dead people, love—is nothing but lust, the thirst to possess another's body. For them, it all boils down to one thing: a man sees a woman, she pleases him. He doesn't know her heart at all, but her face, figure, walk, and laughter attract him. He wants to see this woman, be with her, touch her. And that's when the illness called 'earthly love'

Ice

begins: the man seeks to acquire the woman, he gives her gifts, courts her, swears his love, promises to love her and no one else. She begins to take some interest in him, then she feels sympathy for him, then she starts to think that this is the very person she's been waiting for. Finally they become so close that they are ready to commit the so-called 'act of love.' Hiding away in a bedroom, they undress and lie down on the bed. The man kisses the woman, plays with her breasts; he falls on top of her, thrusts his member in her, pants and groans. She moans, at first from pain, then from lust. The man ejects his seed into the woman's womb. And they fall asleep in sweat, emptied and exhausted. Then they begin to live together, they have children. The passion gradually leaves them. They turn into machines: he makes money, she cooks and cleans. Sometimes they live like this until their very death. Or they fall in love with others. They separate and recall the past with anger. They swear loyalty to their newly chosen man or woman. They start a new family, have new children. And again they become machines. This disease is called earthly love. For us this is the greatest evil. Because we, the chosen ones, know an entirely different love. It is as large as the sky, and as sublime as the Primordial Light. It is not based on external attraction. It is deep and strong. You, Khram, have felt a small dose of this love. You have barely touched it. It was but the first ray of the great Sun that touched your heart. The Sun called the Divine Love of Light."

I wanted to ask him something, but he suddenly reached his hand out to me and took my hands in his. I didn't even have time to speak; he closed his eyes. He seemed to be asleep.

Suddenly, my heart felt—ping.

And just like that time on the train, everything swam. Only this was stronger. Like I dove headfirst into a whirlpool—I saw stars. It was as though he'd shot me in the heart.

Part II

Then something entirely different began. I felt that he was leading my heart step by step up a staircase. It beat against every step. But each time it beat in a different way, each step was completely different, made of some entirely different material.

It was so sweet and terrifying that I just died of happiness.

He kept dragging my little heart along.

Higher and higher.

It was sweeter and sweeter.

And then—that was it! The last step. The sweetest of all.

And I suddenly understood with my heart that there were only twenty-three of these steps.

But I hadn't counted them. I just understood with my heart.

Then he stopped. And I—was just sitting there, as I had been. Everything was swimming around me, but my heart was burning like a flame. I couldn't talk.

Then he said to me, "Just now I spoke to you in the language of the heart. Previously, everyone spoke only a few words to you with the heart. There are only twenty-three heart words in all. I spoke them all to you. Now you know them all."

I just sat there—I felt so good, I couldn't move. I'd never felt so wonderful in my life. I suddenly understood everything, I began to sob so hard that I was convulsed; I fell down on the floor and howled and wailed and sobbed. Bro got up, patted my head, and said, "Cry, Sister."

I wept. I wept like I'd never wept in my life: my whole insides were turned out.

He called some others over to carry me into the bedroom. I was writhing like an eel in their arms, and tears were spurting out of my eyes!

In the bedroom they undressed me and put me in bed. But I was sobbing so hard I couldn't stop. I'd go numb, numb all

Ice

over until I couldn't feel anything, as though I was just about to die. And then I'd come to—where was I? I'd lie flat on my back in bed. As soon as I'd come around just a little—the tears would start again. And I'd work myself up till I was writhing again. Then I'd howl and weep until I lost consciousness.

I wept this way for seven days.

Then I came to. I lay there a bit. I no longer felt like crying. My heart was at peace. It was glorious! So calm and wonderful. But I was so weak that I couldn't move a finger. I lay there looking out the window. Outside I could see fir trees in the snow. Those firs were so glorious and well proportioned. The snow lay on them and sparkled in the sunshine.

I don't know how long I lay there.

Then a woman came in. She brought me something to drink. I drank.

The old man, Bro, came in. He sat on my bed and held my hand. He said, "Everything's behind you, Khram. Your heart cried from shame at your past life. That is normal. It has happened to each one of us. Henceforth, you will never cry again. You will delight and be joyful. Joyful that you are alive."

And my new life began.

Can I tell the whole story? Of course not. Memory captures only bright and dear moments. But my new life consisted entirely of bright, dear moments.

I spent three years in our Home in the Austrian Alps. Then, when the war came to the mountains as well, we left our Home and made our way to Finland. There, in the forest, on a lake, another Home awaited us. I spent another four years there.

I remember everything: the faces of sisters and brothers, their voices, their eyes, and their hearts, which taught my heart the sacred words.

I remember...

Part II

New blue-eyed, fair-haired people appeared, people whose hearts had been awakened by the ax of ice; they merged into our brotherhood, came to know the joy of awakening, wept tears of heartfelt remorse, discovered the divine language of hearts, and replaced the experienced and mature, those who had already learned all twenty-three words.

Finally a fateful day arrived for me: July 6, 1950.

I rose with the sun, like the other brothers and sisters. Walking out into the meadow in front of the house, we stood in pairs, as always; we embraced and fell to our knees. Our hearts began to speak the sacred language. This continued for several hours. Then we released our embraces. We returned to the house, readied ourselves, and shared our meal.

After our repast, Bro took me aside. He said, "Khram, to-day you will leave our brotherhood. You will go to Russia. And you will search for the living among the dead. In order to awaken them and return them to life. You have traveled a long road with us. You have mastered the language of the heart. You have learned all twenty-three heart words. You are ready to serve our greater goal. I will tell you what you need to know. This tradition lives only on the lips, it does not exist on paper. Listen carefully: In the beginning there was only the Light. And the Light shone in Absolute Emptiness. The Light shone for Itself Alone. The Light consisted of twenty-three thousand light-bearing rays. And we were those rays. Time did not exist. There was only Eternity. In this Eternal Emptiness we shone. And we birthed whole worlds. The worlds filled the Emptiness. Thus was the Universe born. Each time we wanted to create a new world, we formed a Divine Circle of Light from twenty-three thousand rays. All the rays were directed inside the circle,

Ice

and after twenty-three impulses in the center of the circle a new world would be born. These were the stars, planets, and galaxies. Once, when we created a new world, one of its seven planets was covered with water. This was the planet Earth. We had never created such planets before. This was the Light's Great Mistake. For the water on the planet Earth formed a sphere-shaped mirror. As soon as we were reflected in it, we ceased being rays of light and were incarnated in living creatures. We became primitive amoebas that inhabited the boundless ocean. The water carried our tiny, semitransparent bodies, but as before, the Primordial Light lived in us. And as before there were twenty-three thousand of us. But we were scattered across the ocean expanses. Billions of earthly years passed. We evolved together with the other creatures that inhabit the Earth. We became human beings. People multiplied and covered the Earth. They began to live by their minds, enslaving themselves to their flesh. Their lips spoke in the language of the mind, and this language covered the entire visible world like a membrane. People ceased seeing things. They began to think them. Blind and heartless, they became more and more cruel. They created weapons and machines. They killed and birthed, birthed and killed. They turned into walking corpses. Because human beings were our mistake. As was everything living on Earth. And Earth became hell. And we, the dispersed, lived in this hell. We died and were incarnated again, without the strength to tear ourselves away from the Earth that we ourselves had created. As ever, there were twenty-three thousand of us. The Primordial Light lived in our hearts. But our hearts slept, as do billions of human hearts. What could awake them, so that we might understand who we were and what we should do? All the worlds we created before Earth were dead. They hung in the Emptiness like Christmas ornaments, to give us joy.

Part II

The joy of the Primordial Light sang in them. Only the Earth violated this Cosmic Harmony. For it was alive and developing on its own. It developed like an ugly, cancerous tumor. But the Cosmic Harmony cannot be violated for long. A piece of one of the tree ornaments we created fell to the Earth. This was one of the largest meteors ever. And it happened in 1908, in Siberia, near the river. The meteorite was called the Tungus Event. In 1927 a group of learned people formed an expedition to locate it. They arrived at the place, saw the destroyed forests, but they did not find the meteorite. There were fifteen people on this expedition. Among them was one twenty-year-old student, a tow-headed lad with blue eyes. Arriving at the site of the meteorite's landing, he experienced a strange feeling, one that he had never felt before: his heart began to tremble and quiver. As soon as this happened, he fell silent. He stopped conversing with the other members of the expedition. He felt with his heart that the meteorite was somewhere nearby. The energy exuding from the meteorite stunned the youth. In two days that energy turned his life around. The members of the expedition thought that he had gone mad. The expedition left empty-handed. He fell behind. Then he returned to the place where it fell. And he found the meteorite. It was a huge chunk of ice. It had sunk into swampy soil, the putrid water closed over it, hiding it from humans. The youth plunged into the swamp, slipped, and hit his chest hard against the ice. Suddenly, his heart began to speak. He understood everything. He broke off a piece of the ice, put it in his rucksack and went out among people. The ice was heavy, it was difficult to walk. The ice melted. When he arrived at the nearest village, only a small piece of the ice remained, one that fit in the palm of his hand. Approaching the village, he saw a girl sleeping in the grass. She was tow-headed, and her blue eyes were half open. He picked up a stick from the ground, tied the piece of ice to it with a shoelace, and struck the girl with the ice hammer in the chest with all his might. The girl cried out and lost consciousness. He lay down near her and fell asleep. When he woke up, she was sitting nearby and looking at him like a brother. They embraced. Their hearts began speaking to each other. They understood everything. They set off to look for more of their kind."

He was silent for a moment and then added: "I was that youth."

Then Bro continued.

"I have never spoken with you about the goals of our brotherhood. Each of us who fully commands the language of the heart feels them. You are close to this. But we don't have time to wait, for you must leave for Russia as soon as possible, to search for our brothers and sisters there, for those who don't belong to the hellish world, for those in whose hearts the memory of the Light still lives."

He fell silent, and gazed at me.

"What must I do?" I asked.

"You must sift through the human race. Look for the gold in the sand. There are twenty-three thousand of us. No more and no fewer. We are blue-eyed and fair-haired. As soon as all twenty-three thousand are found, as soon as all know the language of the heart, we will stand in a ring and our hearts will pronounce the twenty-three heart words in unison. And in the center of the ring the Primordial Light will arise, the very light that created the worlds. And the mistake will be corrected: Earth will disappear, dissolve in the Light. Our earthly bodies will dissolve together with the world of the Earth. Once again we will become rays of the Primordial Light. We will return to Eternity."

Bro had barely finished speaking when there was a movement in my heart. I FELT everything that he had told me in earthly language. I saw us standing in a circle, holding hands and speaking the heart words.

Bro felt this and he smiled.

"Now, Khram, you know everything."

I was stunned. But one question tormented me.

"What is the ice?"

"It is an ideal Cosmic substance generated by the Primordial Light. Outwardly it resembles earthly ice. In fact, however, its structure is entirely different. If it is shaken, the Music of the Light sings in it. In striking our breastbone, the ice vibrates. These vibrations awaken our hearts."

He said it, and I immediately felt what he was saying. And I understood what ICE was.

"Three of our brothers are in Russia," Bro continued. "They will help you. And together you will accomplish great feats. Commence, Khram."

Thus began the return to my homeland.

The next morning near Lake Inari I crossed the border into the USSR. A passenger car was waiting for me in the forest. Two men in KGB officer uniforms sat in it. One of them silently opened the door of the car, and I got in. We drove off, first along a forest road, then a highway. We traveled in silence. We were stopped by military patrols three times. My companions presented documents to them and they immediately let us pass.

Four hours later we entered Leningrad.

We stopped near a building on Morskoi. One of the officers invited me to follow him. He and I entered the building and climbed to the fourth floor. The officer rang apartment 15, turned, and went back downstairs.

Ice

The door opened. On the threshold stood a blond man of medium height in the uniform of a lieutenant colonel of the state security. He was extremely anxious, but restrained himself with all his might. Keeping his eyes fixed on me, he stepped back into the depths of the apartment. I trembled as well: my heart felt a brother. I closed the door and went to him. The apartment was almost dark because of the closed drapes. Nonetheless, I could make out the blue of his straining eyes.

We embraced and fell to our knees. Our hearts began to speak. This continued until evening. His heart had longed wearily for the sacred, and it trembled violently. But it was fairly inexperienced and knew only six heart words.

Finally we broke our embrace.

Coming to, he said, "My earthly name is Aleksei Ilich Korobov."

His heart name was Adr.

He was silent again, and simply looked at me for a long time. But I was used to it. In our Home the brothers and sisters spoke in earthly language only when absolutely necessary. Then he picked up the telephone receiver and said, "The car."

We went out onto the street. It was already dark.

A chauffeured automobile and guard were waiting next to the entrance. We were taken to Moscow Station. There we boarded the Leningrad–Moscow train and locked ourselves in a sleeping car. Adr placed fruits on the table. But he couldn't eat; he just continued looking at me as before.

I was already hungry and ate a few fruits with pleasure. Then he told me his story. He was a regular officer of the MGB, and in 1947 the Ministry of State Security sent him to Germany on business for GUSIMZ, the Main Directorate of Soviet Property Abroad.

Part II

In Dresden, at a holiday banquet honoring the second anniversary of the victory over Germany, he became closely acquainted with his direct superior, General Lieutenant Vlodzimirsky, who headed the GUSIMZ office. Previously, they had met only in the line of duty. Vlodzimirsky, who was considered a tough, unsociable man at Lubianka, suddenly displayed a great deal of sympathy for Korobov, introducing him to his wife, inviting him to the private house where he usually stayed.

In the town house, he and his wife tied Korobov to a column and hit him with the ice hammer. He lost consciousness. Then they placed him in a hospital where he came to in a separate, guarded ward. On the third day, Vlodzimirsky came to him, lay down in bed, embraced him, and spoke to him with the heart.

Thus did Korobov become Adr.

He asked me about the brotherhood, and I told him everything I knew. From time to time he cried from a feeling of tenderness, embraced me, and pressed my palms to his chest. But I restrained my heart so as not to shake Adr too strongly.

I understood my strength.

In the morning we arrived in Moscow at Leningrad Station. An automobile was waiting for us there.

We drove out of town and a while later arrived at Vlodzimirsky's dacha.

It was a warm, sunny day.

Adr took me by the hand and led me into a large wooden house. Curtains covered the windows. Vlodzimirsky stood in the middle of the living room. He, too, was of medium height and had a compact body; a pair of gold silk pajamas clung to his stocky figure; his thinning dark-blond hair was combed back, and tears of rapture filled his greenish-blue eyes. Even at a distance I could feel his large, warm heart. I quivered in anticipation.

Vlodzimirsky's wife stood a ways off—a thin, lovely woman. But she wasn't one of us, and for this reason I didn't notice her at first.

Vlodzimirsky approached me. His head jerked, his strong hands shook. Making a guttural sound, he lowered himself to his knees and pressed against me.

Adr came up behind me and also pressed against me.

They both began to sob.

Vlodzimirsky's wife also began to cry.

Then Vlodzimirsky swept me up in his arms and carried me to the second floor. There, in the bedroom, he laid me down on a wide couch and began to undress me. Adr and his wife helped him. Then he undressed himself. Vlodzimirsky was truly built like an athlete. He pressed his wide white chest to mine. And our hearts merged. He wasn't a newcomer to the language of the heart and he knew fourteen words.

My small, young, girl's heart immersed itself in his powerful heart. It breathed and throbbed, burned and shuddered.

I had never felt so much with anyone, not even with Bro, the old man.

Our hearts had long been searching for each other. They raged. Time stopped for us . . .

We released our embrace two days later. Our arms were numb and would not obey us, we were so weak we could barely move. But our faces shone with happiness. My new brother was named Kha.

Adr and Vlodzimirsky's wife led us to a bathroom and put

Part II

us in a hot bath. Massaging my numb hands, his wife introduced herself.

"My name is Nastya."

I responded with a warm look.

When we were finally feeling like ourselves, Kha began to speak.

"Khram, there are only four of us in Russia: you, me, Adr, and Yus. Adr and I are high-placed officers of the MGB, the most powerful organization in Russia. Yus is a typist in the Ministry of Machine Construction. I was pounded in 1931 in Baku by brothers who then left with Bro. We found Yus. You know that the ice is the only thing that helps us to find our brothers. All of our efforts are currently directed at procuring a regular supply of the ice, and secretly transporting it abroad where the most active search for our brothers and sisters is being carried out. The Scandinavian countries are the most active of all. In Sweden, one hundred and nineteen of our brothers live in three houses. In Norway there are about fifty. In Finland—almost seventy. Before the war, we had forty-four in Germany. Some of them occupied important positions in the NSDAP and the SS. Unfortunately, everything was more difficult in Russia. Four brothers, employees of the NKVD, perished at the end of the thirties during the 'great purges.' One sister from the Moscow City Committee of the Party was arrested and executed because of a denunciation. Two others died in the siege of Leningrad, I wasn't able to help them. Another one, my closest brother, Umeh, whom we found in 1934, was a colonel general of the tank troops. He died on the front. Thank the Light that this had no effect on the supply of ice. But it is very difficult for us to look for new brothers. You must help us."

"How do they get the ice?" I asked.

Ice

"Before 1936 we organized different expeditions. They were carried out in secret. Each time we hired Siberians, local hunters who crossed the swamps to the place where the meteor fell and sawed off pieces of the ice under terribly difficult conditions, bringing it to a secret place. There they were met by officers of the NKVD. The ice was taken to the train station; it was sent to Moscow in a refrigerator, like valuable cargo. Getting it abroad was much easier. But this method was extremely risky and unreliable. Two expeditions simply disappeared, and another time plain ice was palmed off on us. I decided to radically change the way we acquired the ice. At my initiative and with the help of influential brothers in the Siberian NKVD, a directorate was created with special authority for the raising of the Tungus meteorite. Two brothers, the ones who died in Leningrad, were prominent people in the Academy of Sciences. They established the scientific importance of the project, proving that ice from the meteorite contained unknown chemical compounds capable of revolutionizing chemical weapons. Seven kilometers from the place where it landed we organized a corrective labor camp. The inmates of this small camp retrieve our ice. This is only done in winter, when it is easy to cross the swamps."

"But how do they distinguish our ice from ordinary ice in the winter?"

"We distinguish it, not they." Kha smiled. "Here, in Moscow. They break it up with crowbars where it fell, cut out metric cubes of ice, and drag them back to the camp. There the pieces of ice are loaded onto sleds, and horses carry them across the tundra to Ust-Ilimsk, where they are loaded onto railway cars and taken to Moscow. Here Adr and I enter the cars, and put our hands on the ice. Only about forty percent of it turns out to be our ice."

Part II

"And how much ice is there in the meteorite?"

"According to external estimates—about seventy thousand tons."

"Glory to the Light!" I smiled. "And it doesn't melt?"

"When it fell, the block lodged in the permafrost. The tip is hidden by the swamp. Of course, the upper part of the block melts a bit in summer. But the Siberian summer is short: snap—and it's gone!" Kha smiled in response.

"Thank the Light, there's enough ice to achieve our great goal," added Adr, as he massaged us.

"And who makes the ice hammers?" I asked.

"At first we did it ourselves, but then I realized that each person should do his own job." Kha stuck his strong, handsome head under a stream of water with obvious pleasure. "In one of the *sharashkas*—the closed scientific laboratories where imprisoned scientists work—we established a small department for making the ice hammers. Only three people. They produce five or six hammers a day. We don't need more."

"Don't they ask what the hammers are for?"

"My dear Khram, these are engineers who are serving twenty-five-year sentences for 'wrecking.' They are enemies of the people; they don't have anyone to ask, or any reason to ask. They just have instructions for making the hammers. They have to follow these instructions rigorously if they want to receive their camp rations. The boss of the *sharashka* told them that the ice hammers are needed to strengthen the defensive power of the Soviet state. That's enough for them."

The old scars from the ice hammer could be seen on Kha's wide white chest. I touched them cautiously.

"It's time to go, Khram," he sighed resolutely. "You'll come with me."

We got out of the bath. Adr and Nastya rubbed us down and

helped us dress. Kha arrayed himself in his general's uniform, and they put me in the uniform of a State Security lieutenant. Adr handed me my documents.

"According to your passport you are Varvara Korobova. You are my wife, you live in Leningrad, you and I came here on a work trip. You are employed by the foreign department of the Leningrad GB."

A black automobile waited at the dacha gates. The three of us got in and drove to Moscow. Nastya remained at home.

"Is it hard to live—with one of the empties?" I asked Kha.

"Yes," he nodded, seriously. "But that's the way it has to be."

"Does she know everything?"

"Not everything. But she senses the greatness of our enterprise."

In Moscow we arrived at the massive headquarters of the MGB on Lubianskaya Square. We entered, showed our documents, and proceeded to the third floor. In the hallway, several officers saluted Kha as we passed. He responded listlessly. Soon we entered his huge office where three secretaries stood waiting to greet us. Kha walked past them and threw open the double doors of the office. We followed him, and Adr closed the doors.

Kha tossed a leather dossier on his large desk, turned, and embraced me.

"There are no eavesdropping devices here. How happy I am, Sister! You and I will accomplish great things. You are the only one of us who knows all twenty-three heart words. Your heart is wise, strong, and young. We will tell you what needs to be done."

"I'll do everything, Kha," I said, stroking his athletic shoulders.

Part II

Adr approached me from behind, embraced me, and pressed against me.

"My heart wants yours so dreadfully," he whispered at the nape of my neck, his voice trembling.

"And mine as well, and mine..." Kha muttered warmly.

One of the four black phones rang.

Growling with displeasure, Kha loosed his embrace, walked over to the table, and picked up the receiver.

"Vlodzimirsky here. What? No, Bor, I'm busy. Yes. Well? What do you mean you can't? Bor, why are you fucking around with mummies? He's ready to drop, damnit. As soon as I leave the department, everything falls apart. Inform Serov. Well? So? He actually said that? Jeezus..." He sighed with displeasure, scratched his heavy chin, and chuckled. "You're a bunch of no-goodniks. Viktor Semyonich is right to write about you. All right, bring him over here. You have twenty minutes."

He replaced the receiver and looked at me with his blue-green eyes.

"It's my work, Khram. Forgive me."

I nodded with a smile.

The oak door of the office opened timidly and a balding head poked through.

"Excuse me, Lev Emelianovich?"

"Come on now. Carry on!" said Kha settling at his desk.

A small, thin colonel with an ugly face and a thin black mustache entered the office. Behind him, two hefty lieutenants were dragging a plump man in a tattered, bloody uniform with the epaulettes torn off. The man's face was swelling from the beatings and turning blue. He collapsed helplessly on the rug.

"The best of health to you, Lev Emelianovich." The bald man approached the desk in a half-bow.

"Greetings, Borya." Kha stretched out his hand in a lazy

gesture. "What are you doing violating the rules of subordination? You're shaming us in front of the Leningraders!"

"Lev Emelianovich!" The colonel smiled guiltily, as he noticed Adr and me. "Ah! Hello there, Comrade Korobov!"

They shook hands.

"Now, then, Borya, follow Korobov's example." Kha pulled a cigarette out of a cigarette holder and stuck it in his mouth without lighting it. "He got married. And you're still entangled with actresses."

"Congratulations," the colonel said, offering me his small hand.

"Varvara Korobova," I said, giving him my hand to shake.

"You see what sumptuous young maids they have wandering around 4 Liteiny Prospect? Not like the dried-up vertebrates we have here." Kha directed his gaze to the injured fat man. "So what's going on?"

"The viper has gone stubborn over Shakhnazarov," the colonel said angrily, looking at the fat man. "He gave evidence on Alexeev, he gave evidence on Furman. But with Shakhnazarov—I don't know...that was it. The bastard's forgotten how they sold the motherland to the Japanese together."

Kha nodded, and placed the cigarette in an ashtray.

"Emelianov. Why are you holding back?"

The fat man sniffed, but said nothing.

"Answer, you bloody wrecker, you saboteur!" shouted the colonel. "I'll rip your liver out, you Japanese spy!"

"Now, now, Borya," Kha spoke up calmly. "Sit down over there. In the corner. And hold your tongue."

The colonel quieted down and sat on the chair.

"Pick the general up. And sit him in the armchair," Kha ordered.

Part II

The lieutenants lifted the fat man and sat him down in the chair.

Kha's face suddenly grew sad. He looked at his nails. Then he directed his eyes to the window. There, against the background of a sunny Moscow day, stood the black monument to Dzerzhinsky.

Silence fell in the office.

"Do you remember the Crimea in '40? June, Yalta, the resort?" Kha asked quietly.

The fat man raised his glassy eyes to Kha.

"Your wife, Sasha, isn't that right? She liked to swim in the early morning. So did Nastya and I. One time, the three of us swam out so far that Sasha got a cramp in her leg. She was frightened. But Nastya and I are sea folk. I held her under her back, and Nastya dove down and bit your wife on the calf. And we helped her swim back. As she swam she talked about your son. Pavlik, I think it was, no? He had made a steam locomotive himself from a samovar. The steam engine moved. And Pavlik heated it with pencils. He burned two boxes of colored pencils that you had brought him from Leningrad. Isn't that the way it was?"

The fat man remained stubbornly silent.

Kha stuck the cigarette in his mouth again, but didn't light it.

"At that time I was just a plain old major in the NKVD. They gave me a bonus—a trip to the resort. And you were commander of a whole corps. The legendary Com corps, Emelianov! I looked at you in the dining room and thought: He's as far away from me as the sky itself. And now here you are protecting Shakhnazarov. That louse isn't worth your little finger."

The fat man's chin began to twitch, his round head swayed.

Ice

Tears suddenly burst from his eyes. He grabbed his head in his hands and began to weep loudly.

"Take the general to 301. Let him get some sleep, give him a good meal. Then he'll write it. The way it should be," said Kha, looking out the window.

The colonel, who had grown quiet, nodded to the lieutenants. They grabbed the sobbing Emelianov and led him out of the office. The telephone rang.

"Vlodzimirsky," said Kha, picking up the receiver. "Hello there, Began! Listen, I opened *Pravda* yesterday and couldn't believe my eyes! That's right! Good for you! Those are the kind of cadres Lavrenty Pavlovich has! Our lads! Merkurov should sculpt a bust of you and Amayak now!"

Kha let out a booming laugh.

"Be well, Korobov," said the colonel, stretching out his hand and, glancing at Kha, shaking his head. "There's no one else like our Lev Emelianovich."

"He's got an absolute memory, what do you want?" smiled Adr.

"That's the least of it. He's a genius..." sighed the colonel enviously as he left.

Kha finished his conversation and hung up the phone.

"You have to complete the documents for a work trip. With Radzevsky on the sixth floor. Then we'll go to see Sister Yus."

Adr and I went up to the sixth floor, and a business trip to Magadan was arranged for us. We received our per diem money and documents. We left the building with Kha, got into an automobile, and drove along Vorovskaya Street. Leaving the automobile and driver on the street, we walked through courtyards and ended up at a shabby doorway and then went up to the third floor. Adr knocked on the door. It immediately opened wide, and a tall, elderly woman wearing a pince-nez threw herself on us with a cry. She was literally wailing and shaking with joy.

Adr held her mouth. We entered the apartment. It was large, with four bedrooms, but it was a communal apartment. However, four of the rooms were sealed. As Kha later explained to me, he had Yus's neighbors arrested. That made it easier to meet.

Seeing me, Yus immediately wound her long, gouty, arthritic arms around my shoulders, pressed her large, flaccid breasts to me, and we collapsed on the floor. Adr and Kha embraced in turn, and lowered themselves to their knees.

Despite her age, Yus's heart was childishly inexperienced. It knew only two words. But it imbued them with such strength and desire that I was taken aback. Her heart pined, like a traveler lost in the desert. It drank in my heart desperately, without stop.

Nearly nine hours passed.

Yus's arms parted, and she lay flat on the old parquet.

I felt emptied, but satisfied: I had taught Yus's heart new words.

Yus looked terrible: pale and thin, she lay unmoving, her lilac eyes glassily staring at the ceiling; her dentures stuck out of her slightly open mouth.

But she was alive: I could clearly feel her heavily beating heart.

Kha brought her an oxygen pillow from her room, and placed the rubber tube with its funnel-shaped opening to her grayish lips. Adr opened the valve.

The oxygen gradually brought her around. She sighed with a moan.

They lifted her up and carried her into the room. Adr sprayed water on her face.

Ice

"Maaar-ve-lous," she said, exhausted, and stretched her shaking hand to me.

I took it in mine. Her old fingers were soft and cool. Yus pressed my hand to her chest.

"My child. How I needed you!" she said and smiled with difficulty.

Adr brought us all water and apricots.

We ate the apricots, washing them down with water.

"Tell me about the House," Yus asked me.

I told her. She listened with an expression of almost childlike amazement. When I got to the conversation with Bro and to his travels, tears poured down Yus's wrinkled cheeks.

"What happiness," she said, pressing my hand to her chest. "What happiness to obtain another living heart."

We all embraced.

Then Kha told her about the current plans. A complex task lay ahead of us. Adr and I listened to Kha, holding our breath. But Yus couldn't listen for more than ten seconds: she jumped up, threw herself on me, embraced my legs, pressed against me, muttering tender words, then ran back to the window, and stood there, sniffling and shaking her head.

Her room was a chaotic mess of books and objects, and a German typewriter with a sheet of paper in it rose out of them like a cliff. In her former life, Yus had earned money at home by typing, and during the day she typed at the ministry where she worked. Like all of us, she had no financial problems.

Yus begged Kha to take her on the work trip, but he forbade her.

She began to sob.

"I want to speak with you ..." she whimpered, kissing my knees.

"We need you here," said Kha, embracing her.

Part II

Yus shivered violently. Her dentures clattered and her knees trembled. We calmed her with valerian drops, put her in bed, covered her with a down blanket, and placed a hot water bottle at her feet. Her face shone with bliss.

"I found you, I found you..." her old lips kept whispering. "I just hope my heart doesn't burst."

I kissed her hand.

She looked at me with profound affection and immediately fell into a deep sleep.

We left, got in the car, and in an hour we were at the military aerodrome in Zhukovskoe. An airplane was waiting for us there.

We settled down in the small cabin. The pilot reported to Kha on our state of readiness, and we took off.

It took almost twenty-four hours to reach Magadan: twice we stopped to fuel up, and we spent the night in Krasnoyarsk.

When I flew over Siberia and saw the endless forests sliced by the ribbons of Siberia's great rivers, I thought about the thousands of blue-eyed, fair-haired brothers and sisters living within Russia's unembraceable expanses, daily enacting the mechanical rituals imposed upon them by civilization, unaware of the miracle hiding inside their chests. Their hearts slept. Would they awake? Or, like millions of other hearts, having beaten their allotted time, would they rot in the Russian earth, never knowing the intoxicating might of the heart's language?

In my head I pictured thousands of coffins disappearing into graves scattered with earth; I felt the intolerable immobility of these stopped hearts, the decay of divine heart muscles in the dark, the nimble worms that devoured the powerless flesh. My living heart shuddered and fluttered.

"I must awaken them!" I whispered, looking out upon the ocean of forest swimming below me...

Ice

———

We landed in Magadan early in the morning.

The sun had not yet risen. At the airport, two automobiles and two MGB officers were waiting for us. Four long zinc cases were loaded into one car, and we got into the second.

After driving through the city, which seemed to me no better but no worse than other cities, we turned onto a highway, and after a rather bumpy half-hour ride, we rolled up to the gates of a large corrective labor camp.

The gates opened immediately, and we entered the territory of the camp. There were wood barracks and, in the corner, shining white, stood the sole brick building. We drove up to it. We were met by the camp's administrators—three MGB officers. The camp director, Major Gorbach, gave us a hearty welcome and invited us into the administrative building. But Kha told him that we were extremely pressed for time. Then he fluttered around and gave the order: "Sotnikov, bring them here!"

A dozen or so exhausted, filthy prisoners were soon brought to us. Despite the warm summer weather, they all wore tattered padded coats, felt boots, and hats with earflaps.

"Your people wear felt boots in the summer?" Kha asked Gorbach.

"No, Comrade General. I was holding these in the hard-regime barracks. So I issued winter clothes to them."

"Why did you put them in hard regime?"

"Well . . . it's . . . more reliable."

"You're an asshole," replied the comrade general. Turning to the prisoners, he said, "Take off your hats."

They took off their hats. All of them looked like old men. Four were blonds, one an albino, and two had completely gray hair. Only four had blue eyes, including one of the gray-haired ones.

Part II

"Listen, Major, is your head screwed on right? Haven't had any concussions lately have you?" Kha asked Gorbach.

"I wasn't at the front, Comrade General," answered Gorbach, turning pale.

"Who were you ordered to find?"

"Blonds with light eyes."

"Are you color-blind?"

"No, sir, I can see colors normally."

"What the hell kind of normal is this?" Kha shouted, pointing at one prisoner's gray head. "This one is blond in your opinion?"

"In his testimony he wrote that prior to 1944 he was blond, Comrade General," Gorbach answered, standing at attention.

"You're playing with death, Major," Kha said, throwing a piercing gaze his way. "Where is the place?"

"This way... over here, please." Gorbach pointed at another building.

Kha took a cigarette out of his cigarette case, rolled it between his fingers and sniffed it.

"Take these four here, and follow the instructions."

"And where should the others go?" Gorbach asked timidly.

"To hell." Kha tossed the cigarette on the ground.

Presently we entered the building. The biggest room had been designated for the hammering. The windows were shuttered, three bright lamps burned, and handcuffs were attached to the walls. The four prisoners were pinned to the wall, naked to the waist, their mouths and eyes bound.

One of the zinc cases was brought in. Kha ordered everyone out of the building.

Adr opened the case. It had thick walls and was filled with the dry ice that ice cream is stored in. The ice hammers protruded slightly from under the steaming dry ice. I placed my hands on them. I immediately felt the unseen vibration of the

Ice

heavenly ice. It was divine! My hands trembled, my heart beat greedily: ICE! I hadn't seen it for so long!

Adr put on a pair of gloves, pulled one hammer out, and began his work. He struck the gray-haired man. He turned out to be empty, and quickly died from the blows. Then Kha took the hammer. However, that day we were out of luck: the others were also empties.

Tossing aside the broken hammer, Kha took out a pistol and shot the crippled empties.

"It's not so easy to find our people," said Adr with a tired smile, wiping the sweat from his brow.

"Yet what happiness when we do find them!" I smiled.

We embraced, pieces of ice crunching under our feet. My heart felt every single sliver of ice.

Leaving the building, we heard shots nearby.

"What was that?" Kha asked the major.

"Comrade General, you gave orders that the others were to receive the highest penalty," the major answered.

"You idiot, I said—to hell with them."

"My fault, Comrade General, I didn't understand." Gorbach blinked hard.

Kha waved him away, and went over to the car.

"All of you slobs need to be purged."

In the course of two weeks we traveled to eight camps, and hammered ninety-two people. We found only one living one. He turned out to be a forty-year-old recidivist-thief from Nalchik named Savely Mamonov, known by the nickname "Blast Furnace." The nickname had been given to him for the tattoo on his buttocks: two devils holding shovels of coal. When he walked the devils seemed to be shoveling coal into his anus. But this was not the only tattoo on Blast's chubby, hairy, short-legged body: his torso and arms were covered with mer-

Part II

maids, hearts pierced by knives, spiders, and kissing doves. In the middle of his chest was a tattoo of Stalin. From the blows of the ice hammer the leader's face began to spout profuse amounts of blood. I pressed my ear to that bloodied Stalin and heard, "Shro...Shro...Shro..."

My heart felt the awakening of another heart.

This experience is comparable to nothing else.

Tears of ecstasy spurted from my eyes, and I pressed my bloodied lips to the ugly, coarse, heavily scarred face of our newly acquired brother.

"Hello, Shro."

We cut his fetters and removed the bandage from his mouth. His body slid powerlessly to the floor, his eyes rolled back, and from his lips could be heard a weak, but angry whisper: "Fuckin' cunts."

Then he lost consciousness. Kha and Adr kissed his hands. I cried, touching his gnarly body, which had carried the locked vessel of the Primordial Light inside it. Henceforth this body was destined to live.

A month later, Shro and I were sitting in a restaurant atop the Moscow Hotel near the Kremlin. It was a warm, dry August day. A soft wind rippled the striped tent. We were eating grapes and peaches. Below, the great Russian city stretched out before us. But we weren't looking at it. Shro held my hand in his rough, tattooed hands. Our blue eyes could not part for a second. Even when I placed a grape between Shro's lips, he continued looking at me. We spoke almost no words in earthly language. Yet our hearts trembled. We were prepared to entwine our arms and fall down anywhere—here over Moscow, in the Metro, on the sidewalk, in an entryway, or on a garbage heap. Our feelings were so elevated, however, that self-preservation was part of them.

Ice

We took care of ourselves.

And our hearts.

For this reason we allowed them to speak only in secluded places where there were no living dead.

"Can we still croak?" Shro asked suddenly after a silence of many hours.

"Death doesn't matter anymore," I answered.

"Why?"

"Because we met."

He squinted. Grew ponderous. Then he smiled. His steel teeth sparkled in the sunlight.

"I got it, Sis!" he wheezed. "I got the whole fucking shebang!"

We all understood everything: my young self, awkward Shro, wise Kha, ruthless Adr, and ancient Yus.

We were engaged in a great undertaking.

Time made way for eternity. We passed through time like rays of light through an icy thickness. And we reached the depths . . .

In September and October we visited eighteen camps in Mordovia, Kazakhstan, and western Siberia. Almost two hundred ice hammers were broken on the emaciated breastbones of prisoners, but only two hearts began to speak, pronouncing their names.

"Mir."

"Sofre."

There were now seven of us.

We continued our search among the lower echelons of society. Kha's new arrangements were dictated largely by the times: the repressive state structure was destroying the Soviet elite too quickly and too unpredictably. It was difficult for

Part II

high-placed people to survive the Stalinist meat grinder. No one was certain of his safety; no one was protected from arrest. Even those who drank and sang Georgian songs with Stalin.

For that reason we made no attempt to find our own among the Party and military bosses. The losses of the Thirties and Forties had sobered Kha forever.

But the camps did not resolve the problem of our quest. The few brothers found among them were a paltry reward for the huge risk and painstaking preparations.

Kha and Adr worked out a new search plan: we had to travel to the north of Russia, to Karelia, and the White Sea, to lands rich in fair-haired blue-eyed people.

With the support of his patron, the all-powerful Lavrenty Beria, Kha created a special division within the MGB called "Karelia," purportedly to seek out deserters and German accomplices who had taken refuge in the forests of Karelia. It was a small but mobile subdivision consisting of former SMERSH operatives called upon during the war to fight against German spies and saboteurs. However, in line with traditional NKVD practices, the SMERSH people were largely in the business of fabricating false cases, arresting innocent Red Army soldiers, and beating the necessary evidence out of them—after which the newly minted "German spies" were safely shot.

The sixty-two cutthroat SMERSH operatives Kha chose for the Karelia Special Forces—which reported directly to Beria himself—were prepared to carry out any order. These truly merciless individuals viewed the human race as garbage and received great satisfaction from discharging large numbers of bullets into the backs of heads. Adr led the group.

In April 1951 the division began a secret operation called "Dragnet": arriving in Karelia, in the small town of Loukhi, the operatives set about arresting blue-eyed blonds, both men

Ice

and women. They were taken to Leningrad, where, in the basements of the Big House, Kha, Shro, Sofre, and I hammered them.

It was hard work. Sometimes we had to hammer up to forty people a day. By evening we would collapse from exhaustion. The laboratory where, in the past, three imprisoned engineers prepared the hammers, couldn't handle the volume. Five more workers were added, tripling the production; they worked as much as sixteen hours a day, making thirty hammers daily. The hammers were brought to Leningrad by airplane so that we could pound the white-skinned Karelian breasts in the dusky cellar of the MGB.

Our hands and faces were scarred by shards of flying ice, our hands and arms became iron though our muscles ached and hurt, our nails sometimes bled, and our feet would be swollen from hours of standing still. Kha's wife helped us. She wiped our faces, spattered with Karelian blood, gave us warm water to drink, and massaged our arms and legs. We worked as though possessed: the ice hammers whistled, bones cracked, people moaned and wailed. One floor below us shots rang out incessantly—the empties were being finished off. As always, they comprised ninety-nine percent. Only one percent remained alive. But how much joy we received from each one of a hundred!

Each time I pressed my head against a bloody, quivering chest and heard the flutter of a wakening heart, I forgot about everything else, I cried and shouted with joy, repeating the heart name of the newborn.

"Zu!"

"O!"

"Karf!"

"Yk!"

Part II

"Owb!"

"Yach!"

"Nom!"

They were few and far between. Like nuggets of gold in the earth. But they existed! And they glittered in our work-weary, bloody hands.

The living were immediately taken to the MGB prison hospital, where the doctor, following Kha's instructions, provided the necessary care.

Gradually, their numbers grew.

The special division completed the operation in Loukhi and moved south along the railroad—through Kem, Belomorsk, and Segezh, to Petrozavodsk. While the agents were combing each city, a special train stood at the station, earmarked for the transport of prisoners. After the town had been searched, the train full of fair-haired people departed for Leningrad.

In the course of two and a half months of incessant work we found twenty-two brothers and seventeen sisters.

This was a great Victory for the Light! Russia had turned toward Light-Bearing Eternity.

The Karelia special division was nearing the old Russian port of Petrozavodsk, the capital of Karelia, a large city with a population of 150,000, teeming with blue-eyed, fair-haired residents.

To implement the Dragnet-Petrozavodsk operation, the special division was reinforced with twenty officer agents and fifteen wardens from the Lubianka prison.

Dozens of ice hammers awaited their hour in refrigerators.

But the ominous month of July 1951 approached. The "Doctors' Plot" being fabricated in the bowels of the Lubianka—an alleged plot of doctor-murderers planning to poison Stalin and other Party bigwigs—had turned against the MGB. Abakumov, the minister of state security, was arrested. The threat of a new purge hung over the Lubianka.

Beria's old enemies in the Central Committee and the Ministry of Defense acquired new life. Denunciations of Abakumov's deputies, of whom Kha was one, flooded the Politburo.

Kha decided to halt the Karelian operation.

The special division was called back; an empty train returned to Leningrad.

We had to wait things out, to "sink to the bottom," as Kha said. Adr and I received a month-long vacation and set off for one of the MGB's resorts on the Crimean coast, not far from Evpatoria. Kha and his wife flew to Hungary to vacation on Lake Balaton. Shro lived with Yus. Mir and Sofre spent the summer working at one of the MGB's Young Pioneers camps.

After the cellars of the Big House, it was hard for me to adjust to the hot, indolent Crimea, where everything is designed for primitive Soviet "rest," which involves an almost vegetative existence. Our thirty-nine newly acquired brothers and sisters would not leave me in peace. Hundreds of kilometers away from them I felt their hearts, I remembered each and every name, and I spoke with them.

Adr, understanding my state of mind, tried to help. Early in the morning, before sunrise, we would swim out to the wild cliffs, entwining there and lying still for many hours like ancient lizards.

But Adr's heart wasn't enough for me. I yearned for the prison hospital where all of my brothers and sisters lay. I wanted them. I begged and pleaded, crying.

"It's not possible Khram," Adr whispered to me.

And I beat my useless hands against the cliffs.

Adr ground his teeth in futility.

Part II

Soon something began to happen to me. It started on a Sunday evening, when Adr, who tried in every way possible to help me fight off boredom, decided to take me to the movies. They showed movies on Sundays in a simple summer theater. Instead of the promised new comedy, they began showing *Chapaev* that night. Someone shouted out that they'd already seen *Chapaev* twenty times. An old corpse countered, "No matter, you can watch it for the twenty-first time!"

I had seen *Chapaev* as a girl. At the time the film shook me. I remembered it very well. But this time, when the first scenes began and people appeared on the sheet they used as a screen, I couldn't see them clearly. They were just gray spots, flickering appearances, sputters of light and shadow. At first I thought that the projectionist had made some mistake. But I was able to read the list of captions and names. Everything else swam in front of me. I looked at the audience: everyone watched silently, no one cried out "Focus!" or "Murder the projectionist!"

Adr watched it too.

"Can you see the screen clearly?" I asked him.

"Yes. And you?"

"I can't see anything."

"We're probably sitting too close," he decided. "Let's move farther away."

We got up and moved to the last bench. But for me nothing changed: I still could read the captions, but I couldn't make out anything else. Adr thought that I simply had bad eyesight. When another caption appeared on the screen, he asked, "What does it say?"

"In the White Guard headquarters," I read.

Ice

He grew thoughtful. Next to us a tipsy couple sat kissing. I began watching them. The lust of those corpses seemed so bizarre to me. Watching them kiss was like watching two mechanical dolls. The woman noticed my look.

"Whadderya gawkin' at? Look thata way!" She pointed to the screen, and the man groping her pudgy body laughed.

I turned my eyes toward the screen. Petka was telling Anka how a machine gun worked. All I could see was two quivering dark spots.

"What's this?" Anka asked.

"Those are stocks," the invisible Petka answered.

And the two spots merged.

The audience laughed.

"Let's get out of here," I said, standing up.

Adr and I left. It was a dark southern night. The cicadas chirped. Under the heavy darkness of the acacias and chestnut trees, the odd light shone out of the resort building. We entered the lobby.

Two concierges dozed behind the counter. On the wall above them hung a large picture of Stalin. I had never noticed it before, but something made me look at the portrait. Instead of Stalin in his white tunic, a white-and-brown splotch flecked with gold floated inside the frame.

I stared at the portrait and moved closer. The splotch shimmered and swam.

I squinted, shook my head, and opened my eyes again: it was still the same.

"What's the matter?" asked Adr.

"I don't know." I shook my head.

The concierges had woken up and were watching me with curiosity.

"Who is that?" I asked, staring at the portrait.

Part II

"Stalin," Adr answered tensely.

The concierges exchanged glances.

"Varya, let's go to sleep, you're tired." Adr took my arm.

"Wait a minute." I leaned on the counter and fixed my eyes on the portrait.

Then I turned my gaze to the concierges. They looked at me apprehensively. I noticed a pile of postcards lying on the counter. I picked one up. At the bottom of the postcard "Greetings from the Crimea!" was written in dark blue. Above the caption there was a clump of something greenish red.

"What is this?" I asked Adr.

"Roses," he said as he took me forcefully by the elbow. "Let's go. I beg of you."

I put the postcard down and obeyed.

Climbing the stairs with Adr, I heard the concierges whispering.

"They come here to get drunk."

"What do you expect—the bosses are in Moscow, there's no one to keep them in line."

In the room, Adr embraced me. "Tell me what's happening to you?"

Instead of answering, I got out our passports. I opened them. In the place of where the photographs were glued on I could see only gray ripples. But I could read all the words normally.

I took a little mirror out of my purse and looked at myself. The features of my face swam and merged in the reflection. I directed the mirror toward Adr's face: it was the same. I couldn't see his face in the mirror.

"I can't see pictures. Or reflections," I said, tossing the mirror aside. "I don't know what's happening..."

"You're just tired," said Adr, embracing me. "The last two months have been very hard."

Ice

"They were wonderful." I flopped down on the bed. "It's much harder for me to wait and do nothing."

"Khram, you understand that we can't take the risk."

"I understand everything," I said, and closed my eyes. "That's why I'm putting up with it."

I fell quickly into a deep sleep.

From the moment my heart had been awakened, I hadn't had any dreams. The last vivid, though short, dreams I had had were in the train when we were being transported like cattle from Russia: I dreamed about Mama, Father, the village, and noisy village holidays when we were all together and happy. But everything always broke off in the middle of what was closest and dearest to me, and I would awake in the same terrible train car.

My very last dream had been one night in the filtration camp: I dreamed of a fire—a huge, terrifying fire. Everything was burning all around, people ran hither and thither like shadows. I was looking for our dog Leska. I loved her a great deal. The longer I looked for her, the more clearly I understood that she had burned alive because none of the adults had thought to untie her. They were saving all kinds of sacks, trunks, and horse yokes. The most awful thing in that dream was the feeling of impotence, the impossibility of turning things back. I awoke in tears, crying out, "Leska! Leska!"

Then, that night in the sanatorium, I dreamed again for the first time in eight years. Or, not exactly dreamed, because I didn't see the dream in my head, instead *I felt the dream.*

I was sitting in the garden near the House and touching sister Zher, who was sleeping. It was summer, and the weather was warm and windless. We had just finished speaking with our

Part II

hearts. I loved Zher's heart. It was agile and active, and it was quicker than mine. After two hours of heart conversation my mouth was dry, as always, and my arms were numb and ached a bit. Zher was sleeping like a baby—spread out on her back with her mouth slightly open. Her face exuded a tired bliss. I began touching her small chin. It was covered in tiny freckles. There were even more of them on the bridge of her nose. I touched her nose. Zher's strawberry blond eyelashes didn't even flicker: her sleep was deep. Suddenly I heard a weak whimper behind me. With my heart I felt that my dog Leska stood behind me. I looked around. Furry gray-and-black Leska stood there, panting joyfully, her pink tongue hanging out. Her greenish eyes were bright with joy. My heart trembled with happiness: my beloved Leska was alive, she didn't perish in the fire! A piece of the rope hung around Leska's neck, and the fur on her right side was singed.

"Leska, you're alive!" I exclaimed and stretched toward her.

But the dog suddenly cringed and ran toward the House. I jumped up and followed her at a run, calling her name. Leska ran up the steps, darted into a partly opened door on the south porch, which was entwined with wild grapevines. I ran after her. The porch was empty. It was dim and cool there, as it always was in summer. In the middle there was an armchair, and the old man Bro sat in it. Leska sat nearby. She looked at me attentively. Bro pointed his finger; I turned my head and saw my full-length reflection on the opposite side of the terrace. It was neither a painting nor a photograph, but something striking in its perfectedness: an absolute copy of me. I walked toward my double. But the closer I came, the more strongly I felt the EMPTINESS inside the copy of me. It was pure image, a surface that copied my form. There was nothing at all inside the image. I went closer. The copy of Varka Samsikova was absolute in its exactitude. I examined the smallest pores on the face, the little scar over the eyebrows, the moisture at the corners of the blue eyes, the golden fuzz under the cheekbones, the cracks in the lips, and the birthmark on the neck. My copy also studied me closely. Finally we both turned to Bro. Leska stood up; she whimpered excitedly and her ears perked up as she looked at us.

"Call the dog," Bro said.

"Leska!" I called.

"Leska!" called my copy.

The dog ran first to the copy, sniffed it, yelped, and growling, shrank back and came to me. I sat down and ran my fingers through her fur with pleasure. My copy stood there, smiling, watching us. Leska growled at her again. The copy disappeared.

"Why did the dog recognize you?" Bro asked.

"She felt me," I answered.

"Yes. The dog is alive, as are all animals. She saw you with her heart, not her eyes. But the living dead see the world with their eyes, and only with their eyes. The world that the heart sees is different. Khram, you are ready to see the world with the heart."

I awoke. I opened my eyes.

It was morning.

The world was the same as yesterday. I lay in our bed. Adr wasn't in the room. I rubbed my eyes and sat up. Then I took a shower, pulled myself together, dressed, and left the room.

I went downstairs and walked into the cafeteria where visitors ate breakfast, and froze in astonishment: instead of people, MACHINES MADE OF MEAT sat at the tables! They were

Part II

ABSOLUTELY dead! There was not a drop of life in their ugly, gloomily worried bodies. They devoured food: some in glum concentration, others in an energetic flurry, some with mechanical indifference.

A couple sat at our table. They were eating living fruits: pears, cherries, and peaches.

But these marvelous peaches could not confer even the teensiest bit of life to their bodies!

Why were they eating them? It was so amusing!

I began to laugh.

Everyone stopped eating and stared. Their faces turned toward me. For the first time in my life I didn't see human faces. These were the muzzles and snouts of meat machines.

Suddenly the mass of dead meat was pierced by a ray of light: Adr was crossing the cafeteria, heading toward me. He was COMPLETELY DIFFERENT! He was alive. He was not a machine. He was my BROTHER. He had a HEART. It shone with the Primordial Light.

I moved to meet him. And we embraced amid the world of monsters.

Snickers crawled across the bodies of the meat machines like worms. One of the machines that was chewing opened her mouth and spoke in a loud voice: "And they say that no one in the MGB knows how to love!"

The cafeteria filled with the greasy laughter of meat machines...

From that day on, I began to see with the heart.

A veil fell from the world, a veil stretched over it by meat machines. I no longer saw only the surface of things. I could now see their essence.

This doesn't mean that I was blind. I saw objects and was perfectly well oriented in space. But images of any kind—

paintings, photographs, movies, sculpture—disappeared from my life forever. Paintings became merely canvases covered with paint; on the movie screen all I saw was the play of splotches of light.

I could see a person or a thing from the inside with my heart. I knew their history.

This revelation was equal only to the awakening of my heart from the blows of the ice hammer.

After those blows, however, my heart simply awoke and began to feel; but now I knew how to KNOW.

I calmed down.

There was no reason for me to worry.

The month of vacation passed.

In Moscow, Ignatiev was appointed to replace the arrested security minister Abakumov. He was a Party functionary completely new to Lubianka and therefore he was very unpredictable. But his first deputy was Golidze—one of Beria's protégés and an old friend of Kha's. That reassured us. Under Golidze's cover we would be able to complete the search operation for the living in Karelia.

Kha recalled us from the Crimea. We flew into a wet, September capital, ready to accomplish new feats in the name of the Light . . .

But the unforeseen happened.

Ignatiev, who began investigating "Abakumov's criminal activity," received a denunciation from the deputy director of the camp where the precious Tungus ice was extracted. MGB Lieutenant Voloshin wrote that Abakumov established "Camp No. 312/500 for the extraction of ice no one needs, under inhumanly hard conditions of permafrost, in order to provide for

Japanese spies who made their way onto the territory of the USSR and caused harm to our toiling people."

Most likely, Voloshin simply decided to use another purge to receive a new appointment or promotion for his "vigilance."

Despite its obvious absurdity, the denunciation had its effect: work in the camp was directed to cease. Fortunately, Ignatiev appointed an investigatory commission headed by Colonel Ivanov from the Interior Ministry's Main Financial Directorate. Ivanov was indebted to Kha, who had saved him from arrest in 1939.

Kha made Ivanov include Adr and me in the commission, as secretaries.

Just before the trip, Kha called Ivanov and us into his office. We stood before his massive desk.

"Fly, eagles, fly," he directed us, thrusting an unlit cigarette between his stern, handsome lips. "Sort it out—the what and how of it. You are meticulous guys. Dig down deep into the earth, like wild boars."

"But Comrade Lieutenant General, it's the permafrost zone," said Adr, smiling tactfully.

"What a fucking joker." Kha pierced him with a quick glance, and struck the table with his finger. "I want everything turned inside out! Is that clear?"

"Yes sir!" we answered in unison.

"I have a suspicion"—Kha looked out the window, squinting, holding the pause—"that this Lieutenant Voloshin is himself a Japanese spy."

"Do you . . . really think so, Comrade Lieutenant General?" asked Ivanov cautiously.

"Just a hunch. He's muddying the waters, the fiend. While he himself is up to his dirty old tricks. There's a shitload of them out there in the tundra. That samurai breed is entrenched.

Ice

So many agents, even a lazy SOB could rack them in. In the Forties we arrested so many, and they just kept crawling over from the Far East, the bastards. So keep your eyes open Ivanov. Don't make a mistake."

Kha gave Ivanov a significant look. And Ivanov made no mistake.

He knew that Vlodzimirsky was Beria's man, and not the fallen Abakumov's. And Beria was closest of all to Stalin. That meant it was worth obeying the hint.

As soon as we arrived at Camp No. 312/500, buried in snow and strafed by icy winds, Ivanov ordered Lieutenant Voloshin arrested.

In the middle of the deep polar night, under the light of three kerosene lamps in a log barracks, Voloshin was placed naked on his back on a bench and tied down. Ivanov, a thorough man, had brought along two of his broad-shouldered lieutenants, strongmen from the operations department. One lieutenant sat on Voloshin's chest, while the other one set about lashing his genitals with a small whip.

Voloshin howled in the night.

His howl was heard by 518 prisoners hiding in their barracks and awaiting the verdict of the Moscow commission: they hadn't worked for a month at that point. This scared them.

The camp director had been drinking in his house for the last month.

"Tell us what you know, Voloshin, tell us everything," said Ivanov as he calmly worked on his well-groomed nails with a little file.

I sat with a piece of paper, ready to write down the testimony of the accused. Adr walked back and forth along the wall.

The pockmarked lieutenant took pleasure in whipping

Voloshin on his fast-swelling groin, muttering, "Talk, you fucker.... Talk, you fucker..."

Voloshin howled for about three hours. He lost consciousness a number of times and we brought him to by pouring water on him and rubbing him with snow. After that, he admitted that back in 1941, as a fifteen-year-old youth in a remote Siberian village, he was contacted and recruited by Japanese counterintelligence. When, choking on tears and mucus, he signed the "statement" compiled by Ivanov and transcribed by me, his hand shook and I could see his essence with my heart. His entire meat-machine being was filled with the image of his mother. He knew he was signing his own death sentence. At that moment, the meat machine in him was filled with the image of his mother—a simple Siberian peasant. His mother sat in his head, like a stone core, repeating the same thing over and over: "I borned you in torture, I borned you in torture..."

With that stone mama in his head, he would have signed anything.

The next morning a troika of horses wrapped in blankets drove a handcuffed Voloshin, two prison escorts, and a lanky field warden with a briefcase. The briefcase held the report of the investigating commission and the testimony of Lieutenant Voloshin.

We stayed on in the camp, awaiting the arrival of a comfortable automobile with a heater.

Ivanov and the lieutenants went on a drinking binge with the director of the camp, who was so elated that things had turned out well that he was ready to kiss their feet.

Adr and I ordered the sleigh to be readied and we went "for a ride." In fact, it was clear WHERE we were drawn.

Leaving the gates of the camp, Adr directed the horse along

Ice

the big road leading to the place where the ICE was mined. The road along which the columns of prisoners transported the mined ice was covered in snow; no one had cleared it for a month. The camp director's well-fed horse had no trouble pulling the sleigh, and we rode along, covered with a bearskin. It was sunny and frosty.

Adr and I felt the ICE with our hearts even in the camp. But now the feeling grew with every step the horse took.

All around lay low mounds covered with sparse growth. The local forest had been destroyed by the blast in 1908 when the meteorite fell, and the new forest was growing in poorly, in clumps. The snow sparkled in the bright sunlight, and squeaked under the sleigh runners.

From the camp to the site of the fall was seven versts.

We drove about three versts and my heart began to quiver. It sensed the ICE, like a compass senses iron ore.

"Faster!" I squeezed Adr's hand.

He lashed the horse. The horse took off and the sleigh whizzed along.

The big road forked around the mounds, crawling in a wide ribbon to another mound and then descending to the pit. We rushed along it.

I closed my eyes. I could already see the ICE with my heart. It loomed before me like a Continent of Light.

The sleigh stopped.

I opened my eyes.

We stood on the edge of the pit. Before us lay an enormous mass of ice, powdered with snow. It sparkled in the sun, giving off a blue tint.

YES! The ice was blue, like our eyes!

At the edges of the ice mass various wood structures had been erected: poles, bridges, shacks for inventory, guard tow-

Part II

ers. All of this was pitiful, wretched, human—it dimmed and was lost to view next to the amazing POWER of the ice.

It was OUR ICE! The ICE sent by the Light, the ICE that struck the breast of the sleeping earth and awoke it.

Our hearts quivered in ECSTASY.

We held hands and descended into the pit. We approached the ice along a wooden bridge. With trembling hands I tore my clothes off until there was nothing on me.

I stepped onto the ice.

A cry of rapture escaped my chest. Tears burst from my eyes. I fell onto the ice, and embraced it. My heart felt and understood this divine mass. A huge heart lay under me. It spoke with me.

Adr undressed as well. I jumped up and stepped toward him. Sobbing with delight, we embraced and fell onto the ice.

Time stopped for us.

When we regained consciousness it was night.

We loosened our embrace.

A black sky bright with stars hung over us. The stars were so low that it seemed you could touch them. Two blurry half circles, tinged with yellow, shone around the huge bright moon. Somewhere far beyond the horizon, the northern lights blazed.

We lay in warm water. We weren't cold at all. Just the opposite—our bodies were burning. We had warmed a crater in the ice that followed the contours of our entwined bodies. A cloud of steam stood over us.

A shot suddenly rang out nearby.

And then another.

Someone cried out: "Hey—ey-eyyyyye!"

I realized they were looking for us.

Ice

We stood up and left our "bath." We found our clothing and dressed. It was time to say farewell to the ice, to return to the cruel world of the meat machines and to our brothers lost among them. We kissed the ice.

Then we set off across the frozen bridges toward the shots and voices.

In Moscow everything worked out well: the results of the investigation satisfied the new minister of state security. Lieutenant Voloshin was shot as a Japanese spy, as were eight of Abakumov's people against whom he'd given evidence under torture. Another "nest of spies" had been liquidated in the system of rehabilitory labor camps.

Camp No. 312/500 began working again; the prisoners' picks rang, the brigadiers shouted, the guard dogs barked, and cubic meters of ICE were transported to the capital. From there they went to other countries where sleeping hearts waited for the awakening blows of the ice hammer.

We worked precisely and with great focus.

In two years, ninety-eight brothers were found.

It was a huge victory for the Light.

But the ill-starred year of 1953 was at hand.

In March, Stalin died.

The next night, Kha convened us at our dacha. Six brothers and six sisters sat in the half dark of the spacious living room, next to the blazing fireplace. Kha sat in a rocking chair. He wore a lilac Chinese robe with silver dragons on it. He fingered rosary beads from Bukhara. Tongues of flame played across his stern, handsome face, and burned in his blue eyes. Kha said, "A redivision of power is about to take place in the USSR. Enormous changes will follow. They will touch many of us. It is imperative to be prepared. We must take care of our brothers, and of the ice. The majority of our people must be sent out of Moscow and Leningrad into the provinces. It will be less dangerous that way. We must begin this work without delay. Adr and I will take on the technical side of things. As far as the quarrying of ice is concerned—it is difficult to predict what may happen. It isn't clear what will become of the camp and the project. They may survive, but they may be closed."

He was silent for a moment and turned his eyes toward me, "Khram, you are the only one of us who knows all the heart words and sees with your heart. What does your heart tell you?"

"Only one thing—something huge and threatening looms over us," I answered honestly.

"What does it resemble?" asked Adr.

"A red wave."

"Then we have to act now."

We were silent for a long time. Then Kha smiled and began to speak.

"This morning I received joyous news—the first shipment of ice arrived in America. Soon we will find out the names of our American brothers!"

Everyone jumped up. We exulted. Throwing off our clothes, we stood in pairs, embraced, pressing chest to chest, we fell to our knees.

The fireplace went out. But our burning hearts quivered in the dark.

The spring and the early part of summer passed in intensive work. In order to send our people to different cities we needed money, a good deal of money. Kha advised us to rob a bank

Ice

collection truck. It was easy for me to follow the vehicle and the people guarding the bag filled with those packets of paper that meat machines value so highly. My heart knew everything about the bank cashier collector—from his collarbone broken in childhood to his passion for playing the accordion. He also loved sniffing women's toes, talking about soccer, and reading books about the war. At just the right moment, when I signaled, Zu shot the vehicle guard, Shro cut the collector's throat, and Mir grabbed the bag of money from his hands.

Half a million rubles was more than enough for moving one hundred people.

This was our main task. At the same time, we accomplished many other things: an emergency store of ice was placed in three refrigerator factories, and we infiltrated our people into a variety of up-and-coming organizations and destroyed the witnesses. In the last case I was absolutely irreplaceable. All I had to do was walk up to the door of an apartment to know who was home and what they were doing. Mir, Zu, and Shro took care of the rest. Almost every day their knives interrupted the meaningless existence of yet another meat machine whose memory could harm us.

We were merciless to the living dead.

And suddenly.

Like the thrust of an unseen sword: on June 26, Beria was arrested.

Heat blew from the Kremlin. The illusions of Beria's cohorts evaporated: some shot themselves, some went on a binge. Others hurriedly wrote denunciations of yesterday's friends.

But Kha remained calm.

"We have managed to do it," he repeated.

Part II

After the arrest of his patron, he, like many MGB generals, became vulnerable. We no longer had any rear guard, no support from above. I begged Kha and Adr to hide.

"We must fight here," Kha objected.

"We have gone through three purges with the help of the Light, and we can make it through this one as well," said Adr, smiling.

My heart was apprehensive. Something was creeping up on us. I raged at them about the coming disaster. But all my arguments shattered against the wall of their courage.

On the other hand, both of them constantly wanted my heart, foreseeing that we had very little time remaining. During the day we worked on business. At night we froze chest to chest, heart to heart.

Their hearts were inexhaustible.

My arms could barely untwine from their necks, my knees trembled, my body blazed.

Kha's wife poured water on me, and slapped my pale cheeks.

I was happy.

During these close, sultry July nights, Kha and Adr learned all twenty-three heart words from my heart.

And they found the Light.

Forever.

On July 17 they were arrested.

It happened during the day. I was sleeping in the old, cluttered apartment belonging to Yus, whom we had sent to the Crimea with two young brothers. My heart woke me. It was in a bad way.

A sense of petrified horror overtook me. I rose, dressed, and went out. I walked through sun-drenched Moscow to Belorussky Station. It was the first time since my return to Russia that I felt a sucking emptiness in my heart.

Ice

I moved like a machine—without feelings or ideas.

Making my way to Belorussky, I stood on the noisy platform, looking at the trains. Then I went to the long-distance ticket window. I waited in line.

"Where are you going?" the cashier asked me.

"I'm going to . . ." It took enormous effort to force myself to think and I decided to go there, where the ICE was, OUR ICE. And where was our divine ICE? In endless Siberia.

"To Siberia," I said firmly, handing money over through the window.

"Now, now, Varvara Fedotovna, why should you pay money for that?" a sarcastic voice spoke into my ear from behind. "We'll send you to Siberia as a business expense."

Two men grabbed me forcefully under my arms.

"Citizen Korobova, you are under arrest," said another voice.

A couple of hours later I was already being interrogated at Lefortovo prison . . .

That day six associates of Beria were arrested, six high-placed generals of the MGB, one of whom was Kha. At the same time, lower rank MGB employees, who were connected to Beria and his people, were also arrested.

"What tied you to general Vlodzimirsky?" was the first question that Investigator Fedotov asked me.

"Nothing tied me to the general," I answered honestly, seeing through Fedotov with my heart: a premature birth in the hay fields, orphaned, a difficult childhood, tears, fights, the navy; he liked water, cognac, having intercourse with fat women and making them repeat swear words, beach volleyball, and thinking about Saturn while defecating; he was afraid of spiders and scissors, of being late to work, of losing documents; he liked stew, remembering People's Commissar Yezhov, making little boats in the spring, the Black Sea port of Gagra, and beating people on the face and kidneys.

"And what is this?" he showed me a photograph.

I still could not see any images. In the middle of the glossy paper two shiny spots merged.

"What is this, I'm asking you?"

"I can't see it," I admitted.

"Are we going to play the fool?" Fedotov wheezed angrily.

"I really cannot see any images on photographs, not only on this one. Over there you have a portrait—I nodded toward a dark patch in a red frame. "I can't see who it is."

Fedotov looked at me angrily. His plump face slowly turned red with blood.

"That is Vladimir Ilich Lenin. Or haven't you heard of him?"

"I've heard of him."

"Is that so?" he clapped his strong hands and laughed nastily.

I said nothing.

"Vlodzimirsky and your husband, Korobov, are friends of Beria. And Beria, just so you know, is an agent of foreign intelligence services. He has already given evidence. About Vlodzimirsky, among others. I'm offering to let you tell us honestly about the criminal activities of Vlodzimirsky and Korobov."

"I didn't know General Vlodzimirsky well."

"You didn't know Vlodzimirsky? But on this photo he's pawing you. Naked."

"I repeat, I wasn't close to General Vlodzimirsky, and didn't know him well. I knew his heart well."

"What?"

Ice

"And this photograph records a moment when our souls spoke in a secret language."

"That means you confess that you were his mistress?"

"By no means. I was his heart sister."

"And you never slept with him, even once?"

"I slept with him many times. But not like an earthly woman would. Rather, like a heart sister. A sister of the Eternal and Primordial Light."

"A sister of Light?" Fedotov laughed maliciously. "What kind of nonsense is this, you stinking cunt? A sister, shit! What holes did he hump you in, you regiment hooker?! You're all from the same goddamn gang, Beria's spies! You made your viper's nest in the MGB, you reptiles! Tell the fucking truth!"

He hit me on the face.

I said nothing. I looked at him.

He rolled up his sleeves, all business.

"You'll remember everything for me in a little while, you rotten cunt."

He came out from around the desk, and grabbed me by the hair with his left hand. Then he began to beat me on the cheeks with a practiced right hand. He probably expected that I would cry out, like the majority of meat-machine women, and covering my face, beg him for mercy.

But I didn't even raise my hands to my face.

I looked him straight in the eyes.

He swung his hand back and slapped me on the cheek even harder. His coarse palms smelled of tobacco, eau de cologne, and old furniture.

"Talk! Talk! Talk!" he said as he slapped.

My head went back and forth, and my ears rang.

But I kept looking straight into his small, piercing pupils.

Part II

He stopped slapping me, and brought his reddening face right up to mine.

"So you're a bold one, are you? I'll turn you into mincemeat, salt and pepper you, and make you eat yourself! Why so quiet, you dried-up cunt?"

Inside he was absolutely happy. His heart sang, and in his bald head orange flares blazed and extinguished.

I said nothing.

During the first two interrogations he shouted and whipped me on the cheeks. Then a second investigator appeared—Revzin. At first he tried to play the "good cop," initiating intimate conversations with me, asking me to "help the organs of state security expose Beria's gang." I spoke only the truth: the brotherhood, Kha and Adr, twenty-three words.

I did this because my heart was absolutely certain that they would not need our secrets. The meat machines didn't see the truth—they looked right through it, they couldn't distinguish the Divine Light.

It was incredibly wonderful to speak the truth, to delight in it.

They swore and laughed.

Finally, they got sick of hearing about the singing of hearts. They undressed me, tied me to a bench, and began to flog me with a rubber plait. They were in no hurry, they took turns: one would flog, while the other shouted or quietly cajoled me to change my mind.

I felt the pain, of course.

But it wasn't like before, when I was a meat machine. Previously, there had been nowhere to escape from the pain. Because the pain was the master of my body. Now my master was the heart. And the pain couldn't reach it. It lived separately. My

263

Ice

heart felt the pain in the form of a red serpent. The serpent crawled over me. But my heart sang, mesmerizing the serpent. When it crawled for too long at a time, my heart shrank, flaring violet. Then I lost consciousness.

They poured water on me.

While I was coming around, they smoked.

Then their simple hands once again took up the plait.

Everything repeated itself.

I said nothing. My heart sang. The red serpent crawled. The water rang.

Then the investigators grew tired.

They took me away to the cell. I fell asleep.

I awoke from a squeak. The door opened, and three people came in: Revzin, a doctor, and some kind of lieutenant colonel. The doctor examined my swollen thighs, blue from blows to the hips and buttocks, nodded professionally, and said, "Everything's fine."

Revzin called two escorts. They grabbed me under the arms and dragged me along the corridor, then up the staircase—way up high, to that very same office. It was light there—rays of sun beat at the window, the crystal inkstand shone, the copper door handle reflected the eyes and buttons of Revzin. And on the wall, in a red frame, an unseen Lenin swirled.

A small, angry Fedotov came in the room with plaits. They again tied me to the bench. They took two whips and and began to whip me simultaneously along my swelling thighs.

Two red serpents began to slither over me. They became orange. Then blindingly yellow. The yellow sun sang in my head.

"Tell us the truth! Tell! Tell! Tell us!"

But I'd already told them the truth.

Part II

What on earth did they want from me?

The amber-colored serpents wound themselves into a wedding ring. They liked being on my body.

Sweat poured into my eyes.

My heart flared in a violet rainbow: it could feel that my body was being destroyed.

And my heart helped my body: my brain turned itself off, and I fainted.

I awoke on the floor.

Nastya Vlodzimirskaya was hanging over me. They were holding her under her arms and by her hair, so her head wouldn't slump down onto her chest. They'd done more than beat her. They'd torn her to shreds.

"Do you confirm it?" some fat major asked her, a man who loved cats, mashed potatoes, and gold watches.

From Nastya's broken mouth a screech sounded. And something dripped on my head.

"There you go!" The major exchanged a joyfully malicious glance with Revzin.

"And you talk about sisters!" Fedotov said, kicking me with a new boot.

"We're not a bunch of dumbbells sitting here, Korobova." Revzin looked down on me. "You forgot that we're professionals. We dig up everything."

"They only spoke English at home," the major told Fedotov confidentially. "Eye gow to sleap, mye swheat ledy!"

They jeered. And their waist belts squeaked.

I closed my eyes.

"Just what do you think you're pretending?" Fedotov kicked me again.

Ice

I opened my eyes. The fat major and Nastya were gone.

"Now then, Korobova, here is your evidence." Revzin brought me some papers covered with childish handwriting. "If you sign, you'll go to the hospital and then to the camp. If you don't sign—you'll go to the other world."

I closed my eyes and whispered, "The purpose of my life is to go to the other world. To Our World...Our Light..."

"Shut up, you bitch! Don't pretend to be crazy!" Fedotov snarled. "Read it to her, Yegor Petrovich."

Revzin mumbled: "I, Korobova Varvara Fedotovna, born in 1929, having established sexual relations with General Lieutenant Vlodzimirsky, L.E., was recruited by him in 1950 as a liaison between the military attaché of the American embassy, Irwin Pierce, and the former minister of the MGB, V.S. Abakumov. My first task was to meet with Pierce on March 8, 1950, at the boat station in Gorky Park and to hand over plans to him—"

"That's not about me," I interrupted.

"It's about you! It's about you, cunt!" Fedotov growled.

"Sign it Korobova, don't play the fool!"

"I'm not Korobova. My true name is—Khram."

I closed my eyes.

And the amber serpents again crawled over me.

I came to on a gynecological chair. There was a terrible aroma of smelling salts in the air.

"She's a virgin," came a voice from between my legs.

The doctor straightened up, began tearing off his rubber gloves. He was large and wore glasses. He was afraid of his mother, of dogs, and of doorbells at night. He loved to tickle his wife until she got hiccups. He loved crabs, billiards, and Stalin.

Part II

"So, what do we do now?" muttered Fedotov just above my ear.

"I don't know." The doctor disappeared.

"I didn't ask you!" Fedotov snapped back angrily.

"Who then? Yourself?" The doctor laughed, clattering his instruments.

A needle pierced my shoulder. I shifted my eyes: the nurse was giving me a shot.

My spread legs were bluish-yellow in color. My abrasions were bleeding.

My eyes filled with moisture. And I felt like sleeping.

"Well, so?" The doctor let out a big yawn.

"To the hospital." Fedotov nodded thoughtfully.

I lay in the prison hospital for a week.

There were six other women in the ward. Two had been tortured, four had pneumonia. They talked constantly among themselves about their relatives, food, and medicine.

I was treated: a perfumed ointment was rubbed into my legs and buttocks.

The doctors and nurses said almost nothing to the prisoners.

I looked out the window and at the women. I knew everything about every one. They weren't interesting to me.

I remembered OUR PEOPLE.

And their HEARTS.

When I got better, they took me back to interrogation.

The office was the same, but the investigator was new. Sheredenko, Ivan Samsonovich. A slim, well-built thirty-five-year-old with a handsome face. More than anything on earth

Ice

he feared dreaming of a white tower and dying at work from a heart attack. He loved hunting, fried eggs with lard, and his daughter, Annushka.

"Varvara Fedotovna, your former investigators were scoundrels. They have already been arrested," he informed me.

"That's not true," I answered. "Fedotov is having lunch right now in the Lubianka cafeteria, and Revzin's walking down the street."

He looked at me attentively.

"Varvara Fedotovna, let's talk as Chekhist to Chekhist."

"I never was a Chekhist. I simply wore your uniform."

"Don't be absurd. You worked with Lieutenant Colonel Korobov..."

"I worked not with him but with his heart. Now it knows all twenty-three words."

"You went on a business trip on the order of the minister of state security, and you visited Camp No. 312/500, where they extract—"

"The Ice sent to us from Space, to awake the living."

"The director of the camp, Major Semichastnykh, was arrested and gave evidence against Colonel Ivanov, you, and your husband. The three of you beat false testimony out of Lieutenant Voloshin in order to hide the true activities of Abakumov and Vlodzimirsky. This was necessary in order to—"

"So that the camp would continue to extract the Divine Ice, which thousands of our brothers and sisters all over the world await. Thousands of ice hammers will be manufactured from this ice, they will strike thousands of breasts, thousands of hearts will awaken and speak. And when there are twenty-three thousand of us, our hearts will pronounce the twenty-three heart words twenty-three times and we will be transformed into Eternal and Primordial Rays of the Light. And

Part II

your dead world will disintegrate. NOTHING AT ALL will be left of it."

He looked at me carefully. Then he pushed a button. An escort entered.

"Take her away," said Investigator Sheredenko.

I was examined by a psychiatrist—a small, round man, with a meaty nose and feminine hands. He was afraid of many things: children, cats, conversations about politics, icicles, his bosses, even old hats, which "stubbornly hint at something." The only things he truly loved were playing backgammon, sleeping, and writing denunciations.

In his soft, female voice he asked me to hold my hands out in front of me, to look at his little hammer, count to twenty, answer a bunch of silly questions. Then he tapped his little hammer on my knees and picked up the receiver of a black telephone.

"Comrade Sheredenko, this is Yurevich. She's absolutely healthy."

After this, Sheredenko spoke with me differently.

"Korobova, two questions: Why didn't you and your husband have sexual relations? And what were you and your husband doing so often at General Vlodzimirsky's dacha?"

"Adr and I didn't need sexual relations. We had heart relations. At Kha's dacha we would engage in conversations of the heart."

"Enough playing the madwoman!" he said, slapping his palm on the table. "When did Vlodzimirsky recruit you and your husband? What were you supposed to do?"

"To awaken brothers and sisters."

"Awaken?" he asked nastily. "I see, you don't want to do this the good way. All right then. We'll awaken you, too."

Ice

He picked up the telephone receiver.

"Savelev, bring the Fruits and Vegetables."

Escort guards appeared. I was taken out into the courtyard. Sheredenko walked after me.

Cars stood in the courtyard, and the sun warmed us.

I was taken to a dark green van with a sign reading: FRESH FRUITS AND VEGETABLES. The escorts and I sat in the back of the van; Sheredenko sat in the front seat with the driver. The van took off. Inside it was dark; light penetrated only through a few cracks.

We drove for a short time, then stopped. The doors opened and the guards took me out. They immediately led me downstairs into a cellar. Sheredenko followed.

We arrived at a metal door with a peephole; the guard knocked on it. The door opened. It smelled of cold. We were met by a mustached overseer wearing a floor-length sheepskin coat. He turned and walked off. We followed him. He opened yet another door. I was pushed into a small, square, empty room. The door slammed shut, the lock clanked. Sheredenko said through the door: "If you get smarter, give us a knock."

The cell was lit by a dim lightbulb. One of the walls of the cell was metallic. A coating of hoarfrost covered it in white.

I sat down in a corner.

In the metallic wall something hummed faintly. Barely audible, it gurgled.

I suddenly realized: a refrigerator.

I closed my eyes.

The cold grew slowly. I didn't resist it.

If the red serpents of my beating had crawled over the surface of my body, the cold made its way inside. It took away my body in parts: the legs, shoulder, back. The last to yield were my hands and fingertips.

All that remained was my heart. It beat more slowly.

I felt that it was the last bastion.

I really wanted to fall into a deep, long, white dream. But something was in the way. Something was bothering me. I couldn't go to sleep. And so I entered a waking reverie. My heart-sight became even sharper. I saw the corridors of the cellar with its guards. Another eight people were sitting in other refrigerators. They were in bad shape because they resisted the cold. Two of them wailed incessantly. Three others danced around on their last legs. The rest simply lay on the floor in an embryonic position.

Time ceased to exist.

There was only the cold. Around my heart.

Sometimes the door opened. And the mustached guard asked me something. I opened my eyes, looked at him. And closed them again.

One time he put a cup of boiling water next to me. He placed a piece of bread nearby. Steam rose from the cup. Then he stopped coming.

The prisoners in the cells changed: meat machines couldn't withstand the cold. They admitted to everything the investigator demanded from them. They were carried out of the cells like frozen chickens.

New ones were herded into the refrigerators. They jumped up and down and wailed.

My heart beat evenly. It existed. On its own. But in order to keep from stopping, it needed work.

And I helped it work.

I constantly surveyed the environs with my heart: I saw the frost, the iron wall, the hallway, the cells, the walls, the rats on

Ice

the garbage heap, the trolleys, the meat machines going to and from work, the pickpocket stealing an old lady's wallet, a drunk falling on the sidewalk, troublemakers with guitars in doorways, a fire at a factory that manufactured irons, a meeting of the Party committee of the automobile-highway institute, sexual acts in a woman's dormitory, a dog run over by a tram, newlyweds leaving the marriage office, a line for noodles, a soccer game, young people strolling in the park, a surgeon sewing up warm skin, the robbery of a food kiosk, a flock of doves, a conductor chewing a sandwich of smoked sausage, invalids at the train station, the streets, the iron wall, the frost.

The city surrounded me on all sides.

The city of meat machines.

And in this dead mixture like red embers burns the hearts of OUR PEOPLE.

Kha.

Adr.

Shro.

Zu.

Mir.

Pa.

Umi.

All of those who remained in Moscow.

I saw them. And spoke with them. Of the Kingdom of Light.

Sheredenko came in.

He talked and shouted. He stamped his heels on the frozen floor. He shook some papers. Blew his nose. I looked at his dead heart. It worked like a pump. It pumped dead blood. Which moved the dead body of Investigator Sheredenko.

I closed my eyes. He disappeared.

Part II

Then I saw OUR PEOPLE again. Their hearts shone. And they swam around me. There were more and more of them. I reached out to more and more new ones, to ones that were far, far away. And finally, I saw the hearts of ALL OUR PEOPLE on this gloomy planet. My square refrigerator glided in space. Around it, their hearts swam like constellations. There were 459 in all. So few! Nevertheless, they shone for me and spoke to me in OUR language.

And I was happy.

My cheeks were painfully cauterized.

I woke up. I was in a hospital ward. The ceiling had six lights. A nurse was putting something on my face. A towel dipped in warm water. The smell of alcohol. The trace of a shot in the crook of my elbow.

Some colonel came in quietly. The nurse and the towel disappeared.

A chair squeaked. And boots.

"How do you feel?"

I closed my eyes. Seeing the world with my heart was so much more pleasant to me.

"Can you talk?"

"About what?" I said with great difficulty. "About the fact that you are afraid of drowning? You almost drowned twice, isn't that so?"

"How do you know?" he smiled awkwardly.

"The first time was in the Urals. You swam out with three boys, fell behind, and at the bridge you got caught in an undertow. Some soldier saved you. He pulled you by the hand and kept saying, 'Hold on, you horse's prick, hold on, you horse's prick...' The second time you almost drowned was in the

Ice

Black Sea. You dove off the piers. Swam up to the shore, as usual. You never swam out to sea from the shore. But a homeless dog dove in after you, the beach favorite. She could feel that you were afraid of drowning, and she swam nearby, barking, trying to help. This caused you to panic. You thrashed your arms about in the water and rushed toward the shore. The dog barked and swam nearby. Fear paralyzed you. You were certain that she wanted to drown you. And you began to choke. You saw your family—your wife in a chaise lounge and your daughter with a ball. They were right nearby. You swallowed salt water, let out bubbles. And suddenly your feet touched bottom. You stood up. Breathing heavily and coughing, you screamed at the dog: 'Get the fuck out of here, you mutt!' You splashed water on her. She came ashore, shook herself off, and ran toward the stand where one-armed Ashot was grilling shish kebab. You stood waist-high in water and spat."

He stiffened. Horror filled his gray-green eyes. He swallowed. Inhaled. Exhaled.

"You need to—"

"What?"

"Eat."

And he left quickly.

For the first time I remembered about food. In the cell and the hospital they pushed bowls with something brown at me. But I didn't eat. I was used to eating only fruits and vegetables. I hadn't eaten bread since '43.

Bread—is a mockery of grain.

What could be worse than bread? Only meat.

Then, I think, for the first time in these two weeks I wanted to eat. I called the nurse.

Part II

"I can't eat kasha or bread. But I would eat some unground grain. Do you have any?"

She left without a word, to tell the colonel. Through the thickness of the brick walls I saw him, slouched over and gloomy, pick up the telephone receiver in his office.

"Grain? Well...give it to her if she asks. Only that? Give her oats."

They brought me oats.

I lay there and chewed.

Then I slept.

That night the colonel came to see me. He closed the door behind him and sat on the edge of the bed.

"I didn't introduce myself earlier," he said quietly.

"There's no need. You are Viktor Nikolaevich Lapitsky."

"I understand, I understand..." He waved his hand. "You know everything about me. And...about everyone, most likely."

I looked at him. He unbuttoned the collar of his tunic, sighed convulsively, and whispered, "Don't be afraid, there aren't any listening devices here. You...can you say whether they'll arrest me or not?"

"I don't know," I answered honestly.

He was silent a moment, then he glanced to the side and whispered hurriedly, "I haven't slept for eight days. Eight! I can't fall asleep. If I take barbital I fall asleep for an hour and then jump up like a madman. There are big changes going on. Arrests being made. They are sweeping away everyone who worked with Beria and Abakumov. But who didn't work with them? You also worked with them?"

"I worked for us."

Ice

"Two of my friends from the third section have been arrested. Maslennikov committed suicide. Maslennikov! You understand? Khrushchev's broom is sweeping clean... Hmm..."

I said nothing. My heart knew what he wanted. He broke into a sweat.

"I've lived through two purges—in '37 and in '48. It was a downright miracle that I didn't fall under the wheel. I just don't have the strength to live through another one. You know, I haven't slept for eight days. Eight!"

"You said that."

"That's right, yes."

"What do you want from me?"

"I...I want...I know—that you are a real spy. A real agent. For whom—I don't know. I think it must be the Americans. But—you're a real, genuine intelligence agent! Not like those fake ones that our strongmen are breaking by the hundreds in order to hand in their cases. I'm offering you a contract: I'll get you out of here, and you help me to go abroad."

"Agreed," I answered quickly.

He was surprised. Wiping the sweat from his brow, he whispered, "No, you have to understand, this isn't some cheap provocation and it's not...not the fantasy of some sleep-deprived Chekhist. I am really proposing this."

"I understand. I told you—I agree."

Lapitsky stared hard at me. Some reason appeared in his feverish eyes.

"I was sure!" he whispered with delight. "I don't know...I don't understand...why, but I was sure!"

I looked at the ceiling. "I was also certain that I would get out of here."

And it was true.

Part II

Colonel Lapitsky took me out of the investigatory isolation unit at Lefortovo on August 18, 1953.

A fine rain was falling. We drove to Kazan Station in the colonel's official car, which he abandoned there forever. Then we got on the commuter train and rode to the Moscow suburb of Bykovo. There, in a dacha belonging to relatives of Yus's sister, lived Shro and Zu.

They greeted me with excitement, but not as someone who had died and been reincarnated: their hearts knew that I was alive.

Having strangled Colonel Lapitsky, we spent two days in heart conversation. My pining heart was unquenchable. I drank and drank my brothers. To the point of exhaustion.

After burying Lapitsky's corpse at nighttime, the next morning we left Moscow.

Three days later at the station in Krasnoyarsk we were met by Aub, Nom, and Re. Adr and I had awakened all of them in the cellar of the Great House.

Thus, I ended up in Siberia.

One dark December morning my heart shuddered from pain twice: in far-off Moscow Kha and Adr were executed. The meat machines had stopped their strong, warm hearts forever.

And we were unable to prevent this.

Six years passed.

I returned to Moscow.

Three brothers had died of natural causes. The old lady Yus had died as well. The Primordial Light, shining in them, was reincarnated in other bodies that had only just appeared on earth. And we were faced with having to find them once again.

The camp that mined the ICE has been disbanded. The professors who substantiated the importance of studying the "Tungus ice phenomenon" were posthumously dubbed pseudo-scientists, and the secret project "Ice" was liquidated. The *sharashka* where they prepared the ice hammers was liquidated as well.

Nonetheless, the brotherhood strengthened and grew. The stores of ice mined during Stalin's time were sufficient for all. In 1959 we were grateful to the prisoners of Camp No. 312/500. With their bricks they laid the foundations necessary for an ice base. Cubometers of ice slept in refrigerators and underground storehouses, awaiting their hour. Part of the ice was sent abroad through the old MGB channels. From the remainder of the ice we made ice hammers.

They were rarely used, since the search for OUR PEOPLE was narrowed. It became more local. Now, without the support of the MGB, we searched for others of us cautiously, meticulously preparing for the hammering. Train stations, movie theaters, restaurants, concert halls, and stores were the main places we searched. We followed people with fair hair and blue eyes, kidnapped them, and hammered them. But more than anywhere else for some reason, we had luck in libraries. Thousands of meat machines were always sitting there, engaged in silent madness: they attentively leafed through sheets of paper covered with letters. This gave them particular pleasure, comparable to nothing else. These thick, worn books were written by long-dead meat machines whose portraits hung ceremoniously on the walls of the libraries. There were millions of books. They were constantly increasing in number, supporting a collective madness that made millions of corpses lean devoutly

Part II

over sheets of dead paper. After reading they became even deader. But amid these petrified figures were some of us as well. In the huge Lenin Library we found eight. We found three in the Library of Foreign Literature. And four in the History Library.

The brotherhood was growing.

By the winter of 1959 there were 118 of us in Russia.

The stormy 1960s arrived.

Time speeded up.

New possibilities arose, new perspectives opened.

Our people began to move up in their jobs, to occupy important positions. The brotherhood again infiltrated the Soviet elite, but this time from below. We had three new brothers in the Council of Ministers and one in the Central Committee of the Communist Party. Sister Chbe became the culture minister of Latvia, brothers Ent and Bo held leadership positions in the Ministry of Foreign Trade, sister Ug married the commander of PVO troops, brother Ne became director of the Malyi Theater.

And most important—Brothers Aub, Nom, and Mir organized a scientific society for the study of TMP: the Tungus Meteorite Phenomenon. It was supported by the Academy of Sciences and subsisted on government money. Expeditions were sent out to the site of the fall almost every year.

Chunks of ice again flowed to Moscow.

We were working.

In the 1970s the brotherhood increased in strength.

Our newly acquired brother Lech became the director of Comecon. The most extraordinary thing was that his daughter turned out to be one of us, as did his grandson. This was the

Ice

first time that we had a living family. Lech, Mart, and Bork became the bulwark of the brotherhood in the Soviet *nomenklatura*. Comecon began to work for us. Thanks to Lech we established close contacts with our people in Eastern Europe. We began to supply ice to them directly, bypassing the complex, conspiratorial channels Kha created under Stalin.

I took up a small management position in Comecon.

This allowed me to travel often to other Socialist countries. I saw the faces of our European brothers. I came to know their hearts. Speaking in different earthly languages, we understood one another perfectly.

We knew WHAT to do and HOW to do it.

The brotherhood grew.

In 1980 there were 718 of us in Russia.

And worldwide—there were 2,405.

The 1980s brought a great deal of fuss and difficulty.

Brezhnev died. Russia's traditional redistribution of power began. Four of our people lost important positions in the Central Committee and the Council of Ministers. Three from Gosplan were demoted. Brother Yot, a well-known functionary of the All-Union Central Soviet of Trade Unions, was kicked out of the Party for "protectionism" (he promoted our people into the leadership of the union too actively). Two brothers from Vneshtorg fell during the campaign against corruption and were given long sentences. Sisters Fed and Ku lost their jobs in the Central Committee of the Komsomol for "amoral behavior." (they were caught during a heart conversation.) And Shro, my loyal and decisive follower, was sentenced for assault with physical injury (one of the people we hammered ran away and denounced him).

Part II

But Lech survived.

And two of us, Uy and Im, became colonels in the KGB.

Ice was extracted and exported to twenty-eight countries.

And the ice hammers struck hearts once again.

Andropov and Chernenko died.

Gorbachev came to power.

The era of glasnost and perestroika began.

The USSR began to disintegrate. Camecon was disbanded. And Lech died almost immediately after that. This was a huge loss for us. Our hearts said ardent farewells to the great Lech. He had done so much for the brotherhood.

The Party lost more and more power in the country. Panic began to overtake the loyal echelons of power: the Soviet *nomenklatura* recognized a mortal danger in the impending democratization, but could do nothing.

Private enterprise appeared. The smartest representatives of the *nomenklatura* began to move into business. Using their old connections, they quickly made a lot of money.

OUR PEOPLE were also able to reorient themselves quickly. It was decided to establish commercial firms, banks, and stock companies.

In August 1991 the USSR fell apart.

By an irony of fate, one day three brothers and I found our-selves on Lubianskaya Square and observed the monument to Dzerzhinsky being dismantled. When it was tied with steel cables and lifted into the air, I remembered my arrest, my refrigerator cell, the interrogations, the amber serpent, the evil faces and dead hearts of the investigators.

The dismantling of the monument was directed by a blond fellow wearing a tank-division helmet. He had blue eyes. We got to know each other, and a few hours later, in a specially equipped cellar, we hammered Sergei. And his heart spoke his true name: Dor.

Thus, Dzerzhinsky helped us to find one of our brothers.

The rapid-fire 1990s took off.

The cheerful and frightening era of Yeltsin began.

For the brotherhood it was a golden time. We managed to do what we had dreamed of: we secured positions in the power structure, established mighty financial structures, and founded a number of joint ventures.

But the main success of the brotherhood was that our brothers infiltrated the highest echelons of power.

In two years, brother Uf, whom we acquired at the end of the 1970s in Leningrad, had managed a meteoric career: from being a docent of the Engineering Economics Institute he became a vice premier in the Russian government. He directed the economic reforms and privatization of state property. The sale of hundreds of plants and factories passed through Uf's hands. In the first half of the 1990s he was, for all intents and purposes, the owner of Russia's real estate.

It is impossible to overestimate his contribution to the brotherhood's quest. Thanks to the redheaded Uf we attained genuine economic freedom. The issue of money was solved for us forever. And on the planet of meat machines money moved everything.

I blessed him. Our strawberry blond Uf.

His small but inexhaustible heart often spoke with mine.

Uf headed a radical wing of the brotherhood. The radicals tried to increase the number of brothers by any means possible in order to live to see the Great Transformation.

Part II

Unlike them, we in the mainstream were not so egotistical and we worked for future generations.

But Uf, with his great economic burst, brought the future closer: by January 1, 2000, there were 18,610 of US in the entire world.

And for the first time I believed that I would LIVE TO SEE IT!

We celebrated the New Year in a small circle at Uf's country home. This was the only acceptable holiday for us of all the meat machine's holidays: after all, each new year brought the hour of the Great Transformation closer.

After a short heart conversation we sat on a rug around a mountain of fruits and ate in silence. For the most part, we tried not to speak in the language of the meat machines.

And suddenly Uf froze with a plum in his hand. His blue-gray eyes squinted, his small, stubborn mouth opened.

"One year and eight months from now, we will become Rays of Light!"

I froze. The others did too.

Uf looked around at us with a piercing gaze. He added decisively: "I know!"

Suddenly his eyes grew moist, his lips trembled, the plum fell from his fingers. Tears flowed down his cheeks.

I ran to him, and embraced him.

Drenched in tears, I began to kiss his freckled hands.

I awoke, as usual, in the morning.

From the gentle touch of sister Tbo. Her hands were stroking my face.

Suddenly I remembered: today was a special day. A day of Greeting.

Ice

I opened my eyes: I saw my spacious bedroom with tender blue walls and a golden ceiling, Tbo's blue-eyed face, her soft hands. Gentle music sounded. Tbo pulled the blanket off me. I turned on my stomach. The sister's hands began to massage my no-longer-young body. Brothers Mef and Por entered silently. Waiting until the massage was over, they lifted me and carried me to the bathroom. There they helped me to empty my intestines and bladder. Then they lowered me into a bath of frothing cow milk. After about ten minutes they took me out, washed off the milk and rubbed my chest with sesame butter, placed a mask of sperm from young meat machines on my face. Sister Vikha arranged my hair and put on my makeup. I moved into the dressing room where Vikha helped me to choose a dress for today.

I always dress in blue for special days. I chose a dress of restrained blue crêpe de chine, a little pillbox hat of blue silk with a blue veil, blue patent-leather boots, and bracelets of turquoise.

They took me into the dining room.

It was a large half circle, decorated in the same golden-blue tones. White roses and lilies stood in four gold vases. Outside the wide windows was a green fir forest.

Presiding over the table set with a gold service, I reached out my hands. Mef and Por immediately wrapped them in warm, moist napkins. Brother Rak served a dish of tropical fruits. One of my six secretaries entered—brother Ga. He began reading the updates.

Listening to him, I ate leisurely.

He finished reading and left.

Having finished my meal, I stretched out my hands again. Once again, two moist napkins carefully wiped them.

They carried me into the hall for heart conversation. It was round, without windows. The walls of the hall were fashioned of blue jasper.

Three naked brothers kneeled in the center of the hall. I lowered myself to my knees next to them. Their arms embraced me.

Our hearts began to speak.

I taught them the words.

But not for long: our embrace ended with a sweet moan, and I was carried into the room of rest.

A quiet room, with soft, golden-blue furniture, it was imbued with Eastern aromas. While I lay in a soft armchair, my hands were massaged. Then I drank tea made of herbs from the Altai.

My secretary entered.

I understood: it was time.

They carried me out of the house. My dark blue bulletproof automobile and two guard vehicles waited in front of the marble porch. It was sunny and there was a springlike freshness in the air. The last bits of snow had retreated, green grass was pushing up on the lawns. A woodpecker tapped on a dry branch. The gardener Eb was restoring a pyramid in the stone garden. A guard with a machine gun strolled by the gates.

They put me in the car.

We drove into Moscow.

The heavy limousine traveled silently, rocking me softly. I looked out the window. I loved the environs of Moscow, that extraordinary combination of wild nature and wild habitation. Here earthly life seems less horrid to me. The road ran through massive stretches of forest, and among the trees one glimpsed the silhouettes of dachas, the same as forty years earlier. In the Moscow suburbs nothing had changed since Stalin's time. The fences had simply grown higher and richer.

Moscow, on the other hand, was completely different. It had spread out. There was too much of it.

Ice

We drove along the Rublev Highway past white prefab buildings. Meat machines think them ugly, preferring houses built of brick. But what is a human house, in fact? A terrifyingly limited space. The incarnation in stone, iron, and glass of the desire to hide from the Cosmos. A coffin. Into which man falls, from his mother's womb.

They all begin their lives in coffins. For they are dead from birth.

I looked at the windows of the prefab building: thousands of identical little coffins.

And in each one a family of meat machines prepared for death.

What happiness that WE are different.

Driving along Mosfilmovskaya Street, the limousine turned toward Sparrow Hills. As always, it was empty and wide open. Only Moscow University rose as a monument to the Stalinist era.

After a few smooth turns, we drove up to our rehabilitation clinic. It was built five years ago. Newly acquired brothers and sisters lay in it. Here we healed their wounds from the ice hammers.

Sister Kharo rolled a wheelchair up to my car. I was helped to sit in it and rolled into the clinic. In the hallways I was greeted by the experienced sisters Mair and Irey. I greeted their hearts with a flare.

"They are ready," Mair informed me.

They took me into the ward.

There, on a large white bed lay three newly acquired hearts. They were exhausted by the crying that had shaken them for an entire week.

My heart began cautiously to pluck at these three awakened hearts.

Part II

In a half a minute I knew everything about them.

When they awoke, I spoke to them.

"Ural, Diar, Mokho. I am Khram. I welcome you. Your hearts wept for seven days. This weeping is in grief and shame for your previous dead life. Now your hearts are cleansed. They will no longer sob. They are ready to love and speak. Now my heart will speak the first word of the most important language to your hearts. The language of the heart."

The three newly acquired looked at me.

And my heart began to speak with them.

Part III

INSTRUCTIONS FOR USING THE **ICE**
HEALTH IMPROVEMENT SYSTEM

1. Unpack the box.

2. Remove the **video helmet, breast plate, mini freezer, computer, and connection cords** from the box.

3. Plug the mini freezer into an electrical outlet immediately in order to keep the **ICE** it contains from melting. Remember that the battery is capable of maintaining the necessary temperature in the mini freezer for **no more than** seventy-two hours!

4. Familiarize yourself with the **counter-indications**; when you are certain that the **ICE** Health Improvement System is not counter-indicated for you, find a quiet, secluded room and lock the door so that no one will disturb you during the session. Bare the upper part of your body, put on the breastplate, and fasten the belts on your back and shoulders. The mechanical striking arm should be positioned to strike exactly in the center

of your breastbone. Open the mini freezer; remove one of the twenty-three **ICE** segments provided. Remove the **ICE** from the plastic packaging and place it in the striking-arm socket, securing it with the **socket latch**. Connect the cords to the **ICE** system. Insert the plug of the computer adapter into an electrical outlet. Sit down in a comfortable position. Relax. Try not to think of extraneous things. Hold the **directional controls** in your right hand. Press the **ON** button. When you are certain that the mechanical arm is positioned so that the **ICE** will strike precisely **in the center** of your breastbone, put the video helmet on your head. The **ICE** Health Improvement System session lasts from two to three hours. If you experience any discomfort during the session, press the **OFF** button, which can be distinguished from the **ON** button by its rough surface.

5. When the session is over, remove the video helmet and the breastplate and disconnect the system from the electrical source. Assume a horizontal position; try to relax and think about eternity. After regaining your calm, get up, detach the **tear-aspirators** from the helmet, wash them in warm water, wipe them dry, and reinsert them into the video helmet.

Counter-Indications

The **ICE** Health Improvement System is **categorically** counter-indicated for individuals with cardiovascular disease, nervous system disorders, or psychiatric conditions; pregnant women, nursing mothers, alcoholics, drug addicts, war invalids, and children under the age of eighteen.

Part III

Warnings

1. We do not recommend more than two sessions in a twenty-four hour period.

2. If you experience discomfort after the session, contact **ICE**. Our doctors and technicians will provide you with the necessary recommendations. Remember that the Health Improvement System is intended for **individual application only.**

3. If you interrupt the session, remove the unused **ICE** from the striking arm **completely.** In order to continue the session you will have to insert a **new ICE** segment.

4. Do not expose the equipment to the effects of direct sunlight, humidity, and low temperatures.

Additional ice ICE to restock your mini freezer may be obtained from authorized ICE dealerships.

COMMENTS AND RECOMMENDATIONS
FROM THE FIRST USERS OF THE
ICE HEALTH IMPROVEMENT SYSTEM

Leonid Batov, 56, film director
     Until recently I was a steadfast, principled enemy of progress and regarded the technological novelties of our century with suspicion. This was not a matter of my having "environmental"

Ice

views, not at all. Rather, it stemmed from the very logic of my life and my art. I led a fairly secluded life, lived in the country, and socialized with a small circle of like-minded people. Once every four years I made a film. My films were termed "elite," "hermetic," and even "arrogantly marginal" by many film critics. They are right: I was always a supporter of elitism in art, of "films that are NOT for everyone." I believed my primary enemy to be Hollywood, that huge McDonald's which overran the world with cinematic "fast food" of dubious quality. My heroes and teachers were Eisenstein, Antonioni, and Hitchcock. Politically speaking, I was an anarchist, a devotee of Bakunin and Kropotkin, who struggled against the faceless machine of the state. I actively supported the Greens, even taking part in two of their actions. I was born and grew up in a totalitarian state and had always experienced a certain inner tension; I expected aggression from without. Why do I speak of my political convictions now? Because everything in man is interconnected. Ethics and aesthetics, food and attitudes toward animals. It was precisely such an inner tension that I experienced when the courier brought me the **ICE** system. Representatives of the manufacturer had called me on several occasions and spent a long time convincing me to accept this gift. At first, naturally, I refused. I was sick and tired of the ads for the system and the hullabaloo surrounding it which has convulsed our mass media in recent months. I repeat: I have never believed in "instant paradise," neither in life nor in art. On the other hand, the shouts of the mass media about the "collapse of the worldwide movie industry" since the system came out, the comparisons of the system to a torpedo capable of sinking Hollywood, elicited a certain professional curiosity. In short, on receiving the box with the system, I had my breakfast, drank my traditional cup of fruit tea, moved my old leather armchair to the middle of the room, sat down, and followed the instructions to the letter. I put on the helmet and pressed the ON button. At first it was pitch dark. But the little hammer with the ice began to strike my chest evenly. A minute passed, then another. I sat there, staring at the dark. The ice hammer pounded away at my chest. There was something touching and amusing about this. I remembered how, in my childhood, when I lived in the provinces, a huge woodpecker inhabited a grove near us. No one had ever seen such an enormous woodpecker—neither father nor the neighbors. Big and black, with white fuzzy claws and a white head. Everyone went to the grove to look at the huge woodpecker. Finally someone said that it was a Canadian woodpecker, that it wasn't native to any part of Russia. Apparently the bird had flown out of the zoo or someone bought it and didn't take care of it. He worked like clockwork, tapping incessantly. And so loud, so resoundingly! I would wake up from his tapping. And I'd run out to watch him. He wasn't afraid of anyone, he was busy with his own affairs. We got so used to the black woodpecker, that we started calling him Stakhanov. And then one of the delinquents from the next street over killed the woodpecker with a stone. And hung him upside down from a tree. I cried so hard. Perhaps it was that very day that I became "green."... And suddenly, remembering the dead woodpecker and staring into the dark, I began to cry. There was such a warm, sharp feeling in my heart, the sort you have only in childhood when you experience everything directly. I felt terribly sorry for the woodpecker and for all living creatures. Tears poured from my eyes. The tear aspirator in the helmet began to work immediately. It was such a pleasant feeling; the tears were sucked up so tenderly. I was trembling all over from this attack of universal compassion. And the little hammer kept on tapping and tapping, and what I felt wasn't a blow but a sort of soft pressure in the middle of my chest. These attacks of compassion for the living rolled over me in waves, like a tide. Every wave ended in tears, which immediately disappeared in the tear aspirators. The little hammer began to strike more rapidly, and the waves came more quickly. An unending avalanche broke over me. A waterfall of compassion. I was utterly convulsed by sobs. It was phenomenal. The last time I cried like that was sixteen years ago, when Mama died. I don't remember how long it lasted—half an hour or perhaps an hour. But I felt no fear or discomfort. On the contrary, it was very pleasant to cry like this, it purified the soul. I gave myself over entirely to these attacks. The crying gradually ended and I calmed down. The hammer tapped so fast that it seemed there was an opening in my chest all the way to my very heart. The feeling of universal compassion was replaced by a feeling of extraordinary peace and bliss. I have NEVER felt so peaceful and well in my life! And at that moment on the inner screen of the helmet an image appeared. Rather, it didn't appear, it flared—bright, wide, and strong. I saw before me the cliffs of an island rising out of the ocean. It rose from the sea like a plateau, almost a perfect circle in form, and was several kilometers across. And I was standing on the edge of this island, holding hands with other naked people standing nearby. A girl held my left hand and an elderly man my right. They, in turn, held hands with other people. And we all formed a huge circle extending along the perimeter of the island. Somehow I understood that there were exactly twenty-three thousand of us in that circle. We stood there, very still. The ocean splashed below. The sun shone at its zenith. The blindingly blue sky spread out over us. We were all naked, blue-eyed, and fair-haired. We all awaited something with the GREATEST reverence. That moment of awaiting the greatest event continued and continued. It seemed that time had stopped. And suddenly something in my heart awoke. And my heart began to speak in a completely different language. It was amazing! My heart was speaking! For the first time in my life I felt my heart SEPARATELY, as an independent organ. It felt all the people standing in the ring, it felt each heart. And all the hearts, all our hearts, all TWENTY-THREE THOUSAND of them, began speaking in unison! They repeated some new words, although they weren't words in the sense of speech, but more like flares of energy. These flares grew, multiplied as if they were constructing an unseen pyramid. And when there were twenty-three of them, the most amazing thing happened. It is impossible to convey in any language. The entire visible world surrounding us suddenly began to melt and grow pale. But it wasn't at all like in the movies, when the frame pales because of a wide-open aperture. The world was actually MELTING, that is, falling apart into atoms and elemental particles. And our bodies along with it. It was INCREDIBLY pleasant: a great relief after decades of earthly life. They disappeared, disappeared, and suddenly a torrent of light

Galina Uvarova, 38, deputy of the State Duma

Yesterday I received an unexpected gift from the **ICE** Company—a system of the same name. The nine-month hubbub around this project resulted in a successful birth—a new child of advanced technology appeared in the world. In the presence of my husband, son, and friends I tried out this "miracle of the XXI century," by means of which its creators intend to "resolve the problem of human discord in our difficult world." Putting on the helmet and turning on the apparatus, I waited. The "miracle ice," loaded in the mechanical hammer, began to

Ice

strike me in the chest. The first minutes passed in silence and darkness. In a state of expectation, in pitch dark, people usually begin to think about things past. For some reason I remembered how my father once took me to the countryside, to see his relatives. I was about ten. These relatives had slaughtered a calf specially for us. His name was Borka. And I saw his head in the larder. I was horrified and scared. I ran out of the larder. At dinner, my country aunt suddenly asked me, smiling, "Now, then, is Borka tasty?" I began to cry. Then I suddenly felt terribly sad. And wearing that damned helmet I began to weep. Apparently the nervous tension of the recent election campaign took its toll. My husband began to pull at my shoulder, but I pushed him away roughly, something I had never permitted myself. The tears flowed even harder, in a regular flood. I simply broke down. When it was all finished, a picture arose—we all stand in a circle, holding hands. Naked. And suddenly everything around begins to disappear. And we turned into rays of light

Sergei Krivosheev, 94, retired

I feel very happy and hopeful after receiving the **ICE** Health Improvement System free of charge. Thanks to it, I feel energetic and optimistic. I tried it on October 18. The details: At 14:30 I connected everything and sat down on a chair. I was assisted by: my son and his wife. At first nothing happened. So I waited. And then I felt a certain agitation, but it was pleasant. Most important, I remembered many things that I had completely forgotten. I remembered 1926, how I went hunting with my father when I was just a boy. It was near Vyshniy Volochek on the lakes. Father and three of his pals and fellow workers were duck hunting. That morning they had shot nearly a boat-ful of ducks. The boat was in the reeds by the shore. I sat in the boat. Our two dogs, Entente and Kolchak, would swim out to retrieve the ducks that had been hit if they fell in the water, or search for them in the reeds. Then the hunters called the dogs to them and I remained alone in the boat with the dead ducks. And who knows why, I began to feel very sorry for the ducks. They were so beautiful. But I understood the scariest thing back then: no one could ever bring them back to life. I cried so hard. I cried and fainted. Then I cried some more. I got very tired. But then I awoke on the shore of an enormous lake. I am standing with some people. And we all pass easily into a very pure light

Andrei Sokolov, 36, temporarily unemployed

All of you weasels should be hung up by your pricks so you don't shit on people. This stinking **ICE** is an invention of kike Freemasons who want to enslave mankind. Russia has already been humiliated, crucified, they want to cut her up and sell her off like bear meat, and now they're out to fuck her over in the mental sphere. They choose the "necessary" people and hand out this shit for free. But I'm not one to take to that immoral dishonesty. This fucking system is opium for the Russian people. They want to get us all hooked on it, and when we turn into retards they'll bring in fucking UN troops and aim their guns at the Kremlin. And we'll all be speaking English. It's a nasty fucking system: first I started crying my eyes out because I remembered how we buried my little sister when she got electrocuted on the farm, and then all kinds of bullshit started—I'm standing around with naked hookers and pederast

Ice

perverts! And no one's ashamed of themselves. Most of all—even I'm not ashamed. And then—everything disappears and there's something like this kind of bright light

Anton Beliavsky, 18, student

On September 10 my sister told me that I was one of two hundred and thirty people to whom the company **ICE** was giving its super system for free. I didn't believe it at first, but my sister showed me the newspaper where it was written. That was cool! I'd heard so much about this system, they were always talking about it on TV, writing in the papers and magazines. I saw a report on the company, on its unusual story, on how they set up a huge plant to manufacture synthetic Tungus ice in Siberia, and how the company is very rich, but the Russian part is only twenty-five percent, and that they want to revolutionize the video and film industries, to destroy the old cinema, and create something really awesome that will make everyone go bananas. They called me, and then delivered the box. My sister and I opened it; there was a computer, a helmet, and a breastplate. Also a kind of briefcase-size freezer with twenty-three pieces of ice. I took off my T-shirt, sat down on the sofa; my sister helped me put on the breastplate. I put a piece of ice in the hammer, connected the computer and the helmet, plugged everything in, put on the helmet, and flipped the system on. The helmet design is really cool, just like Darth Vader's. And it's comfortable inside, really soft. At first nothing happened. The hammer began to thump the ice against my chest, that's all. But it didn't hurt. I relaxed, sat back; it was dark in the helmet, like in a tank. One minute, two, five. Nothing! I was already thinking, okay, it's just another bunch of bullshit. My sister was sit-

Part III

ting next to me, I said, "Mashka, we've been had!" And then
suddenly for some reason I remembered something. I was fourteen years old when I first got asthma. My very first attack was
in the early morning. They were laying down some kind of
pipes outside right under our windows and these jerks started
drilling the asphalt at around five a.m. They had a compressor
for the jackhammer; they turned it on and it began pounding
away rhythmically—trrr, trrr, trrr, trrr! That morning I had a
dream: it was like those jerks started up the compressor and
connected the hose to our window. They were sucking the air
out of our apartment. We had a one-room apartment; Mama
and Mashka slept near the window and I slept on a fold-out cot
near the sideboard. And it was like I woke up and saw that
Mama and little Masha had almost suffocated. They were lying
as though they were dead under that window. And I jump out
of bed and then have to crawl over to them, because I can hardly
breathe myself, and I start shaking them. But they die right
before my eyes. What was so frightening was that I couldn't
help them at all, and that damn compressor was sucking out
the air and blasting away: trrr, trrr, trrr!! So I grab a chair and
throw it at the window. But it doesn't break. I beat my fists
against the glass as hard as I can, but I can't break it. Then
suddenly I realize—that's it! They're both dead! And they will
never be brought back to life. I began to weep—I wept so hard!
Then I began to sob convulsively. So hard and so long that my
sister even got scared. She told me later that my whole body
was wracked by sobs. It went on and on, and then I kind of
started to feel tired, and then completely exhausted. I felt so
good and calm, it was like nothing bothered me, I didn't care
about anything, and I felt totally high inside. And—bam! A
picture lit up: I'm standing on this awesome island. It's so big,

Ice

like a cliff. The sea is all around. Sun, a bright blue sky, incredible fresh air. And I'm standing in a huge circle with naked people, and we're all holding hands like children. And there are lots and lots of us. And then I suddenly realize: there are exactly twenty-three thousand of us. Exactly! And that really kind of hit me—wham! And in my heart there was this kind of sucking feeling, but in a good way, it was sweet. And there was this rush, as though my heart had a pipe in it, and whoosh, it was off with a whistle. Suddenly I could feel the hearts of all of those people. And it was this really strange but cool feeling that all of us are the only ones on earth. And we began to talk with our hearts. But it wasn't any kind of normal conversation, when you tell someone something, and they answer, like: "Who are you?" "I'm Anton." "I'm Volodya, hi." Not like that. It was more like a conversation without words, but really powerful. And then our hearts all began to kind of vibrate: one, two, three...It was so cool! And when it got up to twenty-three—then...I just can't explain it...! Suddenly everything all around began to dissolve, sort of disappear forever, and us too—whoosh! And we melted in this gentle light

Max Alyoshin, 20, anarchist

When I received the **ICE** system, I immediately decided to test it in our commune. It's in this really awesome condemned building. They're going to restore it and then fill it with the bourgeoisie. There's nothing there, not even any electricity. But we solved the problem—at night we hook up to the neighboring kiosk. And so I got into the helmet, turned it on. At first—it was fucking dark and that ice hammer was humping away at my breastbone. It was a real bummer, no rush, no high. Then

Part III

all this bullshit got into my head: really ancient memories. It was like I was still in Elektrostal, just a little guy; in the morning I run out into our yard and there's this incredible fucking winter, snowdrifts, all kinds of kids out with their mamas. And my mother's the groundskeeper. And right near the third entrance door, she's chopping ice with a pickax: whack! whack! whack! A nice sound. And I'm walking around the yard like a goddamn cosmonaut: my grandma put a bunch of clothes on me, so I look like a head of cabbage. I've got felt boots with galoshes on my feet, and the snow crunches under them like sugar. I have a shovel in my hand, and I walk over to a snowdrift and start making a spaceship out of it with my shovel—I dig and dig and Mother keeps on chopping and chopping. And suddenly I need to piss really badly, because I didn't take a leak before going out, because I wanted to go out so bad. And I don't want to go home to piss—walk all the way up to the fourth floor, then Grandma will unpack me, take me to the john, it would all take way too long. So I keep on digging and digging, and Mother keeps on chopping and chopping. And then I start to piss into my felt boots, not even piss, but just let a little out at a time. And my boots are so warm. But then suddenly I feel like shit. I'm digging the deck, and I start whimpering from anger. But Mother chops and smiles at me. And suddenly I begin to cry, fuck, so hard that I can't see anything and I fall into the snowdrift and I cry and cry and cry. But my mother thinks I'm playing. And she keeps on chopping that fucking ice, and I'm wailing till I'm totally exhausted. And I get so tired that I lie there in that fucking snow like I'm in the grave. I can't move a finger. And then suddenly—fuckin' whammo! I'm on an island. An island in the fuckin' ocean. And I'm standing in a circle with twenty-three thousand people who are standing and holding hands, completely quiet. Me, I'm also holding some chick's hand with my left hand and some old guy's with my right. Fuckin' shit, man. Then—whacko-fuckin-bam—there's this jolt in my heart, like a rush—then a second, a third, and on and on to the twenty-third! And whoosh— we're all heading for fuckin' nirvana, we float away and the light

Vladimir Kokh, 38, businessman

In my opinion, the whole thing is very suspect. I experienced only:

1. Pity, yearning, sadness (when for some reason I remembered the time three schoolboys and I threw stones at a cat).

2. Weakness, deadly fatigue (when I stopped crying).

3. Euphoria (when I found myself in a huge circle of similar people, felt heart palpitations, and suddenly began to disappear and everything all around too, becoming light

Oksana Tereshchenko, 27, manager

I really wanted to try out the **ICE** system. Not just because I'd heard a lot about it. Even a long time ago, I think it was about three years back, when the Japanese found the Tungus meteorite, or rather, what was left of it, and Russian and Swedish scientists discovered the "Tungus ice effect," I was very intrigued by this event. This discovery promised a revolution in sensory experience. And for that matter, I liked the whole story of the Tungus meteorite, the fact that it's a huge chunk of ice, ice with an unusual crystalline structure that doesn't exist in nature. Ice, fallen from the sky, a huge chunk, which no one could find, but it turns out that it had been found and quietly chipped away at. Where did that ice go? What happened with it? Who were these people? It's still a mystery. Now that scientists have synthesized this unusual ice, the whole thing is even more interesting. So when they informed me in our office that I was one of the two hundred and thirty initial testers, I was stunned! It was a huge surprise. Our commercial director included me in the list of two hundred and thirty without even asking me. He just saw how I was always surfing the Internet and following the "Tungus effect." And when fate willed that I was among the first testers, he said that I should try out the device here, in our office, in front of our co-workers. And everyone supported the idea! That was it—and so yesterday when I came to work as always at 9:30, I brought the box with me. Everyone was already waiting. In the packing room they moved the bundles over to the wall, placed the director's leather armchair in the middle. Two co-workers helped me put on the breastplate, load the piece of ice in the little hammer, and plug everything in. I connected the helmet, put it on, felt around for the start button with my finger, and pushed it. Right away the hammer began to peck at my chest with the ice. It was dark in the helmet. It was funny and a little ticklish: tuk, tuk, tuk, tuk, like a bird pecking and pecking at me between my breasts! It was funny because I imagined myself from the outside: the manager of the company sitting in a bathing suit and helmet, this thing pecking at her chest, everyone standing around and watching to see what will happen. But nothing happened—it was dark in the helmet. And I began to worry. I don't much like the darkness. And when I sleep alone, I always leave the light on. I've been that way since childhood, since I was about ten, I think. The thing is, my father would drink, and when he'd come home drunk, he'd be rough with my mother. We lived in a military settlement, in a two-room apartment; they slept in the little room, and I slept in the big room.

Ice

And several times I heard my father raping my mother, that is, she didn't want to and he just took her by force, he was so drunk. And she would cry. One time I couldn't stand it; I got up and turned on the light in my room. And my father immediately quieted down. He didn't even get mad at me. And then I just started doing it a lot. And I began to be afraid to sleep in the dark. And when I thought about that, sitting in the dark helmet, I suddenly remembered really vividly an incident from my childhood. One time, it was in the summer, Mama put me down for a nap during the daytime, and went off to the store. I woke up—and there was no one home. The refrigerator was making a knocking noise. It was big and fat-bellied, made a lot of noise, and was always knocking and rocking: knock, knock, knock. I got dressed, went to the door, and it was closed. I went to the window and saw Mama in the yard. She was standing with our neighbor lady. They were talking about something happy, and they were both laughing. I began to beat on the glass and shout: "Mama, Mama!" But she couldn't hear me. And the refrigerator kept on knocking and knocking. And I was wailing and looking at Mama. And the most awful thing was that she couldn't hear me. I felt so sad from this vivid memory that I began to cry. And then I just started wailing out loud, like a little girl. But there was something really pleasant about this weeping, something intimate, a feeling of something you can never bring back. That's why I wasn't embarrassed at all, on the contrary, I cried as openly as I could. It went on for a long time, my heart would stop so sweetly, the tears rolled down and were sucked up somewhere so pleasantly. It was very very sad, but very sweet, too. I was only afraid of one thing: that one of the co-workers would be scared and pull the helmet off me! But they all turned out to be politically correct! So I cried to my heart's content, and the ice hammer kept on tap-

Part III

ping away at my chest. And a kind of astonishing peace set in, really magical, as though my soul had flown above the earth and saw everything and understood that people have no reason to rush around. And it was so amazing that I completely froze still so as not to spoil it, so it wouldn't end. And the peace just floated and floated, and it was like flowers were blooming in my heart. And suddenly a bright, glistening image appeared on the inside screen of the helmet. It was the ocean and a bit of land in that endless blue ocean, and we stood on that land—twenty-three thousand wonderful people! We were all holding hands, forming a huge circle a few kilometers wide. We all felt fine and comfortable standing like that. We were waiting for some decisive moment, something important, I was entirely transformed into the expectation of something, as if God were supposed to come down from the sky to us. And suddenly our hearts seemed to wake up all at once. It was an incredible jolt! As though a huge organ began to play inside us. Our hearts began to sort of sing scales, rising ever higher and higher. This heart singing in unison was unlike anything else. My whole body grew numb and everything flew right out of my head. And the notes kept on going up and up, like a chromatic chord—higher, higher, higher! And when they'd come to the very top, a real miracle occurred. We began to lose our bodies. They just kind of dripped away somewhere, disappeared. And everything all around us as well—the shore, and the waves, the fresh salty sea air—everything was sort of sucked away, like a cloud. There was nothing scary about it, just the opposite, my whole soul welcomed this disappearance joyously. It was an unforgettable moment. I kept on dissolving and dissolving, like a piece of sugar. But not in water. There's light

Ice

Mikhail Zemlianoi, 31, journalist

There can no longer be any doubt that a new era has dawned: today we are living in the age of the **ICE** system. Yesterday we still lived in the age of the cinema. The moment when I stood in the circle and suddenly began to disappear, when there appeared a shining light

Anastasia Smirnova, 53, organic chemist, professor

The Tungus Ice Phenomenon (TIP) interested me immediately, as it did many scientists. My imagination was fired by the entirely new crystalline structure of this cosmic ice formation, which fell on Siberia nearly a hundred years ago. Our entire department made a model of this complex multifaceted design out of cardboard, painted it the color of ice, and hung it from the chandelier. It spun and turned above our head, its facets sparkling, promising a scientific revolution. And it has come. The discovery made by Samsonova, Endkvist, and Kameyami means more than the Nobel Prize and international recognition put together. The discovery of SEK vibrations is the bridge into the future of new biotechnologies. The **ICE** system is merely the first sign. It is a trial balloon released by a human genius. I was not surprised that I ended up as one of the two hundred and thirty lucky ones. On receiving the system, the entire section tested it out every day. But I was the first. And I can honestly say: It is amazing! At first there were tears and extraordinarily intense childhood memories; then emptiness, peace, and flight! And what a flight it was! It was something like a collective orgasm, and I felt that the light

Part III

Nikolai Barybin, priest

Our world is truly tumbling straight into the devil's jaws. This so-called **ICE** system is yet another hellish invention hastening the fall of contemporary urban civilization. On receiving this "Greek gift" from the company **ICE**, I initially wanted to turn it down, since my Russian Orthodox heart whispered to me, "This **ICE** comes from the Evil One." As a pastor, however, I am obligated to know the enemy in person. I honestly tried this system on myself. At first I felt a terrible fear, which turned to grief. But what was the object of my grief? It is shameful to say—it was a broken bicycle. It happened when I was ten years old. This incident had completely vanished from my memory, but the **ICE** system reminded me of it painfully. Then a spell of absolute depravity ensued: I saw myself naked in an enormous circle of "the chosen," standing above the world and awaiting a miracle. But it was not the Lord's mercy they awaited, not repentance, not the absolution of sin, not the advent of the Kingdom of God. They simply yearned to be transformed into streams of light

Kazbek Achekoev, 82, retired

When the Soviet Union existed and our Republic was part of the USSR, there was a movie theater in our regional center. I worked there almost thirty-four years as a film technician. I showed movies to the people. And I quite respected the cinema myself. I never understood and still don't understand the theater—what's it for? But I quite respected the cinema. My favorite films were—you couldn't count them all! There were lots. But my most favorite were genuine comedies. And my favorite comic movie actors were Charlie Chaplin, Mister Pitkin, Louis de Funès, Fernandel, Yuri Nikulin, Georgi Vitsin, Zhenia

Ice

Morgunov, Dzhigarkhanian, Etush, and Arkady Raikin. This is our gold mine. But when the USSR died, and the Republic received its independence, the movies went downhill. There were hardly any new films. And then the war began. No one was up to movies. My wife and I took our sons and went into the mountains to our relatives. We lived there six years and eight months. But my son Rizvan died anyway. And my grandson Shamil disappeared. When we returned to the regional center, everything had been destroyed. The movie theater was a hospital. But life began to settle down. We got electricity again. They started getting things in order. And my grandson Bislan suddenly told me that I had won some new equipment through the newspaper. He had written us all down on the application and sent it to the offices. And six months later the answer came: Kazbek Achekoev. The company delivered the equipment right to our house. We all looked at it. And I said, "but what does it do?" Bislan said, "It's a new technological miracle. First of all, it shows you movies right in your eyes. Second, it makes you feel really good." I said, "You go and try it out on yourself." But Bislan replied, "Grandfather, you are the person who won it; you have to be the first to try it." I said, "I don't see so well, and I'm farsighted." He read the instructions and said, "Your farsightedness is within the norm. Everything will be fine." I said, "No, I'm too old for these experiments." My sons tried to persuade me. I kept on refusing. Then our neighbor Umar came over, and said, "Kazbek, you spent your whole life showing us movies, now it's your turn to watch." Well, I agreed. They sat me down in a chair, took off my shirt, put this thing on my chest, and put a piece of ice in it, like a bullet in a gun. And put a helmet on my head. Then that ice began to shoot me in the chest. But they didn't show anything in the helmet. I asked, "Bislan, why aren't they showing anything here?" And he said,

"Grandfather, be patient." Well, I sat there quietly. That ice kept on shooting me and shooting me. I sat there. There was nothing to do—so I started thinking about the movies, remembering things. How I showed the movies, what films I showed, different bits of them. And then for some reason I remembered the Great Patriotic War. We were new recruits, we were first sent to the Kharkov area and then to Viazma. This was in September 1941. The Germans had cut off the head of two of our foot-soldier divisions, and we began to retreat. There were about two hundred guys left from our regiment. And when the dawn broke, we began to escape the encirclement through the swamps. And we ended up right under their machine guns. The Germans were waiting for us. Right in front of my eyes they killed everyone around who was walking. They just cut them down like hay. And a bullet took a chip off my rifle butt and I fell into the swamp. Everyone who remained alive also fell in the swamp. And just lay there. The Germans watched to see if anyone moved and they killed them right off. There were three machine guns that shot dead-on and in short rounds—only five bullets: bang! bang! bang! bang! bang! Not more. Then they'd wait, and again: bang! bang! bang! bang! bang! Some of our guys began to quietly crawl through the swamp, but the Germans killed them right away. Because they could see everything in their binoculars. Everyone around me died. Two guys who were wounded cried. I realized that I had to pretend to be dead and lie there until nighttime—then crawl out. It was first thing in the morning, about six o'clock. I closed my eyes and lay there. The Germans shot at anyone who moved. They killed everyone off. But I lay there and didn't even breathe. My face was halfway in the swamp water, but the left side was above water. And so I'd breathe this way: I'd suck a little bit of air in through my nose and let it out into the water through

Ice

my mouth. The Germans settled down. Then suddenly: bang! bang! bang! bang! bang! And I'm still lying there. And the sun began to bake. Somewhere over there the battle was going on. Someone would rush through that swamp again, and they just cut them down and cut them down with the machine guns. Well, then I got good and scared. I wasn't even nineteen at the time. I was lying there with corpses all around me. And suddenly a frog came of out of the water and jumped onto my hand. Right next to my face. And I could see that one of its feet was torn off. A bullet must have torn it off. And it sat there on my fist, breathing and looking at me. And I looked at it. And I felt so sorry for myself and for that frog that tears began to pour from my eyes. And I began to cry—like I'd never cried before. Stronger and stronger. And then suddenly—whoosh! I'm suddenly standing somewhere naked, bare naked, people are holding me by the hand, and it's so nice, and sort of free, and we're singing, and then everything begins to sort of flow, and that was it, and nothing, and only light

Viktor Evseev, 44, butcher

I heard before that they'd manufactured this artificial ice which, when you pound someone in the chest with it, awakes various cardiac centers. And then suddenly—I received this system for free, they had some advertising campaign. And I tried it. It's pretty interesting. Although it takes a long time. At the end, there's this great high, we all stand in a circle and suddenly—whoosh! And we disappear in light

Part III

Lia Mamonova, 22, saleswoman

This is really...something. I don't know how to put it. At first it's all as dark as dark can be, quiet as the grave, just this mechanical arm banging at your chest like a jackhammer. Then there's a kind of compassion in your soul, you feel this sort of sucking sadness. And immediately there's all these pitiful thoughts that get into your head, like—everything sucks, people are shit, life is hard, and that kind of stuff. After that I saw a maternity ward where there's a whole room full of newborns abandoned by their mothers. And it was like, I went there at night and stood there. And they were all sleeping. And I felt so sorry for them that I just started blubbering buckets. And I'm like sobbing and sobbing, I can't stop. I see their tiny little feet and hands and I just wept. And I cried so long and hard that I fell on the floor and fainted—bam! I couldn't stand it. And I really just lost consciousness there from helplessness, or I just fell asleep. And when I woke up—we were standing this uninhabited island and there were twenty-three thousand of us. And everyone was naked. But we weren't screwing, just standing and waiting. And suddenly God came down right from the sky and took us. That light

Anatoly Omo, 27, Web designer

This is a real cult thing. New. Radically new. This isn't any "Health Improvement System," but a new-generation simulator. Which the company **ICE** is pushing hard. Cool controls, awesome picture. Fucking amazing quest. Complete effect of being there. Plus the **ICE** itself with its super qualities, which there's been so much buzz about in the media. The **ICE** is fifty percent of the effect. The high makes you want more. Right away. But in sober daylight you realize—this is the start of an

Ice

enormous new platform. Until now, we've just been floating, playing with our sweet little games: Quake, Myth, Sub Command, Aliens Versus Predator. Now we've arrived on the shore and stepped barefoot onto genuine **ICE**. Ouch! I feel like saying, Fuckin' fantastic: we've arrived! We stand in a brotherly circle and transform into light

Anya Shengelaya, 33, poetess

It is divine in all senses! It prepares us for death, for the transition to other worlds. I haven't felt such excitement for a long time, haven't forgotten myself, haven't disconnected so completely from our squalid, gray reality. Our earthly life—is a preparation for death, for transformation, for great journeys. Like dolls, we are forced to doze in our earthly membranes until the Higher Powers awaken us in our graves and resurrect us. As Lao-tzu said, "He who cannot love death, does not love life." This marvelous apparatus teaches us to love death. And it actually does improve health. Because truly healthy people are those who are not afraid of death, who await it as deliverance, who yearn for awakening and the beginning of a new birth, in other worlds. In one instant we all shone with the light

Part IV

A ray of sun crawled across the boy's bare shoulder.

A plastic clock with a laughing wolf ticked loudly on a stool. The breeze coming through a half-open window fluttered a semitransparent curtain. Down in the courtyard, a dog barked.

The boy slept, his mouth open. The green head of a plush dinosaur stuck out from under the edge of his blanket.

The sunbeam slipped over the boy's plump cheek. Illuminated the edge of his nose.

His lips twitched. The bridge of his nose wrinkled. He sneezed and opened his eyes. He closed them again. He yawned and stretched, pushing back the blanket with his feet. The dinosaur fell on the rug. The boy sat up. He scratched his shaggy head and called out, "Mom!"

No one answered.

He looked down. The dinosaur lay belly-up between a slipper and a water pistol. The boy dangled his legs off the bed. Yawned again. He slid off the bed and shuffled into the kitchen.

There was no one there. An orange lay on the table; there was a note under it. Rising on his tiptoes, the boy pulled the note out from under the orange. The orange rolled across the table, fell off, and rolled on across the floor.

Moving his lips and toes, the boy sounded out the syllables: "Bee...hoooome...ve...ry...sooooon."

He put the note back on the table. He squatted and looked around. The orange lay under the sideboard.

The boy farted. He stood up and shuffled into the bathroom. He pulled his underwear down and peed for a long time, moving his lips. He pulled up his underwear and walked to the sink. He pushed a wooden box over and climbed up on it. He rinsed his mouth out. Looked at his toothbrush and then held it under the water. The water began to wash the toothpaste off the brush.

"Cats and dogs..." muttered the boy and shook the brush.

The toothpaste fell in the sink. The boy splashed water on it.

"Catsndogs, catsndogs, catsndogs, sail away, begone!"

He washed the brush and put it in a glass. He jumped off the box. Ran to the kitchen. Looked under the cupboard and shook his fist at the orange.

"You scoundrel!"

He opened the refrigerator and took out a chocolate-covered cream-cheese roll and opened the wrapping. Bit off a piece. Chewing, he walked into Mama's room. Picked up the TV remote. Sat on the floor and turned on the television. Eating the cream-cheese roll, he flipped through the programs. He licked his fingers and wiped them off on his T-shirt.

"There." The boy crawled over to a shelf with video-cassettes, and pulled one out. "Dinosaurs. Stop."

He began to put the cassette into the VCR, but suddenly noticed a new object. A blue cardboard box with the large white letters I C E stood in the corner. The box was open. The boy went over to look at it. There were some blue objects in it.

Part IV

The boy picked up the one on top. It was a helmet. He looked at it from all sides, and then put it on his head. It was dark in the helmet.

"OOO-boom-boom-boom-boom-boom!" The boy shot a machine-gun round with his two fingers.

He took off the helmet and put it on a chair. He pulled the breastplate out of the box, turned it this way and that, and tossed it on the floor.

"Nuh-uh..."

He took a blue case out of the box. The cord on the case reached over to the wall outlet. A blue light burned on the side of the case. The boy put the case on the floor. He touched the button. He farted.

He pushed the lock button.

The case opened. Inside, in soft blue plastic cells lay a single piece of ice. Twenty-two sections were empty.

"A 'frigerator..."

The boy picked up the piece.

"Cold."

The ice was packed in a frosty piece of cellophane. The boy picked at the blue strip, then pulled on it. The strip tore open the cellophane package. He pressed out the ice into his hand. Examined it. Licked it one or twice.

"Not ice cream."

The phone rang. The boy picked up the receiver.

"Hello. She's not home. I don't know."

He replaced the receiver. He tapped the ice on it.

"The ice froze stiff. It came over to warm up."

He tapped the ice against the glass of the sideboard.

"It's me, ice!"

Sucking on the ice, he went into his room. There in the corner, on a wooden stand for CDs, stood little plastic figures of

Ice

Superman, an X-Man, and a Transformer. The boy put the ice between them.

"Hey, dudes, I'm ice, I came to see you!"

He picked up the Transformer, who held a laser spear in his hand. He jabbed the ice with the end of the spear.

"Ice, hey ice, who are you?"

He answered with the ice's voice: "I'm cold!"

He asked with the voice of the X-Man: "What do you need, cold ice?"

He answered with the voice of the ice: "Warm me up!"

Outside, dogs began barking.

The boy looked at the window. He scowled.

"Aha! Again!"

He ran out on the balcony. It was warm and sunny. Down below, three stray dogs were barking at a Doberman walking with his bespectacled owner. The Doberman ignored them.

"Catsndogs!" the boy exclaimed, raising his fist at the dogs.

He went back to his room. The ice was lying under a Transformer's spear.

"Get out of here, you fat ice!" the boy roared and stabbed the ice with the spear.

The ice skittered onto the rug. The boy sat down next to it. He whined in a high voice, "Be nice to me, I'm cold!"

He picked up the ice in two fingers and crawled across the rug with it, squeaking and whimpering. He bumped into the stuffed dinosaur.

"I'm cold!"

"Let's go, ice, I'll warm you up."

He helped the ice to get on the dinosaur's back. He crawled with the dinosaur over to the bed. He helped the dinosaur clamber onto the bed. He put the dinosaur on his pillow and

Part IV

placed the ice next to it. He covered them with his blanket and roared: "You'll be warm here, ice."

He remembered the orange. He ran into the kitchen.

The ice lay next to the dinosaur, jutting out from under the blanket. The sunlight shone on its wet surface.